DANGER CLOSE

DELTA FORCE ECHO: AN INIQUUS ACTION ADVENTURE ROMANCE (BOOK THREE)

FIONA QUINN

DANGER CLOSE

AN INIQUUS ACTION ADVENTURE ROMANCE

Book Three

Fiona Quinn

THE WORLD OF INIQUUS

Ubicumque, Quoties. Quidquid

Iniquus - /i'ni/kwus/ our strength is unequalled, our tactics unfair – we stretch the law to its breaking point. We do whatever is necessary to bring the enemy down.

THE LYNX SERIES

Weakest Lynx

Missing Lynx

Chain Lynx

Cuff Lynx

Gulf Lynx

Hyper Lynx

STRIKE FORCE

In Too DEEP

JACK Be Quick

InstiGATOR

Uncommon Enemies

Wasp

Relic

Deadlock

Thorn

FBI Joint Task Force

Open Secret

Cold Red

Even Odds

Kate Hamilton Mysteries

Mine

Yours

Ours

Cerberus Tactical K9 Team Alpha

Survival Instinct

Protective Instinct

Defender's Instinct

Delta Force Echo

Danger Signs

Danger Zone

Danger Close

This list was created in 2021. For an up-to-date list, please visit FionaQuinnBooks.com

If you prefer to read the Iniquus World in chronological order you will find a full list at the end of this book.

DEDICATION

This book is dedicated to my friend
Judith Rocchiccilioli.
Life is an adventure, thank you for traveling along with me.

THE TEAM

Delta Force: G Squadron (clandestine), Echo (reconnaissance)

Lieutenant Colonel Burnside
Josiah Landry (T-Rex) Echo One
Tyler Newcomb (Ty) Echo Two, K9 handler for Rory
Jeopardy — Echo Three
Nitro — Echo Four
Uncle – Echo Five
Timothy Nathan Hale (Havoc) — Echo Six
Dice – Echo Seven

Intelligence

Johnna White, CIA
Javeed Hasan, DIA
Damian (Deimos) Prescott, Special Agent in Charge, FBI
Calvin Hock, FBI analyst
Colonel Tan, Pentagon (army)

THE TEAM CONTINUED

Asymmetric Warfare Group

Lieutenant Colonel Arnold, Asymmetric Warfare Group
Rosetta Jetteau Vargas (Jett)
Renée
Deepak
Scott
Tink
Peter

1
———

Fort Bragg, North Carolina

Friday, Zero Seven Thirty

Havoc's heart picked up the pace. This was a simulation, but it made no difference. He acted "as if."

As if the information offered in the briefing room was the real deal.

As if the imperiled women and children inside this particleboard and cinderblock training structure weren't just photographs stapled onto cardboard cutouts.

As if there was an actual cache of weaponry and explosives that trained insurgent fighters would use against Delta Force Echo even if it meant killing everyone inside the structure and out, friend and foe alike.

Standing outside the shoot house, stacked with his Echo brothers waiting for their breacher to open their path into the building, the "as if" part was crucial. It trained the mind to show up for a job. To be functional in life-or-death scenarios—flexible, adaptable, and steady.

The mind and the body had to work dependably in unison.

Each brother was a cog in a greater machine. One man not squared away…yeah, that's all it took—a forgotten step, a trigger finger that was slow to the pull. Lives and mission outcomes were on the line.

They weren't playing in the kiddie leagues. Every mission that required a Delta Force team's involvement was edge-of-disaster.

No wiggle room for mistakes.

And that's why they practiced.

They practiced in the morning when they were bright with energy.

They practiced through hunger. Through fatigue. Through needing a damned bathroom break.

"As if" meant that Havoc's armpits were damp.

His heart pounded against his breastbone.

There was a hitch in his breath.

He knew from experience that what he privately referred to as "stage fright" would disappear once they moved through the door, whether via a twist of an unlocked knob, a well-placed boot alongside the latch, or Nitro with his blast strips.

Then, Havoc would be a rising tide.

He'd flow with the current past the inoffensive. And when Havoc came up against an obstacle, he'd *crush* it.

He was a force of nature, baby.

Laughter winked momentarily into Havoc's eyes at that thought.

Master Chief T-Rex Landry signaled Nitro to the front, calling, "Breacher up."

Today's scenario's threat matrix included the possibility of children, which negated the team's use of C4.

C4 was the kind of explosive Nitro slapped into place on most breaches with its concussive bang.

The goal of a C4 breach was to stun and gun.

Team Echo wanted to overwhelm the enemies' senses. Without noise-cancelling ear protection in place, those on the interior would be rendered deaf with ringing ears. The targets could call warnings and commands all day; no one would hear them.

The interior would fill with particulates and smoke. The shock rendered even the most hard-core frozen in place as their brains scrambled to understand, process, and decide.

In those first moments of relative safety, Echo could swarm the interior and gain control of those inside before their enemies' minds and bodies could get into gear.

Mere seconds—but life or death seconds that Echo would use to their advantage, boosting their chances at the desired outcome.

Nitro, a born pyro, was a master of the nuanced charge. Too little, and no one was going anywhere. Too much? Well, that meant nobody and nothing was left for the team to deal with. Nitro worked the Goldilocks angle, trying to get it just right. While everyone on the team trained to breach, Nitro finessed it better than anyone Havoc had ever served with.

Today, Nitro worked his least favorite breach, water.

Loud, for sure, a water breach wasn't a stealthy way to enter the building. But it also didn't have the C4 teeth rattle.

Once Nitro blasted the door, success was all about swiftness and violence of action.

Today's scenario—a family held hostage.

At T-Rex's command, Nitro jogged forward. He laid his equipment on the ground in a uniform fashion. A few meters of det cord, two bags of saline drip, 100MPH tape (the military's version of good old duct tape.)

Nitro reached out to touch the door. Metal.

He examined the hinges and the locks.

Nitro sent a look to T-Rex that read, "reinforced, should I keep going with the I.V. bags?"

T-Rex gave him a thumbs up. The goal was access. They didn't need to take the door completely off the hinges, though it was preferred.

Det cord was the explosive. But it was a fast explosion. It tended to cut, and that was a problem. Sure, sometimes a slice had its place. But here, they needed a push. The kind of push that would lessen the chance of harming kids.

Nitro turned away from T-Rex and slapped saline bags onto the door with double-sided adhesive. He spooled the det cord around the corner to where Echo stacked and crouched away from the shock wave. Though it should be minimal, still, it could impact hearing or shake their brains.

No one had time for that.

Rory, the team's military K9, was last in the stack. His handler, Ty, held tight to Rory's collar behind Havoc. Trained as a force multiplier, Rory had a nose for finding munitions, a jaw that exerted over two hundred pounds of pressure, and athleticism that was a joy to see.

But also harsh stink breath.

"Rory, back off." Crouched on one knee, the toe of his left foot curled under ready to push Havoc into go-mode, Havoc lifted his elbow, pressing Rory back just as a glob of saliva dripped from Rory's lips down the sole of Havoc's boot.

Havoc scuffed his boot into the dirt, so there was nothing slippery to make him lose his footing when Havoc raced into the shoot house.

Like the rest of the team, Rory was dressed for battle. His ear protection and doggy goggles made him look badass, which was good for frightening the enemy into submission. His K9 ballistic vest would protect him from stab wounds and most gunfire. Uncle

Sam wanted to safeguard their K9 investments. After all, it was about a hundred grand to purchase and train a military war dog.

But Echo wanted to protect Rory like any of their team members. On too many missions to count, Rory was the difference between an op that ended with a raised glass and cheer at the pub instead of a trip home in a flag-wrapped pine box.

Rory trained hard, just like the team did.

With a hand on Rory's collar, Ty took a step back.

"Breacher has control," Nitro whispered into his comms. "Breach 3…2…1…"

The stack lowered their crouch and waited for the boom.

"Fail breach." Nitro mic-ed.

Havoc lifted out of his semi-squat.

Rory pleaded in a high-pitched whine to let him run in and bite the bad guy.

With a hand signal from Ty, Rory calmed the whines to heavy panting. It was an essential skill that Rory could pull back his impatience—even if it was his very favorite thing in the world to do—bite the target.

But any noise could bring unwanted eyes to a window.

It could turn a surprise into an I-see-you-coming.

Squirters might run out the back door to hide in the landscape, thwarting capture.

Rifles might be aimed and ready.

Silence was key.

"Breacher has control." Came over his headset. "Breach 3…2…"

Havoc squatted with his shoulder pressed to the outside cement blocks of the kill house.

"…1"

The *boom* that followed was loud but didn't reach the level of C4.

Even with their noise-canceling ear protection, those blasts could make Havoc's ears ring to the point of distraction. And distraction wasn't allowed.

They worked their hand signals and moved.

To Havoc, it was like being a force of nature. Water after a heavy downpour, rumbling forward, sweeping destruction in its path.

No stopping it. No stopping *him*.

The team stepped through the threshold. The door was concave where the I.V. bags had been taped. As the metal rounded into a convex scoop from the blast concussion, it tore the barricade from the hinges and merely fell to the side.

The men moved as one into the house, peeling off, clearing rooms.

Havoc was first man coming to the end of a hall where the line of sight was clear, but the room was out of his visual field. He took an extra-long step. Balancing and pivoting on the ball of his foot as his right leg swung around to align him with that hidden corner.

He didn't need to think. Havoc's brain, primed for action-reaction, had sent thousands upon thousands of rounds into targets, both paper and enemy flesh. Havoc had shot until he'd built up a permanent callous between his thumb and forefinger, hard as a rock.

His firearm came up, and Havoc double tapped the three inches of bad guy head that peaked out from behind the child's curls.

Havoc glided forward, grabbed the digital image of the child, slung it over his shoulder as he evacuated "her" from the shooter house, and got the image to safety.

Ten seconds later, the airhorn blew.

The team stopped and looked up at their evaluators, who had been watching them from the roosts above.

"Too slow. We need to shave another thirty seconds off your entrance. Nitro, what happened to your breaching charge?"

Before Nitro could answer, a woman's shadow stretched across the floorboards.

There stood Johnna White, CIA.

Ty moaned and wiped a hand over his face. He'd been hand-picked by White for a psy-ops mission a few months back that included him wooing an asset.

The Echo brothers all raised their fingers to point to Havoc.

"Why Havoc?" White asked.

"To be honest, ma'am," Ty said, "he's the only one left in Echo who's still single. If you need a Casanova for your next op, he's your man."

"Actually," she said, "there *is* a woman involved in this mission." She sent Havoc a wink. She'd hung out with special forces operators long enough that she knew how to give as good as she got. But this time, her face was tense with concern. "Time is tight. I'm sorry to pull you away from your fun and games. But I need to read you into this mission. And I need you winging into position. Now."

2

Jett

Arslanbob, Kyrgyzstan

Friday, Eighteen Thirty hours

Jett heard a noisy group of men below her on the mountain trail. What might be construed as a trail, anyway. In this rocky stretch between the tree lines, it was more of a rambling bit of ground that the cattle kicked free of stones. Locals from the village that nestled on the valley floor followed this trek up to the Walnut Forest. According to the legend recounted in Jett's Kyrgyzstan tourist book, this forest was planted accidentally when a Greek guy failed to realize the sack of walnuts draped over his back had a hole in the corner.

Mildly reminiscent of the American Johnny Appleseed folklore, Jett mused.

If it was a true story, that Greek guy had tipped back a few too many ouzos because the trees grew in a thick grove in this part of Kyrgyzstan.

The walnuts that fell were used as currency for a cluster of families that had little else. A day's worth of gathering was weighed in at the shop and traded for rice. That part reminded Jett of the Gold Rush out West when the panhandlers brought their findings to the store to be weighed and traded for supplies.

Though, gold was actual currency but walnuts? Not so much.

So maybe not exactly like the Gold Rush except for the poverty and the quest for survival.

Tracing her binoculars toward the echo of voices, Jett's focus landed on a horse with a blanket thrown over its back, led by a guy in dress pants, sandals, and a pressed white shirt with 1970s-styled long collar points.

Weird.

Jett crouched; binoculars raised. Five more men rounded into view. They weren't nearly as spiffily dressed. They wore loose jeans and ripped t-shirts with their sandals. Not great shoes for this terrain. Not great clothing choices for this altitude with the sun now over the horizon and the evening air already chilling to the point that Jett had tugged on a fleece pullover. From their clothing, she thought that they were probably from the nearby city rather than the village below.

The male population in this part of the country was sparse. The male heads of households mostly went to Russia to find work and send money back to their families.

So a group of six at this hour with no supply packs…

Just strange.

Jett watched their behaviors through her binocular lenses.

They were a nervous bunch. All six huddled together, their shoulders drawn up toward their ears. Yeah, nerves rather than cold, Jett thought.

As Jett watched, she tried to figure out what the heck they were doing. Looking for something. Lost child? Lost animal? Jett hadn't seen anything other than a few scrambling forest critters for the last three days.

Even though their arms were thin and gangly, six were a lot of men with her as the lone woman in the middle of nowhere.

Well, the outer edge of nowhere. Jett only had about another half-hour—forty-five minutes hike to get down to the guest house where she was renting a room.

Jett had been looking forward to getting this pack off, unlacing her boots, and flopping across the bed. She had a crick in her neck that was radiating up to the occipital ridge, where it was a dull ache that pounded with each step.

She was mildly concerned that she'd missed a tick carrying encephalitis. Jett tried to talk herself out of the idea that her brain was swelling, though she did have many of the symptoms, feeling mildly flu-like, weak, and tired. But so many other things could just as easily make her feel bad. Sleeping on rocks all week, for example.

With zilch by way of meds and medical facilities nearby—or heck, anywhere in this country, really—anything that went wrong with her physical body meant abandoning her post just like her operational partner, Renée, had after a viper bit her above her boot, sinking its fangs into her protective gators.

Renée, or a substitute, would be back in another week to join in the hunt. Until then, Jett was on her own.

Yes, forty-five minutes tops, and she'd make herself a cup of tea, tip back a couple of painkillers, relax. She just needed to get through this one last leg of her trek.

This was the stretch of her descent that didn't have cover. The bald part of the mountain.

Jett made her way toward two massive boulders that rested in the middle of an otherwise wide-open stretch. They'd probably rolled into place a thousand years ago. She'd passed them when she'd wended her way up the mountain last Sunday. Jett had thought they looked a little like those heads on Easter Island, but these boulders had turned their backs on the world as they bent inward, busily gossiping.

That image had tickled her.

But now, she was in a situation where things weren't particularly funny. She was glad to move into the wedge of protective space between them.

The space between the two giant boulders formed a circle about arms breadth and had a smooth surface. There were no good handholds for getting herself to the top. Freeclimbing from this point would be impossible. If she could just get herself off the ground a good four or five feet, she thought the surface above her reach looked more inviting for grips. The proximity of the rocks would make for a quick scramble to the top. About twenty feet high, it would have been just enough to make her feel like she had the advantage in a fight.

But alas and alack… Jett didn't see a way up.

The stone was still warm from today's sun, so Jett wasn't worried about the rocks absorbing her body heat, at least for now. And the break from the frigid winds that liked to race down the side of the mountain at this time of day was appreciated.

She'd wait for the men to pass on by. If that didn't happen, Jett could wait for the sun to go down, and under the protective blanket of darkness, she could slink past the pack of men using her night vision goggles.

Yup, out in the open with six men felt like a hassle that she would just as soon avoid, she thought as she shucked her pack, then touched the pommel of her hunting knife in its sheath on her hip.

Just be patient, she told herself, let the group pass out of sight. Then Jett would finish her trek down to the guest house where she rented a room. Tonight she'd be in a bed. Jett closed her eyes and breathed in, imagining the luxury of her goat skin-covered straw mattress. While Jett enjoyed being out in nature and didn't mind sleeping in the wilds for long stretches, as was often required with her job, she also didn't mind the luxury of a mattress and a soft pillow under head.

The group's laughter would erupt every once in a while, helping Jett keep track of the men's movements. They were a slow-moving blob of a group like they had a reason to get somewhere, and yet… Yeah, their pace didn't make sense to her.

The men were very close now. And very nervous. That laughter wasn't jovial as much as it was a group trying to find courage by teasing each other.

Out here? Really? What could make them act like that?

"Stop," one called out. "She has to come down this way. And it must be soon, or it'll be too dark. Me? I say we sit by the boulders where she can't see us and wait."

Jett strained to understand their words. Thankfully, they spoke Russian amongst themselves instead of Kyrgyz, though the men used a unique accent and cadence that was hard for Jett to follow. While Jett spoke Russian like a native, here in Kyrgyzstan, Jett could communicate best with the older generations who were educated under the USSR school system. Even so, with concentration and a little imagination, Jett was able to piece the ideas together.

"She," they'd said. Jett definitely picked up on the fact that they were waiting for a female.

And that…even taking into account that she was in a foreign land with very different societal norms, it still felt…off.

"I can't hide a horse," the voice complained.

Jett wished she had some visual vantage point. They were here at the boulders now. She wouldn't risk exposing herself.

Six. That *was* a lot. Her palms slicked with sweat.

Maybe the person they were waiting for would come. If she came from the same direction as Jett had descended, would this female see her? Would she give Jett's position away? That might depend on the amount of sunlight left. And the female's disposition.

Jett was dressed in digital camo pants that helped her to blend into the rocky setting. Her fleece was a pale boulder gray. Jett pulled the hood up over her hair and cinched it down tight. In the dusk, if she was still, Jett might be missed.

"Look how bright the red blanket is. It's too visible. Take it off the horse. We can sit on it while we wait."

"When she comes, we'll snatch it up for the ride down the mountain."

Snatch? Was that the correct verb? Jett's mind went to a lost child who might be cold and tired. Had the family sent the young bucks up into the mountains to get her?

Jett dismissed that thought. The vibe didn't fit.

Putting her hands against the solidity of the rock, Jett tried to slow her breath, wishing that her heart wasn't banging so loudly in her chest, distracting her. Jett was having a hard enough time making out the meanings of their conversation. Add in the wind, which whipped at the men's words and carried them down toward the valley floor, and Jett was left straining to gather the information before it blew away.

"It's a good place. Anywhere she comes down the mountains, we can see her from here. We can better surprise her if she walks by, and we spring up. She'll be closer to us and easier to grab."

Jett ran a long string of cusswords through her mind. These guys were up to no good concerning some female.

And here, Jett stood aware of the impending attack. Now, she had a decision to make.

And it sucked big-time.

Jett had a personal moral compulsion to protect the female.

But in doing so, Jett might have to hurt, or heck, even kill these men. Jett hadn't seen weapons but that didn't mean anything. Were they trained fighters?

This was *not* how this evening was supposed to go. She'd promised herself tea and a bed.

Yeah, if she did anything to engage, the mission, at least the part of the mission that Jett was involved with, would be done. And the mission came first.

Jett closed her eyes and exhaled.

...and the mission came first.

Jett knew that she *couldn't* intervene on the part of the person they were waiting to ambush. And that so sucked.

Please don't come down the mountain, whoever you are.

"The old woman said that she came from the hills every Friday night and spent Saturday doing her laundry and getting ready for another week on the mountain."

Wait. What?

That was *Jett's* pattern of behavior.

Jett didn't like patterns. But in this case, she was following orders.

A chill ran down her back.

"I think that you should give this up. What if she is not from here? What then?"

"The old grandmother said that the woman was not married. Not married means I can make a claim."

"I was in the taxi with you when you delivered her, Marat. She will put up a fight."

"They always do."

"Yes, but the other women do not look as strong. This woman, she was built like a man. She had muscles."

"Maybe our friend here enjoys men?"

There was a crack of sound like someone being slapped. Hard.

"No ring, no scarf. She is for taking. I think she is beautiful. And sturdy. Modest as she should be. She didn't speak to either of us in the cab. She simply handed me the paper with the instructions. A quiet woman. A silent woman. These are desirable qualities."

Jett thought back to her taxi ride from the city to the guest house. It had been months ago. There had been two men sitting in the front while she sat in the back. There had been nothing that stood out to her by way of physical features. She couldn't remember what they looked like. But apparently, she'd made an impression. Enough so that they went and spoke to the elderly woman Jett rented the room from. That must be the old woman they mentioned.

"Your mother will think she is sickly."

"Why do you say that, Imal?"

"She has beautiful black hair, but her skin is as white as curdled milk. She looks like uncooked dough. Pale. And she is skinny. What good is a skinny woman? Skinny women don't make healthy babies."

"And these women are too sharp for a pleasant ride."

The men laughed deep, gasping laughs.

After the hilarity died down, the man whom Jett thought must be at the helm of this event, the one leading the horse with the pressed shirt, Marat, said, "I don't know. I think she'll be okay after I bring her to my family's compound. After she eats enough goat meat and frybread. Perhaps she is poor. Too poor to eat properly. I guess there is pity in my heart for such a woman. Me? I am thinking that despite being too thin, she seems strong enough for doing the chores."

"It's best when they are a more tender age. Much younger. A schoolgirl."

"This woman is old. She might even be thirty. No ring on her finger. What kind of woman is not married by the time she's this age? Her family must be filled with shame."

"You don't think it will be shameful to have such an old woman, Marat?"

"I've kept my eye out for a younger girl. But this woman is the one I choose. When we have her, she will cry for a day or two, and then all will be fine."

"We have to find her first."

"And get her off this mountain."

"I've been thinking about this. It will not be enough to just place her on the horse. I think we should roll her up in the blanket."

"How will she straddle the horse, Imal?"

"We drape her over Marat's lap. He will hold her in place."

"Then how does Marat ride the horse? She's a woman, not a goat."

"Imal, you grab the reins and lead the horse down to the taxi. After we put her inside the car, there won't be enough room for all of us. Two in front. Three in the back. The woman goes across your laps, holding her down in the back. I will ride the horse back to its home and thank Burhas for loaning her to us."

Jett recognized that name. Burhas ran a shop on the side of the road about a mile from the guest house. Jett had no idea where he lived.

"All right. Yes. I think that is the way we should do it."

"The police? What if they see us?"

"They aren't strangers. I'll go talk with them."

"Promise them a present. Some sweets from the feast."

"It will be fine, don't worry about the police. They all know how these things work."

There was a *pleck, pleck* sound as someone was picking up pebbles and throwing them.

Long minutes went by. Long enough that the setting sun was making progress. It wouldn't be much more time before it was dark and safe for Jett to circle around these guys, go to her guest house, and ask the elderly woman living there what this was all about.

Jett focused on the small sounds to hear if anyone thought about circling to her side of the boulders.

The horse stomped its hoof into the stones. It whinnied and snorted as a gust of wind roared down from the snow-covered summit.

Jett wished she could see the horse up close. If it were a trained horse, Jett could vault onto its back, give it a smack on its rump, and power down the mountain.

The thought came and went. Horse thievery meant jail time, and it would be six native voices against her in a country where, apparently, police would turn their back on a kidnapping in exchange for some sweets. What was up with the chores and his mother? Jett was so lost, she thought she probably wasn't understanding the men's conversation correctly.

"We must have missed her."

"How is that possible? We started at the old woman's house."

"Where is your horse?"

Perfect, here it was, peering right at Jett. Bony and old with knock knees and missing teeth. It might be okay to get a child up or down the mountain, but this mare certainly wasn't going to outrun a person.

Jett made shooing motions with her hand.

The horse farted long and loud.

The men giggled.

"Pull the beast back around, so it isn't right there to make the woman wary."

Jett shooed again.

The horse stretched its neck out to snuffle her. Then turned and pushed its butt toward Jett.

Pulling her ruck into place on her shoulders, Jett belted the straps tight around her hips and sternum. She knew where this was heading. And fight or no fight, Jett couldn't lose the data and equipment in her pack.

Sure enough, there was a gangly guy in a yellow t-shirt, staring wide-eyed at Jett from between the horse's ears. His mouth was agape, stammering nonsensically.

Taking advantage of the surprise, Jett put her hands on the rump of the horse, spread her legs, and leaped astride as she'd done since she was a bitty child on her babushka's ranch.

Jett could feel the horse's apathy and arthritis between her thighs as she kicked her heel to make the beast move.

The beast *didn't* move.

Jett let curse words string out with her exhale. She just wanted to lay on the goat skin bed and drink tea. She was cold. And tired. And her head was freaking pounding.

Okay, option number two.

Pressing into her hands as they splayed across the horse's bony butt, Jett popped her feet under her and stood on the horse's back.

"She's here. I have her here!"

Okay, confirmation—*she* was the target. Jett would figure out the how and why later.

Six against one. If she couldn't get to the top of the boulder, she'd *have* to fight.

One thing Jett had determined, this wasn't an official act on the part of the government, or the men wouldn't be worried about the police.

Nor were they from the Zoric family, or they wouldn't have mentioned the need to bribe the cops.

There were the weird details about the chores, and the sweets… Jett had questions. The first and most important being—would this somehow blow her op?

Bending her legs, Jett used the added height of standing on the horse's back to jump up. Grabbing a ridge on the rock, Jett dangled over the group gathering below her, their eyes wide with surprise.

The men jumped and tried to grab at her ankles and pull her back down.

Jett's mind was back on her cliff climbing lessons with her parents, hearing them in her ear, coaching her as she clambered away from the men's hands.

Dangling from a handhold, Jett brought her feet up to either side of the boulder's tube-like structure. Jett started up, using a climbing technique of pressing outward as she frog-hopped her feet, settled them, reached up, and pressed out again.

Now that she was in the narrowed chimney between the boulders, this wasn't a challenging climb. Well, it wouldn't be if she didn't have a thirty-pound backpack cutting into her shoulders.

The group below was trying to angle the horse back so one of the men could stand on it as Jett had.

Jett got herself wedged into the space well enough that she could reach into her thigh pocket and pull out one of the rounded pebbles she collected and kept there for her slingshot. She pitched the stone at the horse with enough of a sting to make the mare angry but not enough to do her harm.

The horse bucked and tugged. The men stepped back.

This was a land of riders. It wouldn't take the men long to get the horse under control and use the mare to reach Jett.

Jett pulled another pebble from her pocket and zinged the horse in the rump.

The horse took off with more energy than Jett could have imagined.

Jett scrambled to the top and looked over the edge. If the men followed her, she'd dispatch them one at a time back over the side of the boulder.

One at a time was fair, she thought as reached for her sheath and pulled out her hunting knife with its razor-sharp edge.

$$3$$

Havoc
Fort Bragg, North Carolina

Friday, Zero Eight Hundred Hours

Delta Force Echo swarmed into the briefing room with its banks of monitors and antiseptic design. Pulling out the khaki-colored roller chairs, their eyes scanned over the array of professionals seated at the front of the U-shaped table formation.

A cadre of officials sat there with stoic faces.

Havoc spotted retired Delta Force Echo member Damian "Deimos" Prescott, now a special agent in charge with the FBI. Their eyes locked as they gave each other a nod of recognition.

The last time Havoc saw Deimos, he'd used those FBI credentials to save Delta Force from an infiltration plot. What was he doing here now? Had they failed to dig out the root of the problem?

Johnna White stood front and center. "Lots of information to hand you, gentlemen. Lots at stake. A quick rundown of those present. I'm Johnna White, and this is my assistant." She pointed to a mousy-looking woman standing in the corner.

The no-named assistant seemed nervous, positioned on the balls of her feet, ready to spring forward on command.

"Colonel Tan, Pentagon. Special Agent in Charge, Damian Prescott, FBI. Calvin Hock, communications specialist, FBI. Lieutenant Colonel Arnold, Asymmetric Warfare Group. Javeed Hasan, DIA"

The men settled into silence.

"First an update on your London trip safeguarding Senator Blankenship. Following the blast and rescue in Beirut, the senator has been at the TJ Monroe Center in Texas, receiving care. Announcements concerning her condition aren't yet available to the public. While the senator maintains her privacy, she and her family wish to extend their heartfelt gratitude for keeping her alive in the Beirut catastrophe. I'm sure you know that T-Rex, Havoc, and Ty are being considered for commendations for their valor during that mission."

Rory, laying under the table next to Ty, thumped his tail on the ground as if applauding. That lightened the mood a bit. But grim was the overall feel from those who showed up for this brief.

"Interestingly, this next mission has a tie into the issues you had in England on the Blankenship protection mission."

Echo leaned in.

The team had been protecting Senator Blankenship on a trip that stopped first in London. There, a group disguised as environmental activists had attempted to make headlines. First, they tried to kill their imbed reporter, Remi Taleb, who was shadowing the trip along with Blankenship's aide. Next, they aimed for the senator.

To what end? Some kind of kidnapping? Assassination? Echo hadn't been told.

"The reason I'm allowed to share this portion of information with you is its connection to the mission we're about to send you out on." She spread her fingers and pushed them into the surface of the table. "We're reading you into a series of events because you might brush up against evidence that would help us connect dots. If you didn't know to look, Echo might walk right by vital information. Information that could thwart one of the biggest and most dangerous issues the military may face in modern warfare."

White paused and let that last phrase grab hold of their attention and imaginations.

"So to focus you," she continued. "This is a search and rescue mission, but let's start with England."

White tapped her computer, and an image came up of T-Rex and Havoc protecting Senator Blankenship as they escaped a violent crowd.

The team had all escaped. Bumps and scrapes were the worst of it. Thankfully.

That attack in England was the second event on a mission that seemed chock full of improbable events.

Hopefully, that wouldn't be true of this operation.

"We believe," White said, tapping her computer to pull up a map of South-Central Asia and the Middle East, "that the person who developed the crowd that attacked the senator was the Zoric family. The family originates from Slovakia, but now they live and operate throughout the southeastern portions of the old USSR countries." White swirled her red laser point across the map. "As well as the Middle East – Lebanon, where you just finished up your assignment. Syria, in the past, though not as much in play since ISIS moved in. Afghanistan, mainly for the poppies. And that's our first lecture for the day. Colonel Tan, if you would." White stretched the laser pen to Tan.

"Gentlemen," he acknowledged Echo. "As the United States and our allies exited Afghanistan, the Taliban quickly gained control. As everyone here is aware, the narco-economy was one of the biggest sources of income for groups such as ISIS and other insurgents, that along with slavery and conflict relics. The allied troops tried but failed to eradicate this stream of income. Importantly, we know that over the twenty years that we were in country, opium cultivation increased. Poppy farming hectares expanded almost thirty-fold. With the troops gone, and the Taliban's power dependent on the will of tribal leaders, we anticipate that this situation might be even more dangerous to world stability than the terrorists themselves, creating a global health crisis. The connection to the Senator Blankenship mission? The Zoric family."

He paused while he looked at the map, then he flicked on the laser pointer. "The Zoric family has interests laced throughout this region. They are supporters of militants in Lebanon. Senator Blankenship was supposed to deliver messages of hope and support from the United States. These messages would not have been well received by certain factions in Beirut. To this end, Scotland Yard is investigating individuals associated with the Zoric family for their efforts in thwarting the senator from delivering her remarks. And this makes sense. The senator was off U.S. soil, visiting an allied nation. These plans were simple and had the potential to be incredibly effective. Had everything not turned in our favor, I can easily see how the senator might just disappear. With the Lebanon trip thwarted, all eyes would be on England. And that would have been quite the coup for the Zorics. It was close. Outstanding effort."

Echo gave a nod accepting the remarks.

"The Zoric family has been doing an excellent job of running under the radar. Though you might have read about an FBI sting that scooped up an entire branch of the family in the Washington D.C. area. It's been what, almost two years ago now?" Tan focused on Deimos and gave him a nod.

Havoc wondered if Deimos had been involved in that case or

if Tan was merely acknowledging the FBI's success in dealing with the family.

"One thing we do know about the Zoric family is that they are associated with crime families that proliferated under the USSR. Now that the USSR is no longer intact, the families have slotted their specialties. They try to stay in their own lane so as not to step on toes and get into mafia-style wars."

"And the Zoric specialty is heroin?" T-Rex asked.

"No, the Zorics have bigger plans," White said. "They use narcotics to fund those plans. You will be briefed on that momentarily."

Tan moved the red dot over the map regions as he called them out. "Specific to the Zoric family, they have drug routes all in this Central Asian area: Turkmenistan, Uzbekistan, Tajikistan, Kyrgyzstan. Places that are black holes to most Americans. They simply don't exist in most people's awareness, no one's paying attention. These routes lead into Europe." He swept the laser up to the west. "These into China." He moved the dot from Afghanistan north through Tajikistan, where he swirled the laser over Kyrgyzstan then east to China. Lastly." Tan drew the laser across Turkey into the Mediterranean. "This is the route to get the drugs onto ships headed for North America."

"Where are we deploying?" T-Rex asked.

White stood up. "Colonel, if I may."

Tan nodded.

"Kyrgyzstan." She scrolled and tapped to bring up a map showing the boundaries of the country. "Afghanistan is here in the south of the map, Tajikistan is the next country to the north then here into Kyrgyzstan. The proximity to the opiates is an opportunity for smugglers to move the heroin into the world market. Kyrgyzstan was part of the ancient Silk Road. It has long been a trade route, so it makes sense that smuggling would become part of that country's economy. With the fall of the USSR, the trafficking issues have become major national security headaches. Politico-criminal clans are growing in strength. Bribery. Corruption. Collusion. This means that the authorities are part of the illegal smuggling structure. Power protects and is enriched by the drug trade." White sat down.

Tan took the pointer back. "Criminal organizations, like the Zoric family, are ramping up their efforts to move narcotics from Afghanistan to produce money for their enterprises and destabilize first-world countries. It's believed that sixty thousand kilos of heroin move through Kyrgyzstan each year. That number is expected to grow exponentially now that the Taliban is in power in Afghanistan."

"The search and rescue has to do with drug trafficking?" T-Rex asked.

Tan lifted his chin. "This mission has to do with the Zoric family. This drug information is provided to you so that you understand that the Zoric family is operating in the country on various projects. The drugs are their largest money makers. The Zorics have a symbiotic relationship with Kyrgyzstan officials from the local police on up the chain. Your expectation should be that no official will offer you help or cooperation. Indeed, *if* you're discovered operating in their country, you can expect very bad things to go down. Since you will be without communications systems, for the most part, it is imperative that you do what Delta Force does best—think on your feet and roll with the punches."

Dropping into territory where they weren't welcome wasn't new to Echo, but no communications systems? Havoc's brows drew together.

"What is the Zoric's end goal?" T-Rex asked.

"World domination," White said as if those words had laid there on the tip of her tongue, waiting for the opportunity to spring free.

Havoc focused on White to see if there was a gleam in her eye to show she was teasing, but no. Her face said that was precisely their goal.

Tan's phone buzzed in his pocket. He looked down at it briefly then raised his brows at White. White nodded, and Tan left. Havoc assumed that there had been some kind of communication between them beforehand, that Tan spoke first because he was due elsewhere.

"Drugs aren't your goal," White said as the door shut behind Tan. "We simply wanted you to understand that this is *not* a country where we have sway. Relationships are transactional. Unpredictable. It's unwise and unsafe to trust anyone. For anything. And with that being said, I would like to introduce Calvin Hock, FBI communications expert. He's going to tell you about an event that happened on U.S. soil in a joint operation between Iniquus Security's Strike Force and the FBI. I am aware that you all know Strike Force from their intervention at Fort Bragg."

Echo nodded.

"Calvin is fine. Call me Calvin," the man said as he stood. "I'm not part of or privy to your mission." He swiped his hand down his tie. "I won't be addressing that. But I do have some background. I'm here because Ms. White thought the story I'm about to share might give you a solid understanding of why the FBI, the DIA, the CIA, and others are all scrambling." He licked his lips. "Everyone who knows about this…we're all…scrambling."

Calvin was an interesting-looking character. He reminded Havoc of a childhood book that he'd loved when he was a little kid. In this book, the pages were cut into three sections so the head, the torso, and the legs could be mixed and matched to make funny images.

Calvin had a professorial countenance with a substantial amount of wiry hair. He looked like he was churning through an enormous amount of data that he stored in his over-sized head. Deep-set lines mapped his forehead. And he looked like he'd swallowed something acidic.

From the neck down, Calvin was built like a marathoner. His body was much younger looking than his face. It didn't fit together. And that, in Havoc's mind, made him memorable and therefore not a great person to have out in the field.

Calvin's gaze scanned across the room to the whiteboard. "Can I use that?" he asked.

Burnside opened his hand by way of invitation. So far, Echo's commanding officer, Lieutenant Colonel Burnside, had sat in scowling silence.

"Two years ago," Calvin said, "Strike Force was working with the FBI to find a group of Somali nationals that had disappeared on American soil. The whys and wherefores of that case are not important to this story. Basic background: An American group called the D.O.A. corralled the Somalis and brought them to an underground mine to hold them hostage. Unfortunately, the mine gases, trapped in pockets, were lethal to both the captors and the captees. It was nearly lethal for Strike Force as well." Calvin pulled the top off the whiteboard marker, pressed it back on with a click, pulled it back off, looking like he was trying to line his thoughts up. And looking grim.

"In Strike Force's attempt to rescue the Somalis, two of their members were shot outside of the mine entrance. Those who went into the mine were able to escape before the gas suffocated them. All the Strike Force members needed medical attention except for their communications guy, Blaze, who was at Iniquus Headquarters monitoring the op, and their puzzler, Lynx, who was off campus during the incident. Strike Force radioed for medical help. They believed that Blaze had informed them of a ten-minute ETA for the paramedics. Strike Force members were *not*, in fact, communicating with Blaze or anyone from Iniquus. The team had radioed in their change of coordinates but their transmission, having been intercepted, was not received by Blaze. No one at Iniquus knew their location or that life-or-death injuries had been sustained by Strike Force members."

"What did Blaze hear?" Dice asked.

"Static." Calvin frowned. "Without comms, Panther Force deployed to track them down."

"But someone was communicating with Strike Force?" T-Rex asked.

"Bingo." Calvin pointed at T-Rex.

Havoc was a little lost. If he had been communicating with one of his teammates, he sure would know if someone else started addressing the team over the comms. They'd know their communications were compromised.

"Since this was an FBI-contracted op, I headed the team that tried to figure out what happened," Calvin said. "The ramifications for law enforcement, the military, well, everyone really, are *dire*."

The door popped open. A man with an arm full of files seemed startled to find a room full of people. He pulled his head back, looked at the number over the door, turned, and closed the door with, "my apologies."

"Deep fakes are on the horizon," Calvin said. "Photographs that have been photoshopped, we're familiar with. A guy on Tik Tok kept putting up videos that never said they were of the high-status actor Tom Corbine, but everyone sure *thought* they were. Imagine a guy who is a Tom Corbine impersonator. He developed the body movements—the gesticulations and what have you—and his facial expressions. Then a guy, a filmmaker, videos the impersonator doing short scenes—washing dishes and the like. The filmmaker goes back to his editing room, looks through footage of the actor, finds examples of the actor making the same face as the impersonator. The film editor then cuts the face from the rest of the actor's footage. Are you following me? The filmmaker cut out the real actor's face from video footage and… I think the term is 'sewing.' He sewed a video of the real actor's face onto the video of the impersonator's face. And it is nearly impossible to tell that it is a deep fake." Calvin twirled the marker in the air. "I tell you that story to show you how easy it would be for someone to deep fake sound technology. If a bad actor taped Blaze communicating—'Wilco. Affirmative. I read you loud and clear.' The bad actor could simply record that, tap a button, and insert Blaze responding."

"Only for things he's said, though, right?" Ty asked.

"No." Calvin shook his head emphatically. "Once the computer has enough of a voice sample, the bad actor could speak into a mic, the mic would filter through the program to replicate the inflection, accent, tone, etcetera, and it will sound to the listener as if they are hearing Blaze in real-time."

"But they had an open line between their communications and the team, right? How would that work?" T-Rex leaned forward, his focus sharp.

"That's where this thing gets really interesting in a dystopic-kind of way," Calvin said.

Havoc was grinding his back teeth while he took this in. His mind wanted to spin forward with all the ramifications of communications glitches that meant command had no idea what was happening, and teams were misinformed while on a life-threatening mission like what had happened to Strike Force—a team that was the same size as Echo.

"The speculation is that the whole episode was created on purpose by the external forces. We conjecture that the entire incident, all the deaths, was to test a means of hijacking communications. We are investigating the Zorics possible connection to the case of the mine. Evidence in hand suggests the Zorics hired Omega Security to help carry out the ground game."

"Omega operatives were the shooters?" Havoc asked.

Omega Security were American mercenaries who created more problems than they solved for special forces in theater around the world.

"Yes, that's right. Our speculation is," Calvin continued, "that the entire incident had nothing to do with those who were captured. Nothing to do with those who did the kidnapping and pulled everyone down into the mine. It had everything to do with *testing* a system on a group of military professionals. What we know about Iniquus Security is that they fill their ranks with ex-special forces operators. Striker Rheas leads Strike Force. He had been in SEAL Team Six. Their team has other retired SEALs, Marine Raiders, and so forth, all highly capable, highly prepared, and equipped with the best that can be had. It makes sense that if an enemy were testing their system that this would show them if their capabilities were enough to thwart the mission."

"Some kind of jammer?" T-Rex asked. "That would make sense with the static that Blaze received. But that would make no sense with the deep fake that you've described."

"So much worse than just a jammer." Calvin started drawing on the whiteboard. "This blob is a satellite. Sorry. My art skills haven't improved since kindergarten. But here is a communications satellite." He tapped his drawing. "Strike Force was using satellite communications that were encrypted end to end. The communications went up." He drew arrows on the board. "But were rerouted to the rogue actors." He licked his lips and inhaled, looking at his drawing. "The intended recipient, Blaze, got static."

"Wait," T-Rex said. "Communications are call and response. The words are encrypted. How would the players know how to respond?"

Calvin waggled a finger in the air. "This isn't someone with a radio set playing around. This is *highly* sophisticated. They have to have AI systems that could unencrypt in real-time. We believe they took samples of Blaze's voice. They fed that information into an AI system that replicates voices. When the response was a typical 'wilco' or 'roger,' they simply played that. When there was more, they could have someone speak into the computer mic. The computer would change the speaker's voice to sound like Blaze's voice. We have the stored communications from the incident. We were able to put it through our own AI analysis. The generated voice is indistinguishable from the authentic speaker."

The men's postures were rigid as they focused. Looking at the blob on the white board, it seemed innocuous, the ramifications of these capabilities could create world chaos.

"Back to my picture. A signal goes up to a transponder. There it is cleaned, amplified, and retransmitted. You all know how this works. Don't mean to dummy this down. But I want to make sure… well, anyway." He shook his head as if changing gears. "If a rogue actor wants to intercept a communication, all they need is the satellites' location, which is easy enough to find with an online search. They figure out the input frequency. Then they need to generate more power for their transmissions to override an authentic transmission to the satellite."

White took a step forward. "That's what we want you to be on the lookout for, the antenna that would allow the," she looked over at Calvin, "rogue actor, if you will, to push out enough juice that it could take over the satellite."

"Is this what happened in Ukraine when Russia was involved in the incursion?" T-Rex asked. "They experienced a communication dead zone."

"We believe that's what happened to the communications then. *And* since. We think the Zorics are quietly testing different scenarios, getting ready for some big event. We want to take them down before their plan unfolds," Calvin concluded.

"High priority on that," White said. "This is *not* just true of troops and militaries that could be impacted but, say, commercial planes. A few have gone missing in the last few years. Poof. And we think it has to do with someone gaining control of the satellites and miscommunicating with the pilots. The same is true of US Navy ships having collisions in the open oceans, and more recently, a sub grounding in the South China Sea. The satellites inform our GPS technologies. We follow the GPS readings. Especially when we don't have landmarks, we trust that the coordinates given are accurate. They may be far from accurate if tampered with by rogue players."

The tension in the room amplified with each new piece of information. This capability would be catastrophic to world order.

"Now," White said, "think this through. Troops are monitored via complex computer algorithms associated with GPS. This helps prevent friendly fire incidents. If someone is controlling the satellite and the GPS coordinates, what havoc could ensue?"

White looked over at Havoc. "Not the good kind like you bring. I mean the destructive apocalyptic kind."

Havoc's face was frozen as he churned over these ideas.

"As we're out on a separate mission, we're to keep an eye out for massive radio towers?" T-Rex said.

"Maybe." Calvin blinked. "Actually, we're not sure what it is they're using. But a tower and a dish would be my best guess."

We need you to save the world by looking for *something*. We just don't know what it is you're looking for…

That was one heck of a challenging mission.

But White had started with "this is a search and rescue." Just who were they going after?

4

JETT

Arslanbob, Kyrgyzstan

Friday, Twenty-One Thirty Hours

The men had expected a fight, planned for it, and worked to gather their courage.

The horse made sense to Jett, she guessed. None of them—or even all of them working as a group—were in any kind of physical shape to carry her, kicking and fighting, down the mountain on a forty-minute trek.

But, once she was up on top of the boulder, they were out of ideas. The frigid wind quickly turned them around. The descending night finished off any lingering good-idea fairies that might have been flitting around their pea brains. They tramped down the mountain, heads hanging low.

Forty minutes was the amount of time it took Jett to get back to the guest house. Granted, she was making her way down using night vision goggles, but still, she was pretty fast.

The mare they borrowed was a sad specimen, and Jett wasn't

convinced that even the horse could have made it with her hundred and thirty pounds on its back, let alone another hundred and thirty-ish for that guy, Marat, to hold her, bound up like an infant in a bunting blanket, across his lap.

Yeah, that horse just didn't have it in her.

Jett vaguely wondered if that horse was running the mountains of Kyrgyzstan after Jett spooked the mare by throwing pebbles or if it knew where its oats were found and raced back down to the guy at the walnut shop.

And here, Jett had thought of that man as someone she was friendly with. For sure, Jett had to market there. There were no other options in this part of the country. Jett would just pretend none of this ever happened. But she'd go armed with her knife from now on.

The woman who ran the guest house was more troubling. Did the hostess know what the men were up to when she told them about Jett's schedule and route?

Shoot, even Jett wasn't sure what the men were up to. According to the men, she was going to cry, fight, then agree. They'd feed her frybread. There were chores involved. All Jett wanted to do was check her body for a tick that might have infected her with a terrible disease, leaving her with a sore neck and throbbing head.

Jett simply wanted to take some pain meds and go to bed.

But bed wouldn't be safe if the men were staging to snag her there.

Jett didn't have options. Tomorrow, she had to be there to send her postcard. It was Jett's signal to her handler, letting her handler know she was safe and what grid she'd be searching next.

Perhaps they would send a message regarding the status of her search partner, Renée.

It had been better with the two of them working the same task. Easier. Safer.

This week alone on the mountain had taxed Jett physically and emotionally.

Bed was calling.

Thinking that she'd have to sit up all night watching for kidnappers wasn't appealing. Nor was sleeping on the roof.

Jett had decided to confront the elderly woman. Figure out what had happened on the mountain with that pack of men. Then, Jett would make a decision on how to proceed.

Reaching up to massage her neck and the back of her head, she whispered, "Please don't be encephalitis." Jett wouldn't be this paranoid had Renée not just been poisoned by a viper.

In the last communication, Jett was told that if not Renée, someone would be sent so that Jett wouldn't be alone in the field. Buddy system and all that. Hopefully, it would be someone good —someone who knew their way around mountainous terrain, someone who didn't gripe the whole time. The only thing worse than being out on a mission alone was being out on a mission with a whiner.

Carefully approaching the ancient house, Jett found her host feeding sticks into the clay oven in the garden. A tea pot sat on a trivet. A glance at the wood pile told Jett that the woman had used up most of what fuel Jett had purchased last Saturday. There was still enough for them to cook their breakfast.

With no one else around, Jett made noises as she went through the gate so as not to startle the woman as she muttered over her task.

The woman looked up and nodded, then gestured toward the kettle as steam shot out of its spout.

"Yes, thank you. I'm going to take my pack in. I'll be just a moment," Jett said in Russian. With her hand on the pommel of her hunting knife, Jett moved slowly through the kitchen door, clearing each room in the simple cottage. When she got to her room, Jett unlocked the bolt, pushed her way in, and shucked the pack to slide it under the bed. She pulled out her suitcase and noticed that the lock was still locked, and the ribbon she had allowed to drape out of the case was still an exact one-inch length. Spycraft 101: laying traps to see where people had gone and what they had done in her absence.

Pulling off her boots, her heavy wool socks, and sock liners, Jett wiggled her toes, feeling relief. She took a moment to think of a strategy for asking about the men's ambush on the mountain. As Jett shoved her feet into her yellow shower shoes, Jett decided to tell the story and ask straight out what that was all about.

Of all the things the men had said, bribing the police with a mere sweet to turn their heads on a kidnapping was the thing that made Jett feel the most vulnerable. After all, with Renée out of the picture, there was no one to get messages out that help was needed.

She could just—poof—disappear.

On the day the viper bit Renée, there was a horseback-riding tour group moving through the area. Jett and Renée had kept their eye on them throughout the day, tracking their movements through their binoculars. When Renée slipped on the rock, frightening the snake, it sprang at her, sinking its fangs into her calf muscle.

Jett killed and bagged the snake for the doctors to identify, then she sprinted across the fields to intersect the tourists. One of the Kyrgyz men peeled off to help get Renée back down the mountain to a shop with a phone. Luck. Sheer happy luck.

Over the months Jett had been traipsing the mountains, Jett's seeing anyone was a rarity over a certain elevation.

Jett was unprepared for the melancholy that swept over her as she thought about the potential bad outcome from today. To be lost. In need. And no one would know unless somehow she had pressed the SOS button on her sat phone. But that was last-ditch because it would blow her op.

Well, there were the postcards that she sent out each Saturday. They went somewhere. Ostensibly, someone at the AWG was paying attention.

Jett had been recruited seven years ago by the Asymmetric Warfare Group (AWG)—a division of the Army based out of Fort Meade in Maryland—when Jett decided to move on to a new challenge after years of being a smokejumper out west.

Yes, she worked for the most advanced, out-of-the-box thinking specialists in the United States armed forces, and still, their only communication with the mothership AWG, was old-school postcards.

The AWG dealt with rogue weirdness. And this mission was the motherlode of weirdness. Their team of six mock scientists, divided into three "research teams," were hunting for a thing. A big thing. But no one knew what the "thing" was.

Let's say the men successfully dragged me off the mountain, Jett thought, and they took me to god knows where. No postcard from me would arrive this week to my AWG commander.

If Jett's postcard failed to show up, someone with the AWG would come and check things out, go out to her last grid to look around. In Jett's experience, while search and rescue was the application of science, it almost always came down to dumb luck, like the tourists riding horses out to nomadic yurts at the perfect time to help Renée when she needed them. It was a little bit like a miracle.

Jett slapped her knees and stood, time to go find out if it was safe to sleep tonight.

"Tetushka," Jett said, moving through the door to the garden. Tetushka meant 'auntie' in Russian, and that was the name Jett's host asked Jett to call her. "Something very strange happened to me today."

The old woman wrapped a piece of leather around the kettle

handle and poured tea into two cups. She came and sat with Jett. "Tell me."

Jett decided to just lay it out, what the men said, how she had responded. How the men left, almost in tears, without having captured the horse.

"The horse will find its way home. Don't let that bother you."

"Good. I'm glad. But the men? Will they come here?" Jett watched very closely to see how the woman would respond. Not the words, but her eyes and her face. Honestly, she looked grief-stricken.

"You are safe in the house. It's only out in the streets or out in the open like on the mountain that you're at risk."

Jett scowled.

"The men didn't come to speak to me. A woman, a young woman, approached me as I was making bread a few days ago. She talked to me about you. She seemed to know who you were but not how to find you. I believed she was a friend or someone that you worked with on your science. Had it been the men, I would have said nothing."

Jett blew across the top of her cup to cool the tea.

"Come look." Tetushka placed her cup on the oven, lifted the oil lamp, then moved into the house.

When Jett caught up, the host was standing, looking at a picture of a woman.

"She's beautiful," Jett said.

Tetushka put a hand over her heart. "My only child. My daughter. She is long dead. She was traditionally kidnapped and forced to be a bride."

Traditionally kidnapped? Yes, it sounded like the men were moving through a traditional rite of passage. They'd mentioned their families preparing a feast.

"Kidnapping a bride—this is an old tradition. A guy grabs his friends, and they steal a woman off the streets. He takes her back to the mother and aunts to convince her that she should marry the guy. In rural areas, nearly half of all weddings happen by kidnapping the bride. This is on the rise."

"But isn't that a violation of Islam?"

"Yes."

"And is it lawful?"

"No. Here, tradition is the most important thing. More than religion. More than law. This is an ancient tradition."

"Ancient?" The people of Kyrgyzstan were nomadic herding families. Would they just swoop into a family group, grab up a girl, and ride off with her? Would the families allow that?

"Not so ancient, truly," Tetushka said. "I spoke with my mother about this before she died. I am an old woman. My mother, she was born in 1908. She remembers well what life was like before the USSR. And before the USSR, things were very bad for young girls. The families would work to have a bride's price. The marriages were arranged. The girls were married very young. They were considered women and marriageable once their moon cycles began. The young girls were given to older men. My mother was only twelve when she was given to my father, who was almost fifty. Since my mother didn't have much in the way of a dowry, and they had many, many girls in the family, her parents, my grandparents, felt that this marriage was the best that they could do for her. Fortunately, my mother was not fertile. She did not get pregnant until she was in her late twenties. I was her only child."

"Is that how you got married, too?" Jett leaned her shoulder into the wall. Exhaustion slackened the muscles in her face. Her bed was calling to her, but Jett didn't feel safe.

"No, right after my mother's marriage, that system no longer existed. Things changed when we became part of the USSR. The USSR wanted good things for girls, but this led to bad things in the end."

"Yes? Can you tell me about that?"

"No marriages before the age of fifteen."

"That's similar to laws where I come from. But typically, our brides are much older."

"That is what happened here. The USSR and tradition butted heads like the mountain rams. Under the USSR, both boys and girls were encouraged to go to high school and college. I know you will not believe me, but I went to school to become a lawyer. Oh, so many years ago." Tetushka curled her fingers to bid Jett follow her back out to the garden. "Higher education isn't what happened before the USSR made the new rules. Girls stayed home and worked with their mothers learning to do womanly tasks. Schooling was not so important. There was also the change in the money. There was no family money—no more dowry."

"What do you mean there was no family money?"

"It went to the collective good. No family gathered wealth. No wealth, no bride price. Even ugly girls, girls with rotten teeth or slow brains could find a husband if there was a big enough dowry. A big enough dowry and someone would step up." Tetushka smoothed her skirt and squatted on the outdoor mat with her cup of tea balanced on her bent knee.

Jett did the same. "A dowry helped a girl with rotting teeth find a husband. I see. But why did this butt heads with tradition? How does this have anything to do with kidnapping women for marriage?"

"I will tell you what happened to me. When I finished secondary school, I went off to the city to attend college, to study. There, I met a man that I fell in love with. We were so happy when we were together. I was so excited about spending my life with him. But..." She looked off into the distance. "We went home so that my parents could meet him. My parents said no. They had already selected a man for me, and the families had agreed. My parents forced me to marry their selection, and I was not able to return to school. I never saw the man I loved again."

"Did you consider this kidnapping? Didn't the guy you were in love with try to help you?"

"Kidnapping? No. I conceded to my parents' wishes. Girls in my country are taught obedience. It is deep within our souls that we must obey. I felt I had no choice. My dear friend, Aida, from college, was much more brazen, courageous, and strong. Aida was my friend who came to my home to see me and find out what happened so that she could tell my beloved. My friend and I grew up together and knew each other very well. When Aida went back to school and told the tale to her boyfriend, Aida, and the man she wished to marry, came up with a plan. He and his friends pretended to kidnap Aida from the streets in front of everyone. There were rumors that this was done in other parts of the country. They say that the tradition of bride kidnappings comes from the time of Khan when there was tribal thievery. But I am old enough to remember the truth."

"Your friend Aida told her boyfriend to kidnap her?"

"Yes. Yes. And take her to his family's compound to stay the night with him. A woman who sleeps with a man out of the marriage was considered dishonored. No man would marry an unclean bride. Aida came to visit after all was done. She told me how the elderly men from Aida's husband's family went to tell Aida's parents what had occurred. The parents arranged for the man to marry Aida to keep the peace and to preserve her honor. The parents weren't happy that had happened, but what could they do? My friend lived a long life with the man she loved."

"And your husband from the arranged marriage?"

"Was a harsh man. A violent worthless man. I should have had the courage to do what Aida did. Then maybe my life would have been different. The kidnappings, over time, became the way that things are now done here in my country. No longer the way it was originally in place—a means to get around an arranged marriage —but just that a man saw a woman he wanted, and he and his friends snatched her from the streets."

"Okay, so much of what the men on the mountain were saying makes sense to me now. I don't think they realize I'm American, and the story would have unfolded badly."

"I wish for this to stop. The women who are kidnapped into marriage, they are more unhappy. Their faces are sad like mine was. And they commit suicide more. My daughter—" the woman gestured toward the house to remind Jett that she'd seen her daughters' photograph. "This happened to my beautiful Chynara. She could not stand the man who kidnapped her, and she killed herself. We went after her to try to have her returned to us. But she had agreed and wed. They gave me a goat. I wanted my daughter."

"I'm sorry for your loss."

The old woman stared into her tea with a deep frown.

"Is this your marriage home? Did Chynara grow up here?"

"This is the home that belonged to my parents. I lived in Osh with my husband. Thirty years ago, Kyrgyz and Uzbeks fought in the city of Osh. A group of Kyrgyz demanded that an Uzbek collective farm be given to them. The Uzbeks said no. There was violence. Friends came to my apartment. Pounding on my door, they said I should leave with my daughter. So I did. I gathered what I could grab at a moment's notice. Pictures, what little I had of value. I piled it onto a cloth with a few clothes. I put all the food I could into a pot with a lid. I tied the lid down with my husband's belt."

"Where was your husband?"

"Drinking vodka. Always drinking vodka with the men."

"I'm sorry to interrupt you. You were gathering your things."

"I tied the corners of the cloth together. I put this on my head. I hugged the pot in my arms. My Chynara grabbed blankets. A thoughtful child. Yes. This was good. Very good. We raced into the streets, and my neighbor slowed his car. We piled in with his family, and he drove us into the countryside. We were afraid to light a fire, so all of us huddled beneath the blankets my daughter brought with us. We shared our body warmth. Then I went home. My husband had been shot dead. My home was burned to the ground. I was free of the bad marriage, but I was not free from poverty. I returned here to my childhood home and helped my mother until she died, and then I was here with my daughter."

"Have you seen anything in this area that would make you feel afraid?"

"How is this?" Tetushka canted her head.

"Maybe people who are outsiders coming into the area?"

"Like you?"

"I'm not violent," Jett said with a shrug. "I'm here to figure out what's happening to the weather and how we should protect the Walnut Forest from burning."

"When you find this, will you come tell me?"

"I will," Jett promised, feeling terrible for her lie.

"This isn't a place where many come. Though, some tourists want to hike to the waterfalls. And they want to see the Walnut Forest. But they come, and they go again right away. I think they spook at night."

A shutter ran down Jett's spine.

"Yes, see? You are susceptible to the spooks."

"Is there a specific spook, or is it just … What is it that makes people feel afraid?"

"Did you know that this is where they think the black plague originated?"

"No. I… didn't."

"Many bad things. When I was a child, my school friends died so easily. We did not have the children's shots yet. But in my mother's time. Back in World War I, there was a very bad flu.

They call this a pandemic. The sickness was all over the world. People died just one after the other."

"I've studied this." Jett nodded. "We call it the Spanish flu."

"There was a whole village of people who got sick with this. With everyone so ill, there was no one left who was able to help. No one to cook the food. No one to pump the water from the wells. No wood was gathered for warmth. They all died. Every single one of them. We knew this was happening, but my family was sick, too. Me, I hear this story, and it makes me stay away from the hills at night. The ghosts."

"From the village?" Jett pulled her brows together.

"They were not given the proper burials. The prayers weren't said. So evil was allowed in. The village was no longer clean and sacred. The bodies were left to be eaten by the bugs and scavenger animals. It is a village of skeletons. Then, there was a great landslide that sealed off the roadway. Allah made sure that no one would accidentally drive by and be haunted."

"Oh." Jett was hearing this story for the first time. She'd take out a map in the morning and have Tetushka show her all of the haunted areas. They might be places that Jett should avoid. And they might just be the areas that she and her fellow AWG operators should investigate.

Jett said softly, "I have to camp in the mountains when I do my science."

"Ah, well, you should leave a letter for your loved ones in case you don't come back."

5

Fort Bragg, North Carolina

Friday, Ten Forty Hours

White thanked Calvin, and he nodded to the room, gathered his keys and notepad, and left.

Havoc still didn't have much to go on in terms of this new assignment. Search and rescue, Kyrgyzstan, no comms, with a background of doomsday.

White nodded to the person introduced merely as White's assistant. That person walked around laying manila envelopes in front of each man with their call signs Sharpied across the top.

"These are your cover personas. You'll have time to memorize them on the plane." She pointed to the corner of the room at a pile of varied travel bags. "I've packed you up based on mission needs and the role that you're playing."

She tapped her laptop, and six pictures were arrayed across the screen, three females, three males. "We divided these six Asymmetric Warfare Group operators into three teams." She nodded toward Lieutenant Colonel Arnold in his crisp uniform. "All of these operators have science backgrounds and were given scientific tasks to perform, data to collect, so that they had cover for being in country."

Havoc focused on the DIA guy, Hasan. He looked like he was there to listen not offer insights. Compared to his FBI and AWG counterparts, this guy didn't look official. His hair was collar-length and brushed straight back. He had a European slickness to him that stuck out as odd in this Army base setting.

Though Havoc, Ty, and T-Rex had been clean-cut and shaven for their mission protecting Senator Blankenship, their team usually went for the long hair and full beards of the hot spots where they would have to drop and blend. As a blond, Havoc had a tough time with the blending and often ended up dying the hair on his head and his facial hair dark brown. Havoc rubbed a hand over his short-cropped hair, blond for the moment.

With the pointer dancing over the six pictures, White said, "Split into three groups, our operators have been scouring the Chatkal Mountains of Kyrgyzstan for the means by which the satellites are being compromised. Again, we don't know what it is they're looking for other than big."

The men shifted in their seats.

"Let me clarify the situation on the ground. There is no GPS, no internet connectivity, no cell phones in this area of the world. You will only communicate through satellite as a last-ditch effort to survive, and then you will speak in code. I'll go over that in a bit. We kept in touch with the three AWG teams via postcards. Each Saturday, the postcards are sent. They follow a code to let us know their status and which grid they're working on next."

"Search parameters weren't defined at the outset?" T-Rex asked

"They were," Arnold replied, squinting toward Echo's master

chief, sending the message that T-Rex was stepping close to the boundaries.

T-Rex didn't care. If he was sending his team out, T-Rex was asking the questions that needed to be asked. That's how Delta Force trained. Everyone put their thoughts and concerns on the table to be reviewed. Experience had taught them that sharing their thoughts and using this hive mind strategy to explore potential potholes or cliff edges in their new assignments made their missions safer and more productive.

"We also gave the teams latitude to make decisions," Arnold continued. "If, for example, there were conditions that made it better to postpone, such as severe weather, or maybe there was a reason to skip and go back to a grid location—a landslide, unrest, a wolf pack moving through. So we leave it to those on the ground to know best how to navigate within their deployment area."

"Which means that if this is search and rescue," T-Rex said, "we can't assume they were working within a specified area."

"Correct. All we have to go on is their postcards, sent once a week on a Saturday. On these cards—couched as updates to a friend staying just to the south in Jalal-Abad—the teams indicate their physical and mental state, any need for supplies or resources, the grid area they accomplished with a score for how thoroughly they think they searched it. Those numbers haven't been constructive in that they don't know what they're looking for other than big and in an improbable place. If you please." Arnold held out an open palm, and White handed him the laser pointer.

It reminded Havoc of camp where they would pass the "talking stick." The person who held the baton was the only one allowed to speak.

Arnold stared at the screen for an overlong moment, then lifted his pointer and circled the top two female's pictures. "This is Jett. And Renée." He turned toward Echo. "Jett is still in the field. Eight days ago, on Thursday the sixteenth, Renée was bitten by a viper, was evacuated off the mountain, and is receiving medical care."

White leaned forward. "Vipers in the area, be aware. I'll go over some of the other creepy crawlies and furries with sharp teeth, so you're forewarned before you go." She smiled her wicked smile.

Arnold waited for a moment to see if White had finished, then continued. "Each of the teams comes down from their work area on a Friday night, preferably. They stay at local accommodations to speak to, be seen by, and develop rapport with the locals to see if the folks living in that area have useful information to pass along."

"The operators speak Kyrgyz?" T-Rex asked.

"Russian. This works for the most part, especially with the over-fifty population, which is the group that we would focus on. Renée is not returning to this assignment." He looked at Havoc. "When you get to Jett, tell her that Renée and her doctors think that the damage to her muscles needs more time to recover—if, indeed, she were able to fully recover."

Havoc noticed that he was picked out for that bit of information. Looked like he was assigned to Jett. "She's operating on the mountain in a male-centered socio-political system alone?" Havoc asked, surprised. From this photograph, if she were appropriately dressed, she probably could pass for a local, except, perhaps, that she had fairer skin coloration.

Havoc knew for sure he'd be sticking out like a sore thumb. He hoped his mission story was backpacking college grad or something reasonable.

Arnold turned back to the screen. "This is Deepak on the left and Scott on the right. Deepak was exfiltrated for medical reasons on Sunday the fifth. Deepak's issues had nothing to do with the environment, so I'll leave the reasons to privacy. Scott is accompanied by a military working dog, a German shepherd Rottweiler mix. I'm told this is a 'shepweiler.' His name is 'Digger.' As of the fifth, all was well with Digger and Scott."

Rory thumped his tail approvingly, and Ty chuckled.

"Scott was supposed to have sent a postcard out on Saturday the eleventh, thirteen days ago. He also missed sending a postcard last Saturday, the eighteenth. The teams were instructed to get information out as soon as possible if they missed the drop. That way, if there were an issue on the mountain, and they were a day or two behind, we wouldn't pull together a Delta Force team to go in after them." Arnold stopped to scowl. "We sent in Deepak's replacement, another AWG operator."

"What date was this?" T-Rex asked.

"The replacement rented a room at the guest house serving as base for Scott on Friday the tenth and stayed until the eighteenth. He did some day hikes in various directions and found no signs of Scott or K9 Digger. We pulled that operator back out. People just hanging out in this area is not common and would call too much attention. We didn't want another single person heading up the mountainside looking for Scott. This calls for a team."

T-Rex pulled up a calendar on his phone. "If he were in the backcountry, he could have run into issues as many as eighteen days ago. Twenty days from the point when we can get boots on the ground." T-Rex leaned forward. "Are they equipped for that length of time in the backcountry?"

"It depends on how they ration," Arnold said. "Where the issue took place. What the problem is. In Scott's case, something might have happened on his way back on that Friday night, and he was only impeded two weeks ago."

"But that might actually be worse," Nitro said.

Arnold raised his eyebrows in a question, asking Nitro what he meant.

"If a guy goes down at the beginning of his rations, he's

sparing with what's in his pack. A man is coming off the mountain, and he chows down on the last of his food and isn't cautious with his water because that's excess weight. A one-week pack might be fine for three belly-pinching weeks. An 'I'll be home by dinner' pack might well be empty. He'll be eating his lip balm."

Arnold's jaw clenched, and he stood perfectly still, then seemed to shake off the thought that had momentarily paralyzed him.

The seemingly novel idea that it was the state of the operator's supplies that mattered to survival and not the time downrange made Havoc think that Arnold hadn't spent much time in the field. Havoc would need to keep that in mind when he was making decisions on this mission.

Lieutenant Colonel Arnold coughed into his fist then pointed the laser again. "The last photograph is a husband-and-wife team, Peter and Tina. Tina goes by 'Tink.' Their last postcard came in on the thirtieth of last month. They missed the card due to be sent on the fourth. Nearly a month ago. We sent an operator to their guest house, but they found no signs of the couple. After a week, we pulled that operator out. Then there was Deepak's illness that needed exfil and Renée's incident. Things were getting too hot in this area. Too many eyes were starting to focus on the unusual traffic."

"Jett is acting as a lone operator searching her grid and has been following protocols?" T-Rex asked. "As far as we know, she's fine?"

"Affirmative," White said.

"Scott and K9 Digger are acting alone and disappeared. You've left them out there for possibly three weeks without support," T-Rex continued.

"Again, we can't swarm the area. There are very few visitors," White said without an ounce of defensiveness. "We decided to send you all in." White moved her feet wider and shifted to balance her weight. "All of you will stick out as foreigners. There is no blending. I've provisionally divided your team up. Of course, I have every respect for your leadership, Master Chief Landry." She caught his eye. "Master Chief, if you need anything changed, I'm willing to consult with you."

Havoc thought that was politically expedient, but that she didn't mean anything beyond she would listen to T-Rex and nod her head. White was a logistical micro-manager. Heck, Ty said in his last mission with White, she'd even bought his underwear and socks. Granted, she was outstanding at her job. White expertly manipulated the puzzle pieces, trying to leverage the best advantage for the team going in.

White shifted to take in all of Echo. "The language in this region is primarily Russian. Since T-Rex, Ty, and Havoc speak Russian, I made these decisions. I want at least one fluent speaker on each team."

She focused on Havoc. "You will operate alone. You're simply performing a well-check on Jett. You're a friend of her family. Since you were traveling in the region, you said you'd be happy to swing by and drop off some gifts from home. I have them wrapped and packed for you. You don't know what the family sent. There's no food, alcohol, explosives, and so forth, so you need not worry about that going through customs. Once you make contact, you'll tell Jett about Renée and bring Jett to Jalal-Abad. That's the nearest city. We've set up a TOC—tactical operations center—in an apartment there. Now, we're trying to get you in place as fast as we can. You need to be there before Monday morning. I know that window is short. If we can't get you in place until Monday, we'll wait for Jett's postcard to arrive in Jalal-Abad and figure out what area she's working this next week. You'll have to catch up to her."

"Yes, ma'am." Sure, Havoc could ramble up and down a

mountain grid trying to find the woman who was trained to not be found. Already Havoc didn't love this planning.

"Two-man team, Ty with K9 Rory and Nitro, will go after Scott," White continued. "The rest of you will be searching for Peter and Tink. I'm leaving it up to you, T-Rex. You may want to split that team further to spread your search wider. But with the limited number of operators, I feel I can get into the country under these circumstances without floating up any red flags, we'll work with what we have. Please, let's not make this op last longer than six months. That's the amount of time you can be in-country without a visa."

T-Rex frowned. "Is that a possibility?"

"Not if you do your jobs properly." White's swipe didn't go over well. She probably read that in Echo's posture because she added, "No. We can't leave you there that long. It's too obvious. Our sending you in at all is problematic. Anything we do could further compromise this operation. Now, because of local laws, very few people have gun permits in Kyrgyzstan. Those who have them usually have hunting rifles. The only way to get a gun in your hand is on a sanctioned hunt, and the government has shut that down to allow the animal populations to rebound. All that's to say, like in England when you were protecting Senator Blankenship, there are no guns on this mission."

"Yeah, and that went really well, didn't it?" Nitro muttered under his breath.

White heard. "Can you imagine if Echo had shot someone? Better that you used your other skills. And that's what we're asking of you here and now. If you get eyes on our people, we'll revisit our strategy. Right now, you're tourists. You're hiking."

"And I'm the family friend. Wouldn't it be easier if Jett were married to me? We've operated in a lot of Muslim countries and a single man looking for a single woman—" Havoc shook his head.

Talk about raising people's awareness. That might be the thing that brought all the eyes to the situation.

"We can't run that scenario," White said. "First, Jett didn't know that she had a husband and would have spoken to people as a single female. Second, once a woman is married, they display their marital status. In this area, typically, the wife wears a scarf over her hair, we could get around that because Jett is from America and doesn't choose to wear a scarf, but then, she'd definitely have on a wedding ring. So…"

"Okay, I get that." Havoc stroked at his chin where his beard was just starting to grow back in from his clean-cut look, providing security for Senator Blankenship. But since the men in Kyrgyzstan had little or no facial hair, it looked like he'd be back to shaving. "I'm just wondering if a single man going after a single woman will cause issues."

"We're going to lean into the DIA on this one." She looked over at Hasan. "I have limited understanding of the culture."

Hasan nodded. "As long as you aren't sleeping in the same room, my understanding is that it's all right."

"But we think that the female is still operating?" T-Rex asked. "So it might be that only the guest house where Havoc knocks on the door would have any interaction with him."

"Right, we think that she's at the guest house. We hope that Havoc can swing by, tell Jett that she's needed at the TOC in Jalal-Abad, and take a taxi back to the apartment we've set up as a support venue, waiting for their next orders." She turned toward Havoc. "Got it?"

"And if I don't find her there?"

"Well, then we have bigger problems, don't we?" White's eyebrows were raised so high they were almost to her hairline. "That could mean that all of our operators were found and wiped off the slate."

6

———

Raleigh-Durham International Airport, North Carolina

Friday, Fourteen-Twenty Hours

Havoc swiped his ticket and sauntered down the jet bridge to board the plane to New York. There, he'd catch another flight to Amsterdam and then the third leg directly into Jalal-Abad, Kyrgyzstan, where Havoc would hire a car.

White told them that the Echo operators weren't seated together on the flights. She'd scrambled last minute to get them onto the first flight out. Her goal when arranging their boarding passes was to give the men enough legroom. Most of the guys on Echo were well over six feet tall. Nitro, their smallest and scrappiest, got last available. Sucked to be him. Havoc wondered just how bad Nitro's seat was going to be in the back of the plane.

As master chief, T-Rex got the lone business class seat that was available and had already boarded. Ty got the bulkhead to help accommodate Rory. It was Pentagon policy that the military K9s always outranked their handler. So if rank was determinate,

Rory was afforded the better placements. Rory never flew in the hold like many pets do. This caliber of military working dog needed to be under the control of the handler at all times. There was just too much of a chance that something stupid could happen to the detriment of everyone.

As Havoc made his way down the aisle, wearing the clothing that Johnna White chose for his cover, Havoc felt conspicuous. White had good fashion sense; it just wasn't Havoc's style. Havoc was more of a comfort seeker, a jeans and flannel shirts kind of guy. These pants were a little tighter than he liked them. His shirt had buttons and no stretch. While they fit comfortably across his shoulders, they were overly tight around his biceps.

Havoc didn't like to have his range of movement restricted, both for comfort's sake, and because he didn't want to be bound when explosive action was required. But White was right to dress them for this leg of their trip as monied businessmen. They got treated with a bit better service, waved through TSA without having to remove their loafers.

Loafers.

Havoc couldn't remember the last time he'd worn loafers. High school for his cousin's wedding, maybe. Havoc liked his boots. And boots were the one concession that White had afforded them. They were allowed to use non-tactical hiking boots from their own closets. There was no time to break in new footwear before they were hoofing it up and down the mountains. The Army, after all, survived and thrived based on the condition of their feet.

Havoc made his way past T-Rex and Ty without acknowledging them, sidling toward his place. White had finagled an emergency door seat for Havoc on the right, and Jeopardy mirrored him on the left. Jeopardy was sitting next to a mother with an infant in her lap. It looked like she hadn't sprung for an extra ticket to have a car seat next to her, so she'd be holding the baby the whole trip. Sitting in the middle chair—talk about restriction of movement—that looked like a nightmare for the woman.

Jeopardy held up his noise-canceling headphones and shook them at Havoc. Havoc nodded and pulled his set from the pack before he shoved his bag into the overhead bin.

Havoc nodded at the woman sitting in his row, and she got out to let Havoc slide in to take his seat. She looked chatty. Hopefully, the earphones would do the trick, letting her know he wasn't interested in small talk. Havoc needed the time on the flights for work. He'd wait until the plane took off before he pulled the headphones on.

The woman followed him into their row, jostling her way back into her seat, all smiles, with impossibly long purple fingernails stroking through her hair.

It was bar pick-up behavior, and Havoc just wasn't interested.

He had work to do.

"Hi there," she said with a smile.

Havoc lifted his chin, acknowledging her and not getting involved. White had created code-protected files for them to study. And Havoc needed to practice his new persona. He needed to think beyond what White had given him and flesh out a whole life for himself in case anyone were to ask.

And someone might just ask.

"I'm a little nervous about flying. The last time didn't go so well," she told Havoc as he pulled his seatbelt into place. She was obviously trying to hook him into a conversation. Her opener begged for a "Why, what happened?"

Havoc gave her another nod but nothing else. The infant started squalling next to Jeopardy. If Havoc had to pick, Jeopardy had the easier spot.

"I was traveling with my emotional support squirrel, Pearl."

Havoc blinked. What?

She put her hand on his arm. "Not that I really need emotional support. My hobby is wildlife rescue. Pearl was brought in as a baby after she fell from her nest. I carried Pearl around in my hoody pocket to keep her warm and safe. She had to go everywhere with me. They take lots of time and attention. Like, for example, baby squirrels need a bottle every three hours. Anyway, I couldn't find anyone willing to do that for her." The woman sighed as if it showed the depravity of modern man not to want to get up twice in the night to feed a random squirrel. "So there I was, traveling with Miss Pearl the Squirrel in my pocket."

Havoc's brows pulled in tight. This story was going to end badly. Havoc heard this kind of tale from women as an opening gambit when they wanted to engender sympathy and kind feelings.

And that was Havoc being jaded.

It seemed to Havoc that there was a dating playbook, and the women he met followed along. After a while, they all seemed to melt into the same persona. Havoc was bored with it. And a little jealous that he was the last single man on Delta Force Echo. He'd like to get off the dating merry-go-round. He thought settling down was the next step. With his last birthday, something seemed to shift around for him. Thirty-two, not an old man, yet. Still, it seemed like a door opened. Sadly, readiness for a wife and jaded over dating were poor relationship buddies.

Havoc tried to bubble up some enthusiasm for this woman. It wasn't a bad opening story. He was kind of intrigued by someone walking around like a kangaroo mama with a rodent in her front pocket.

"When Pearl needed to use the bathroom, she would climb out of my hoody pocket, scamper down my leg and do what she needed to on the ground by my shoe. I just put a napkin down to absorb her body waste. I mean, she was this tiny little squirrel. It wasn't like she could make a huge mess. Then I'd put the napkin in a plastic bag. When Pearl was making her way cautiously down my leg, my seatmate on that flight freaked out." The woman sighed. "Yeah, that didn't go very well. Pearl went and hid somewhere, and she was never found. Probably, she curled up all cozy in someone's carry-on bag, and they took her home with them. Surprise!" She smiled, then frowned.

Havoc focused on her hoody pocket. It looked flat, unpopulated by rescued woodland animals. But he asked anyway. "Got anything with you today? Baby skunk?"

She squeezed Havoc's arm and laughed as if that were the best joke.

"Last time I flew," Havoc said, "a flock of birds tried to steal the meat sandwiches from the schoolgirls who were traveling with us."

"That's…unlikely."

"I thought the same. Put a guy's eye out."

"What?"

"Animals and planes are a bad combination." Havoc thought he'd just outweirded her. She was back to batting her lashes, but this time it was less flirtatious and more about confusion. Havoc took advantage of the lull in conversation to put his earphones over his ears and turned to the window.

Havoc watched the workers ready the plane, thinking about the mission.

In his mind, he was back in the briefing room, picking through the information they'd been given. "You said no comms?" T-Rex had asked.

White had circled her laser on the map. "First, in this area, there's no internet."

Havoc had frequently been on missions where comms were difficult. Satellites had kept everyone in contact, at least intermittently. But White was satellite averse.

"The terrain is mountainous. Radio is line of sight. Satellite can be traced even when encrypted. It's high-end to have a sat phone in this region. Since you'd likely be the only ones operating a sat phone, you'd be pinpointed instantly."

"The AWG operators didn't have sat phones with them in the field?" T-Rex had asked.

"They did," White countered, "but with the instructions that they were to only be turned on and used in a life-or-death situation. As far as we know, none of the AWG operators turned them on. But as you've been apprised, that simply doesn't mean anything. It could be that if the teams were close enough to our jackpot, that the calls might have been monitored and absorbed. 'Absorbed' is how I frame the message going up to the satellite but not going back down to the intended recipient. They could have been calling for help night and day, and we might just be unaware. And worse, they may have been told help was on the way, like what happened to Strike Force, and yet, no one arrives. Or, they could have been rerouted to head in the wrong direction. Or anything, really. We just don't know."

White's assistant had walked around handing out cell phones with their names on a sticky note. "You, too, will have a sat phone for a dire emergency. If you wish to communicate with your TOC, you need to go to a hotel in the city, buy a burner with a local SIM card, and call over an encrypted line. Toss the burner and start again." As the assistant finished handing out the phones, White continued. "Each of you now has a cell phone with appropriate information on it for your cover persona. You'll want to browse the photos, texts, and contacts to familiarize yourselves with the contents should anyone ask. These phones will never be turned on in-country."

"Okay," Dice said. "That should work."

"All right, gentlemen," White said in her stressed-teacher voice. "I get it that spycraft isn't your favorite. But the CIA and

FBI thoroughly trained you. None of this is new. If you're rusty, I suggest you get out the steel wool and polish up your skills."

Havoc was processing the information, speculating what had happened to the three missing AWG operators as the flight attendant went through her safety instructions, the plane's motors revved, and they were taxiing down the runway.

The Asymmetric Warfare Group included some of the brightest minds in the Army. The men and women sent into the field were a unique blend of physical capability and a specific kind of intelligence. They were the people who would observe an issue and come up with the solution, either tactical or material.

Though they'd been apprised that the AWG was being dismantled next year and the operators would be absorbed into other military organizations, Havoc thought that was a mistake. If this communications threat was out there, they needed out-of-the-box brains figuring this out, which took a unique culture that didn't work well within the confines of other military spheres.

That at any point, this Zoric group could simply reroute a plane by screwing with its GPS, make the pilot think that he was still on task through communications, and drive it out into the ocean where it didn't have the fuel to get to safety, was incomprehensible.

Was it possible that satellite manipulation caused the jet's disappearance over the Java Sea? Or the Malaysian craft over the Indian Ocean?

Heck, it could happen to their team as they winged their way to Kyrgyzstan to find the operators who were trying to stop just that.

Stranger things had happened.

As Havoc thought that, the woman sitting next to him released her safety belt, pressed into the armrests, and lifted her body. She focused attentively up the aisle, her face stiff with concentration.

Something stressful was up.

Havoc pulled off his noise cancellation headphones.

The infant hadn't stopped squalling. Jeopardy had his earphones on, and his ball cap pulled down over his eyes, muttering to himself. He was probably memorizing his cover story. Havoc needed to get onto that, too. Since this was only an eighty-minute flight, Havoc would wait until he jetted over the Atlantic to read through the files. His plan had been to start scrolling the phone contacts and texts White had created as cover.

As Havoc observed, the issue that caught his seatmate's attention seemed to be happening between first class and the economy seats at the lavatory. Ty was right there, but he'd have his hand on Rory. On a mission, Ty's job was to facilitate Rory, and that was it. That took full-time attention. The rest of the team dealt with the issues that arose.

The male flight attendant stared hard, sending daggers down the aisle, trying to get his colleague's attention.

The other flight attendant was pushing the drink cart along, unaware of the issue.

Someone touched the woman's elbow and pointed down the aisle.

She turned.

Havoc observed the attendants. Their training included hand signals, so they weren't yelling up and down the plane. Hand signals meant the attendants didn't have to use the intercom to pass along concerning information, thereby reducing panic amongst the passengers.

He'd heard in the news just last week, a plane was rerouted because a woman was yelling, "Don't do that!" Everyone got the "There's a bomb!" bug. The pilot rerouted to the closest available airport. They set down with a full cadre of first responders ready to deal with a bomb. The guy was face down on the tarmac, getting handcuffed. Turned out it was nothing. A misunderstanding. The guy was released from custody and the airline sent out apologies.

Echo didn't have time for that mess. They needed to get to New York and on to Kyrgyzstan before Jett took off into the mountains again on her hunt for something big and odd. There was only a slim window for Havoc to catch up with her.

Back in the mid-seventies, when Delta Force was in its infancy, one of the potential voids the new team was to fill was that of anti-terrorism response on planes. Hijackings were a more prominent thing back then. Delta Force was magic at taking down the bad guys on a plane. But they had weapons in their hands when they did it.

Havoc's mind jumped to the underwear bomber. But then, Rory and his highly trained sniffer were right there. If someone was whipping out explosives in the lavatory, Rory would alert on the scent, and Ty would react.

Because of his training and the real vulnerabilities associated with the lavatory, from setting fires to the potential for bomb parts or weapons hidden within by a member of the crew, Havoc was on high alert.

Delta Force was trained to understand the hand signals used by the various airlines. Havoc sent a quick glance toward his seat-mate, wondering just how they had handled that woman's escaped squirrel. As far as Havoc knew, there were no hand signals for accidental wildlife.

The signal that was sent from the male to the female flight attendant was two hands coming up like a mime pressing against an invisible wall.

That didn't alleviate Havoc's concerns.

"Looks like someone's locked in the toilet. I know this may seem funny, but it's not." The man on the aisle seat turned toward Havoc. "I was on a cruise in Vancouver up in Canada. The lady in the room across from us was about our age, seventies. They had the vacuum toilets on the cruise. The woman flushed her toilet while she was still sitting down, something I never do anymore. Never, not even as a courtesy if you know what I'm saying. Because this lady said she flushed, and it just sort of sucked everything out. She was hollering, and I tried her doorknob. It was unlocked, so I peeked in to see what the commotion was about. There she was, lying on her bed with her pants around her ankles and her intestines dangling down the side of the bed into the little hallway. Imagine if I had stepped on them."

The woman in the middle seat sucked in a gasp of air, clutching the cloth over her heart. "What did you do?"

"I hollered at my wife, and she phoned for help. Now, you might think that I'm telling you a tall tale, but the story made its way into some medical journal. The woman was taken to the hospital. I think she was all right. Yup, just lying there on the bed with her intestines hanging out her butt. I shit you not."

"Just terrible," the middle seat woman said. "You know I read about a woman who did a courtesy flush on a flight, and she was sealed to the toilet. It took them two hours to fly to an airport, get down, and have the maintenance crew turn off the suction. But she made it into the Book of World Records as having the biggest hickey ever."

"Yeah, I read about that at the time, but the media debunked it," the man said.

"Really? Aw, that's a shame. I liked that story. There are worse things to be famous for."

"Worse than getting the world's largest ass hickey and diverting a plane full of people with connections to make?" the man sitting next to her asked. Then he raised his voice. "Hey, if someone's stuck on the toilet because she courtesy flushed, that's her fault, right? She'll just have to weather the storm and wait until we land in New York, right? I mean, my connection is really tight, and I'm supposed to be at a wedding tomorrow. I don't really have time for butt hickey emergencies."

Havoc was watching the flight attendant. She locked the wheels on her cart and made her way up the aisle, balancing herself with a hand on either side of the luggage bins as they hit more turbulence.

Havoc tapped the woman next to him, exited their row, and moved to an empty seat close enough that he could be on hand if there was an issue that needed more training, and honestly, more violence of action.

"Hey, a lady is sitting in that seat. It's not open," the new middle seat guy said.

"Where is she?" Havoc asked.

"Uhm…bathroom. I'd assume."

Female in the bathroom.

Groups had been indoctrinating and training women for decades. 'Female' didn't make this a better scenario.

Havoc caught Ty's gaze. Ty's hand gripped Rory's collar, and he was watching to see if a fur missile was needed.

People were leaning out into the aisle now, trying to gather information.

The stress levels on the plane were on the rise. A little information over the loudspeaker would quell this if it was innocuous.

Havoc watched as the female attendant tapped on the door and introduced herself.

The sound of a woman crying filtered out.

Not jumping to conclusions, that could be anything from embarrassment on one end of the spectrum to a medical issue, to the far end of probable scenarios—a woman psyching herself up for terror activity.

Havoc's gaze settled on the female attendant's hands as she lifted the silver LAVATORY sign just above the red occupied sign. And she pushed the lever to the left to open it from outside. She rattled the doorknob. It didn't open.

The attendant slid the lock shut and open again, rattled again, and stepped back perplexed.

"Why do you think she be in the bathroom crying like that, and they can't get her out?" some woman asked.

"There was that woman not long ago who thought she was having cramps, and she ended up having a baby."

"What?"

"Yeah, had no idea she was pregnant. Just sat down on the airplane toilet, and the baby's head was coming out into that blue water."

"That's just nasty. Was that baby okay after getting dunked like that?"

"Some people on the plane figured it out. I think a NICU nurse and a doctor or something. Yeah, baby's fine."

"That would spin my head around if that happened to me. Baby suddenly squirting out my hoo-haw like that?"

The woman has a point, Havoc thought. He decided to intervene. Though, in general, intervening wasn't a good idea. Sometimes "helpers" were helpful. Sometimes it just clogged things up. But these two attendants looked like they were at wits-end.

Havoc walked forward. "Hey there, I'm an Army Medic. Is there a problem? Can I be of any help?"

The man held up his hands and spread them out as if he were offering the whole situation to Havoc.

"Can you tell me what's going on?" Havoc asked.

"The lady inside was asking for help. Then she started crying. We're not sure what the situation is."

"But it's not the lock. You disengaged the lock. And it still won't open?" Havoc slid the lock closed then open, listening intently for the click of the release. He twisted the knob. So far, that all seemed to work. Then he noticed that the door was a little catawampus. Lifting the doorknob to even the alignment, he tugged outward.

The woman must have been leaning against the door. As it opened, she fell out of the bathroom, grabbing at Havoc's arm as she flailed.

Her eyes rolled back in her head as she collapsed.

Havoc slung his arm around her, trying to trap the woman and ease her down to the ground. He checked for a medical alert bracelet or necklace as he asked for a medical kit. He reached into the back of a nearby seat to grab the safety card and use it to waft some air over the woman. She was red-faced and tear-streaked, but her lids fluttered. As she came to, she looked over her shoulder to the open bathroom door and exhaled heavily. She focused back on Havoc. "Oh man, I need a drink."

"Can you tell me what happened?" Havoc asked, even-toned, then looked over his shoulder to the flight attendant. "A bottle of water, please."

"I was thinking something stronger," the woman muttered. "What happened? I got trapped in the restroom."

"Yes, ma'am."

"I don't like small spaces. Don't like them uh-uh."

Havoc continued to waft air over her face and pressed gently on her shoulder to keep her lying down until he could check her vitals.

"Trapped. You know what I'm saying? Stuck in a bathroom of all places." She slid her hands over her face then into her hair, holding her head. "I couldn't get the door to open. I just remember reading about that woman who got sucked into the toilet all because she courtesy flushed. Two hours is what I read. She was stuck there for two hours while they landed the plane. I couldn't do that. Couldn't. Then, I guess I just plumb passed out."

"Yes, ma'am." Havoc reached for the medical kit the attendant handed over. Pulling out the stethoscope and blood pressure cuff, Havoc assured himself that her vitals were in range before sitting her up slowly. After waiting to make sure that she wasn't still lightheaded, he helped her to her feet.

She moved back to the seat that Havoc had just vacated.

The staff came over the PA system to say they were sorry for any inconvenience, but the issue had been resolved.

Rory took the opportunity to jump onto Ty's lap and look back at everyone. He added two barks to let everyone know he'd been a very good boy and had sat quietly the whole time.

The plane cheered for him.

7

JETT

Arslanbob, Kyrgyzstan

Saturday, Zero Seven Hundred Hours

Jett lay in bed, though she could hear Tetushka outside, muttering as she did when she tried to rouse a spark from the banked coals. There were long kitchen matches inside on a shelf, but they were precious and only used when there was no hope of sparking a new flame from the old.

Everything, every little thing that this woman had was precious. A luxury. It humbled Jett.

Yesterday, with her head pounding, all Jett could think about was the decadent luxury of this straw mattress made smooth with layers of thick goat skins and topped with a fresh blanket. Tetushka was very wealthy to have such a luxury while Jett had slept on the rocky terrain, not even able to stretch her hammock to get off the ground and away from predators; there were no trees on the bald part of the mountain.

Jett had heard the wolves howling their communications over

long distances while they hunted in the twilight. Not having trees meant she didn't have enough fuel to build a protective and warming blaze. She chose a vegetarian MRE that self-heated. She'd hoped that she might be a little safer by not floating cooked meat smells in the wind. Jett had slept fully dressed, with her boots laced tight and her hand on her knife. It didn't comfort her. Sleep was ephemeral.

And so, lying tucked away from the cold mountain winds, with a soft pillow and sturdy walls, had been wonderfully luxurious. And some of the pity that Jett felt when she saw her host struggling around the house lifted. It was a cozy home. A tidy home. And there were worse things in this world.

The clang outside Jett's window meant the tea water was placed on the fire.

When Jett moved, the pounding in her head was still there. The tightness in her neck. If she were home, Jett would head to the doctor. She was getting paranoid, Jett told herself. Now Jett was considering meningitis. She tipped her chin down to test, she seemed to be able to do that okay.

Jett had taken her light and a mirror and searched her entire body last night for ticks or a red bullseye saying she'd had an infected tick bite but found none.

"Come on, girl. Get it together," Jett said aloud as she pulled off her blankets, swung herself around, and shoved her feet into her shower shoes. She'd head to the outhouse, then wash up with the bucket of warmed water and ladle that Tetushka placed behind a vine screen for bathing.

Today, Jett would do the laundry. It was a physical chore. It meant pumping water, ice-cold from deep in the earth, boiling it on the clay oven, then rubbing the fabrics over a ridged board. Rinsing. Wringing. Hanging on the line. Since she'd been here, Jett had taken on the laundry for Tetushka as well as herself. It really was too arduous for a woman at Tetushka's age.

Today, Jett's chores would take longer than usual. Her gear needed extra attention. A few nights ago, Jett was caught in a deluge that had her stuck in one place, drying out her things in the sun. It slowed her down and was ultimately the reason she was walking the bald spot on the mountain near dusk when the men had gone there to take her as a bride.

Jett was just glad to have the shelter and amenities of the guest house to rest and regroup.

While their clothing dried this morning, Jett would ask the neighbor for a ride to the market. She'd buy enough wood and provisions to make sure that her host would be well-fed and comfortable while Jett hiked the mountains looking for...*something.*

Jett helped out because of compassion. And expediency. She wanted Tetushka to see her as a benefit. As a good person. And most of all, as trustworthy and kind. Jett needed the locals to tell her the stories, share the gossip, and possibly stand up for Jett if something happened where she needed an ally.

Jett needed Tetushka to translate local traditions and laws for her—like that bizzaro would-be kidnapping-to-wife scenario.

Did Jett even want to be a wife by choice?

Jett thought that might be nice. Someone to share stories with at the end of a day or the end of a mission; yeah, that would be nice. Someone Jett trusted to have her best interest at the forefront of their mind. Someone who would start making a stink if she suddenly disappeared from off the side of a balding mountain after being rushed to a family compound under duress for a foisted-upon-her wedding. Shoot, had she already been married, those men would never have come after her. Well, not for marriage's sake.

Sadly, though, few possible suitors understood that Jett was busy pursuing her dreams. Gone for long stretches, weeks on assignment often turned into months downrange. Jett was never sure when she'd be called to leap from a plane, where she'd end up, or how long she'd be gone. That's why Jett had no live plants in her apartment.

Jett simply had never met a man who created sparks for her and was supportive and patient with Jett's career. No, that wasn't part of a single foray Jett had made into the dating pool. So Jett put thoughts of a significant someone—a romantic partner or a possible husband—on the shelf. A curiosity to ponder on occasions.

Right now, Jett had other relationships that she was pursuing.

Jett tried to make allies with the neighbor and the shopkeeper. She wondered if the shopkeeper knew why his horse had been borrowed yesterday. Well, Jett wasn't going to play around today. If those men tried to show up and kidnap her, Jett would have her bear spray ready.

And then what will you do in the mountains if the wolves and bears approach?

Yeah, well, hopefully, she wouldn't be trying to dissuade would-be kidnappers.

What a ridiculous thing to do—snatch strange women you knew nothing about off the streets to make them your wife.

With those thoughts churning through her brain, she grabbed her shower kit and slogged toward the latrine to relieve the pressure in her bladder.

On her list of things to do today, Jett mentally added a sit down with Tetushka to ask her hostess about the spooky places like she'd mentioned last night. It seemed to her that if she wanted to do something nefarious, she would choose to do it in a place that everyone shunned out of fear.

After completing her morning hygiene routine, she went to join her hostess near the fire. "Tetushka," Jett folded herself into a cross-legged position on the carpet, where a breakfast of home-made bread, cheese, and hard-boiled eggs with tea had been placed. "When I'm done with my cleaning chores, is it safe for me to go to the neighbors to ask them to take me to the market?"

"If you are with the father, you will be safe. No man would take you in the presence of another man."

That would work out. It was always the male neighbor who let Jett perch on the back of his moped as he bounced them down the pothole-ridden road to the village store. There, he'd wait for Jett and give her a ride back with her purchases piled in the basket strapped precariously to the back of the moped. This cost Jett the equivalent of five dollars in Kyrgyzstani som.

When Jett made the weekly trek to the store, it was mainly to make sure that Tetushka was well stocked. While the average pay for a working male was about two hundred and thirty dollars a month in Kyrgyzstan, women earned less. Certainly, Tetushka made very little. With her clan dead, and no family to help care for her in her elder years, Tetushka got by gathering walnuts in the forest, taking in guests in her guest room, and creating traditional embroidery pieces.

Jett had bought enough of these works of art to supply Tetushka with a year's salary. Jett planned to use these as Christmas gifts. Her family would cherish the beautiful work. Bonus, Jett didn't need to set foot in a mall; she called that a win. Besides, Jett enjoyed the elderly woman, and it brought her pleasure to be able to do something kind.

Along with the rice and fresh produce that Jett bought for Tetushka, Jett had learned to take at least a few pieces of fresh food with her on days when eating yet another MRE was morale-crushing.

Jett had a friend, MaryJo, who was an ultralight trail camper. She took the barest of essentials onto the trails with her fellow minimalists, weighing their bags to see who could thrive with the least. Out there for days on end, MaryJo would pull out a special treat like a single jewel of a tree-ripened mango. The smell, the texture, after days of deprivation, a ripe mango was pure bliss. Until you went without a single bite of fresh foods for days on end, a mango was a mango.

Just like the goatskin-covered straw mattress, typically, such a setup would be make do. But after a week on the rocks? Bliss.

Yes, Jett had learned how true MaryJo's lesson was.

Jett had trained to be the opposite of an ultralightweight hiker. Back in the day, before she joined the Army when Jett was a smokejumper, she would parachute into the wilds near the erupting forest fires with a hundred and ten pounds on her back. Of course, nothing in her pack was anything as luscious as a single bright-gold, tree-ripened mango. The weight in her pack was all about putting out the fire and her own survival: tools, food, water, first aid. The luxury that Jett afforded herself was a couple of rolls of mints in her pocket. When the smoke was thick, the soot covered her head to foot, and there was no way to even brush her teeth without expending precious drinking water, the bright, clean taste of mint revived her weary spirits.

While Jett waited for her tea to cool and for Tetushka to stop her fussing and sit for the meal, she moved to where she'd piled her clothes by the washtub. She patted the pant leg, pulled at the Velcro closure, and found the zippered baggie with the unopened roll of mint candy. She thought she'd gift this roll to her host. It might bring a twinkle to the old woman's eyes. Ever since she'd discussed the incident last night with the mountain, and Tetushka told her the story of her violent, loveless marriage, and then the suicide of her daughter, Jett felt that she'd roused the woman's ghosts. Opened the door to the memories. And Jett felt guilty.

Mint-flavored candies weren't going to tuck the pain back away again. But it might assuage a bit of Jett's guilt.

She offered her gift, then they ate in silence. Human silence, not natural silence. Nature was loud, the winds, the bird calls, occasional bleats from the neighbors' sheep.

It was nice being here, listening to the near-silence, savoring her bread and home-crafted cheese. But Jett had a purpose greater than her own comfort. While she used to jump out of planes to shovel dirt on the forest flames, her job now wasn't much different. She dropped from the sky, with her pack on her back, looking for a spark, and putting out political fires.

To that end, Jett pulled out her tourist map. "Tetushka, can you help me circle the areas near here that are haunted or, for some reason, a place that might be dangerous for me to go while I collect my scientific data?"

Jett moved the map in front of her hostess and gave her a pencil. "We're here. This is the road to the shop. Here is the mosque." Jett reached both of her hands up to massage her neck while the old woman thought about the map.

Tetushka made a circle. "This is where the town died of the flu. But it is long from here." She made another circle. "The people who went to this area had nothing but bad luck. Much bad luck, earthquakes, landslides, and herds that drank the water sickened and died. Families went hungry and died of sickness as their wealth died with the animals." She circled the third place. "When I was a child, this is where the sick people would go and soak in water warmed inside of the earth. 'Hot springs' do you know this word in Russian?"

"Yes, ma'am."

"I remember as a child how I would hold my nose. It smelled like rotten eggs. But those who ached and got into these waters found relief."

"Would you like to go there and soak?" Jett asked.

"Oh, no. No. You see how the road is close, but it's still a difficult trail to get to the waters. Back when people still went there for their health, the town had volunteers to make the path easy for their elders. There were stairs and carefully maintained trails. It was quite nice."

"Except for the smell." Jett grinned.

"Which was awful. I'm just sorry that you can't go. I see that you have been kneading your neck like I knead my bread."

"I've been sleeping on the rocks all week."

"Yes, a shame. You sacrifice much to understand the weather and forest fires. I'm grateful."

Jett pulled out her topo map and compared the two to determine where the hot spring was on her grid. She discovered it was in Deepak and Scott's task area to the east of Jett's last grid. Still, the teams had autonomy concerning what task they took up each week. Jett could do that. She could head over into Deepak and Scott's territory tomorrow, then come Monday, she could work that far section of her own map.

She was required to spend Sundays relaxing between Saturday chores and her Monday trek. Her commander didn't say Jett had to be at the guest house doing her recuperation.

In fact, a soak in a sulfur spring might just make Jett operational. She couldn't very well trek up and down trailless mountains with the cymbal clang of a headache she had going on.

When she talked to the neighbor about going to the shop, Jett would see if she could pay him to take her down the road on Sunday. Jett would just stay mum about heading to the springs lest the neighbor gossip and let that information spread. Jett wanted to relax in the water and not brace her muscles for a possible attack by wandering bands of would-be grooms. She'd give the neighbor a destination a couple of miles east of where the trail was marked on the topo map. That should be safe enough.

Speak of the devil…

The neighbor arrived on his moped, thrusting his neck out so he could look over the fence. "Hi there, American lady." He couldn't pronounce Jett's name, and this is what he'd landed on as a workaround. "I go to the shops now. Will you come with me? I cannot go later today." The neighbor's Russian was halting. He looked old enough that only a part of his education was done under the USSR system. Kyrgyz only became the official language about thirty years ago, and this man might be in his early forties. "If not, I can go again tomorrow."

"Now works for me. I'd appreciate a ride." Jett pulled the money from her pocket, handing it to him with a bit of a bow and a Russian thank you. She reached down to pat the thigh pocket to assure herself that the postcard she'd filled out last night—a funny travel anecdote that covered for her passing information that she gathered from her search parameters, which was nada—was secured in her tactical pants. Jett would have to add a p.s. and include her new plans to head to the far grid away from the bald mountain path.

Today, Jett wrapped her head in a scarf, a symbol of a married woman, lest any other men were on the lookout for a wife to snatch.

8

Jalal-Abad, Kyrgyzstan

Sunday, Zero-Nine-Hundred Hours

The pilot announced they'd soon be landing at Jalal-Abab airport.

Havoc was the only Echo brother on this flight. They'd divided up in Amsterdam, each following White's directives. Nitro and Ty with Rory were flying into Manas International Airport in the far north, farther north than the capital, Bishkek. That was the only airport that visitors could fly into with a pet.

Rory as a "pet" was a stretch. But they didn't want to smuggle Rory over the border, so there they were, thirteen hours from where the AWG had a support apartment set up for this mission.

There was only one flight out of Bishkek to Jalal-Abad each day, and the international flight would be too late arriving to make that connection. So, that team had a thirteen-hour drive ahead of them.

Comparatively, Havoc had it easy. Jett was having her

recovery day at a guest house in the countryside outside of Arslanbob, just two hours away.

Havoc would hire a car to drive him out there, pick Jett up, and drive them back to Jalal-Abad, where they would meet up with the rest of Echo as they trickled in and got to work on the search mission for the three missing AWG "scientists."

As the landing gear whined into place, Havoc studied Jett's picture. And he had been for a long time.

White had put various photographs on Havoc's phone. One thing he had noticed as he flipped through the gallery, Jett smiled a lot. Not a picture smile. Not a pretty-me smile. These were photos of a woman being happy. Tossing laughter over her shoulder, looking out across the lake water with just the tiniest of contented smiles.

Jett rarely wore makeup in these photos, and when she did, it was just a little. Just enough to line up with the formality of the occasion. In these photos, her face was smooth of worry lines or tension. They weren't the cold-stare, and head-on-a-swivel looks that Havoc had expected of an AWG operator who had the balls to be dropped alone in the wilderness and live out of a backpack. He had to erase the G.I. Jane image that he'd somehow settled on in his mind.

Jett looked like a woman at peace. Something he saw in yoga advertising and not out in the world of spycraft and subterfuge.

So maybe she was the Zen master of cloak and dagger?

Granted, White was a manipulative SOB. Havoc thought that in the kindest terms possible. She was a psychological wizard and seemed to have her fingers on the pulse of humanity.

White picked out these pictures with a purpose in mind. She was nothing if not shrewdly calculating—in the best sense of the terms. This was the side of Jett that White wanted others to see if his phone was confiscated and searched. These are the kinds of photos that a family friend would have on his phone with the texts: *See you at 8, Mom made your favorite pumpkin cake—the one with the chocolate chips that you like.* How White knew that was what Havoc enjoyed was beyond his comprehension. But pumpkin cake with chocolate chips was what he asked for every birthday. Havoc thought White might just be a mind reader, a soothsayer, and an oracle rolled into one. But, of course, if that were true, she wouldn't need Echo to go in and find their three "scientists" who were unaccounted for.

Havoc found himself worried about Jett as he stared into her eyes.

Whatever was happening, would Jett be rolled up in it? Could he protect her? There was no macho-man in that thought. Jett was, after all, in a unique elite group of the military. It was more that she was operating solo—and that always had its risks, no matter the skill levels.

The man sitting next to Havoc leaned in, pointing to the photo. "This is your wife?"

"No," Havoc said, practicing his spiel. "Friend of the family."

"Have you told her you love her yet?"

Havoc chuckled. "No, sir, just a family friend."

The man tap-tapped Havoc's arm with a bony finger. "You've been staring at her face for a very long time now. Who does that but a man who is in love?"

Someone who just happens to have a photo up on his phone while he's thinking about other things, Havoc almost said. Truthfully? He'd been absorbing Jett's images into his system since they took off on this third leg of his trip from Fort Bragg to Kyrgyzstan. Havoc told himself it was mission-related; he needed to recognize Jett as soon as he saw her. Jett had no idea he was coming into town, would have no idea that she should act like they were "family friends." He hoped she could just roll with it. But he could easily blow his cover by not picking the right woman to smile at and greet.

He had no idea how to finagle it if things got off to a bad start in front of anyone.

The old man tapped on Havoc's arm again, a little more insistently this time. "I've lived a long time. You can't fool me. I see in your eyes, she is someone special."

"You're right about that. She's very special to me." *Just not for the reason you're imagining.*

"Then, I will give you my best advice, though I know you haven't asked for it. Too many people lead lonely lives because they are protective of their hearts. The heart is strong. It is the muscle that works when all of the other muscles are sleeping. Trust in the strength of your heart. Trust it enough to take a chance on this woman. Be sincere. Be trustworthy. Be strong enough to dare." He patted Havoc's sleeve with his fingers. Gnarled with age, the man's hand was a map of bony ridges and ropey blue veins. A long life lived.

There was no reason to argue with the man that Jett was a stranger, and Havoc was just going to do a well-check to see if she had any idea what had happened to a guy named Scott. So Havoc smiled and said, "Thank you, sir. I'll do that."

The man looked satisfied—like he'd done his duty to bring harmony to the world.

Havoc didn't live in a world of harmony. His life was about blood and sweat and being indefatigable about defeating those that would bring harm. His job was to make sure that men like his seatmate could offer their sage advice and go home to their families to worry about banal things and not whether or not some psycho was going to reroute their plane into an ocean.

Luckily, no psycho had put their finger on that switch; their landing in Kyrgyzstan was uneventful. Havoc pulled his day pack from the overhead bin, the pack that held a passport with his cover name.

This was always a tense time, moving through customs,

facing scrutiny. If the customs official caught on, it was bad all around. Through his body language, Havoc worked to set his face and stature to convey that he was a tired traveler.

Mirroring his fellow passengers' energy, Havoc followed the swarm of deplaning passengers.

As Havoc waited for the crews to unpack the plane, his cell phone pinged with a message. Havoc followed the link to read:

Alert – U.S. Embassy Bishkek, Kyrgyz Republic

Subject: Updates on continued unrest and State of Emergency conditions.

Location: Bishkek

Violence has been reported between rival political factions, which erupted last night in the downtown area. Violence is expected to continue through tonight. Unrest has spread into neighboring suburbs and residential areas.

Former President Baikayev was arrested earlier today outside of Koy Tash. Demonstrations and violence are expected in this area.

U.S. citizens should avoid this area.

We encourage U.S. citizens to follow U.S. Embassy protocols.

Be aware of your surroundings.

Follow all commands by police.

Listen to local news via radio or television to stay updated.

Avoid crowds.

Havoc wondered how this would affect Ty and Nitro.

Luckily, that team was landing north of the capital. Perhaps they could route around any unrest. It would add hours to their journey but getting in place and going after Scott ASAP was the most important thing. T-Rex and the rest of Echo, assigned to search for Peter and Tink, were on a flight landing further to the south. They'd all be together by the end of day at their makeshift headquarters, where they'd listen to Jett's information and prepare their missions.

Havoc slid the phone back in his pocket, staring at the luggage chute that would send out his hiking backpack.

There was his seatmate, the old man with the sage advice. He was sitting in a chair, a small child on each knee, other little ones ran circles around him. An elderly woman rested her hand on his shoulder. Havoc traced her gaze to a man and a woman standing by the luggage conveyor, waiting patiently, their eyes on the kids, making sure they were staying out of mischief.

Havoc found himself smiling at them.

The old man turned and caught Havoc's gaze, then waggled a finger in the air. It said to Havoc, "See? I know what I'm talking about. Just look at my beautiful family."

It was easy for people to recommend marriage. The doing was much harder. Havoc found himself thinking about the squirrel-girl (as he now labeled her in his mind) and what Havoc read as a flirtation. Yeah, her approach was formulaic. Open-ended hook…all of it.

He wasn't sure that there was a better way.

If there were, he'd probably be in a relationship now.

And it wasn't all up to the woman. He wasn't giving it a solid effort. If he was honest with himself, he would say he just found dating life tedious.

Havoc had enough lectures by the Echo wives and his own sisters. They all agreed, Havoc was the problem.

And in the end, Havoc was sure they were right.

He had dated all kinds of women from different walks of life. His friends had tried to set him up—the other Delta Force wives, his mother. The women were friendly, attractive, intelligent, and often he had a good time for a date or two, a month or two.

And then he just felt bored.

He hadn't felt the right spark. There was no fire in his gut telling Havoc that he'd found her, the one meant to be his.

He certainly wasn't going to marry for the sake of checking a box.

And in Havoc's mind, box-checking was what comprised most of domestic life, the inevitable Honey Do lists—cleaning the clothes, going to the market, cooking the food. The drudgery of life, and yet that was what he was supposed to share with a spouse?

Havoc would be living his life as a brother on Delta Force Echo; his wife would do whatever it would be that she pursued as a career. They'd come home to see each other surrounded by the grind of banality. And in his mind, that's what relationships boiled down to—a long list of chores that needed to be done, just to turn around and do them again, and again, and again, out into infinity.

He'd grown up in what his parents described as a "traditional household," and those were his observations.

His stay-at-home mother was always rushing around tending to everyone's needs, except her own. His father came in to eat, to pat his kids on the head, and to tell them that he'd had a rough day, "go play quietly in your rooms."

When Havoc was growing up, his mother would make a list of her children's transgressions. His dad would pull off his belt, and any kid that made the "Mom List" would line up and take their punishment.

Havoc always tried to go first when his dad was pissed that he had to deal with "this crap."

During his whipping, Havoc wouldn't yell and wouldn't cry. That infuriated Havoc's dad—made his father rain down a more brutal punishment. But it also wore his dad out. By the time his dad sent Havoc and his "stoic face" to bed with no dinner, his younger siblings had an easier go of it.

It killed Havoc when his baby sister would come and shove

peanut butter and jelly sandwiches under his door. She'd smoosh them flat, so they fit under the crack. It was a considerable risk. If either of their parents knew she did that, all hell would break loose in the household.

Not that it wasn't the normal state in his house; there were six kids. He was number two behind a sister with intellectual disabilities who liked it best when she sat in the corner, sucking her thumb, with a picture book in her lap.

Dad would do the yard work on Saturdays and tinker with the cars while he smoked and drank beer, listening to the game. While Havoc joined whatever sport he could to be away from it all. The noise, the mess, the seething anger that flowed like molten lava just underneath his parents' skin.

Sunday was church, pot roast at the grandparents', chores, and homework.

His whole life in that house, Havoc never saw secretive love smiles exchanged between his parents. Never saw them kiss or hug. They weren't adversaries, but they weren't friends. They were two people exhausted by the life they'd built. And obviously, they were bored with each other. The only thing they had to say to one another was a game of one-upmanship on how miserably they were treated, how unfair it all was.

And yet, looking from the outside in, his parents were the end-all-be-all of relationship role models.

Havoc promised himself he'd never lead a life like that.

His brothers in Echo were all happily married. They all lived on the same block at Fort Bragg, so the wives could bolster each other while Echo was downrange. All of his brothers were married except Ty and T-Rex. Everyone saw the writing on the wall with those two, though. This last year, both men had found exceptional women to love.

All of the Echo wives and girlfriends had lives, interests, new perspectives to enrich their relationships.

Ty's gal, Kira, for example, held a Ph.D. in humanities. Her job was to translate, restore, and write about centuries-old literary works. That was pretty cool. Uncommon.

Granted, White had manipulated Ty and Kira into a relationship. White had picked Ty out as the "right" love interest to get a Delta Force operator into a specific compound in Tanzania.

White used Ty to manipulate Kira, period. It was a psy-ops that went for the jugular, or maybe an arrow to the heart was a better description. A Cupid's arrow that brought love for tactical expediency.

When that first went down, Kira was just glad that with Ty and Rory's help, she escaped the life-threatening events that she'd been innocently embroiled in. But once she came down from the euphoria that is common after facing a life-or-death situation, well, then you had to contend with the fallout. The fallout here was that Ty lied to her, manipulated her, and saved her from her family. That was a lot to process. Mainly, was it okay to love someone that lied to you? All in all, not a great way to start a relationship.

But they did love each other.

And White helped them get into therapy with a psychologist who had government clearance, so they could openly discuss what happened.

Havoc thought they'd pull through. Anyone who saw them together knew that the love was deep; it was the relationship's foundation that was wobbly. And that would take time to buttress.

T-Rex and Remi were a different story. They worked side by side for most of their mission, then stood shoulder to shoulder to survive. Yeah, that was a different dynamic.

Havoc was starting to see a pattern.

Look at Deimos Prescott. He'd come down to Fort Bragg to take his old place in Echo to help ferret out a spy tasked with taking down Delta Force. Deimos posed with his ex-fiancée

Storm Meyers, and by the end of the mission, they were engaged again.

Now married, she retired from her job in the DIA to have a baby and pursue her other passion, writing and illustrating children's books. It was nice to see.

At the time of the Fort Bragg mission, Havoc thought Storm was retired from the military after terrorists nearly killed her. But it turned out, she was as badass as ever, roaming the world working for the DIA.

Badass…maybe that was the kind of woman that he should be looking for. A risk-taker. A suburban lifestyle rule breaker…

A text buzzed his phone, which he wasn't supposed to use in-country: **This is for awareness. The country is under a level red DO NOT travel advisory. We are in the process of clearing personnel from the U.S. Embassy in Bishkek. ERASE MESSAGE.**

Havoc hoped Ty and Nitro didn't get wound into that mess.

9

———

HAVOC

Arslanbob, Kyrgyzstan

Sunday, Fourteen-Seventeen Hours

The hired car pulled over in front of a house that looked like it had stood in this mountain shadow for over a hundred years.

"We're here?" Havoc asked in Russian. He regularly read Russian language newspapers and listened to books on tape to improve his pronunciation and vocabulary. Languages were perishable. You use it, or you lose it. Luckily, Havoc had T-Rex and Ty to practice with.

"Here, yes?" the driver asked. "I wait, yes? You go back to the city?"

They were out in the countryside, far from shelter or transportation. "Yes, please wait. I'm just going to get my friend, and I'll be right back. I'll go make sure she's here."

"This is the right place. It's the place you told me."

"Yes, sir." Havoc pulled the handle and opened the back door. "I'm sure you delivered me to the right house. I'm just not sure that I had the right address to begin with. So if you wouldn't mind…"

The driver nodded.

Just in case this guy wasn't on the up and up, Havoc dragged his pack out with him, sliding it over one shoulder as he moved to the cottage door.

He knocked.

When an elderly woman edged the door open, Havoc said, "Grandmother, do you speak Russian?"

"Yes."

"I'm looking for a family friend. Her name is Jett." Havoc held up his phone with Jett's picture on it. Then scrolled to an image that White had photoshopped, making it seem as though he and Jett were sitting side by side at a restaurant with others. "My friend?" he asked in Russian.

"Yes. Jett is staying here. But she's gone now."

White said Jett took a required rest day each Sunday. Jett shouldn't have left until tomorrow.

"Uhm, do you know where she went? Jett's mother packed some gifts that she asked me to deliver. I promised Jett's mom that I'd do that."

The woman searched Havoc's face with calculating eyes. Havoc thought she was probably a better lie detector than the polygraph machines they had at the FBI.

Havoc set his pack on the ground and unlaced the top. There, as he knew it would be, was the first of several brightly wrapped gifts. It said Jett on the top. Havoc showed the woman. "This says in English, 'To Jett. Love, Mom'."

The woman now sent her scrutiny toward the taxi driver. This woman was either highly suspicious by nature, or this woman felt protective of Jett.

Finally, she looked back at Havoc.

"She is a brave one."

"Yes, ma'am." *What did that mean?*

"She had a bad headache. Her neck was sore from sleeping with the rocks."

"I'm sorry to hear that. Are you sure Jett isn't here? May I say hello?"

"She is doing science. She will figure out why the weather is changing and how to protect the Walnut Forest from fires. Then, she will come and explain it to me."

"Yes, ma'am."

The woman's gaze slid past Havoc, past the street, to the expanse of wilderness that rose into mountain terrain. "Jett never tells me where she's going in the mountains. I have seen the samples she brings down. She drills pieces out of the trees to look at how much water they have gotten over time."

"Yes, ma'am. That's her job."

"But I may have made a mistake. And if I have, then it is good that you're here."

"Oh? How can I help?"

"There is a spring that smells of rotten eggs. People in my youth used to go there to soak and feel better. I mentioned this to her."

"Okay."

"We have no doctors here."

"Do you think she went to soak in the spring to feel better?"

The woman laced her fingers and pressed her knotted hands under her chin. "She finished all of her chores, packed her backpack, and told me goodbye this morning. Jett said that she'd see me Friday as usual. Yes, I think I made a mistake in telling her about the healing waters. It's bad there. There's evil in that valley. I don't think she understood what I was trying to explain to her. It's her brave heart that wasn't listening. This spring is in an area that is filled with dark spirits. She didn't seem to believe me when I told her this. I showed her on the map where the dangers were."

"From the dark spirits. But you went to the waters when you were a child?" Yup, this is precisely the kind of thing that Havoc would get curious about. It was Mystery 101; where there were stories of scary monsters, it was usually a criminal trying to keep folks away. "When did the bad spirits begin?"

"Oh, a very long time ago. About when my child was born."

Havoc would guess that was probably fifty years ago, and that probably wasn't a good clue. "I see. Well, I should go check on Jett then. Is it far? Could I walk?" He pulled his topo map from his pack and showed her where her house was located. Where the road to the village ran.

She twisted it this way and that, trying to see clearly. Then lifted a finger, pointing at a blue water feature.

"There? That's pretty far from your house. Much too far to walk. How would Jett get there?" It would have him doubling back toward Jalal-Abad.

"The neighbor has a motorbike. He took her."

"Yes, ma'am. When did she go?"

"After lunch. Two hours ago? Yes, about two hours ago."

"Thank you for your time." Havoc offered a respectful bow and stepped back two steps before he turned and headed toward the taxi.

"Not right place?" the man asked as Havoc slid inside.

"This was the right place, but she went for a hike. Can you take me here?" Havoc leaned forward with his finger on the blue oval.

The taxi driver looked at the map. "No good." He waggled his finger at Havoc. "Haunted."

"Oh." Havoc wondered if the driver meant to offer a word of caution or if he was refusing to take Havoc there?

Havoc handed him a wad of cash. "This pays for my route here. I will pay you more to take me to this place."

The driver accepted the money and put the car into gear with a deep scowl on his face.

Havoc leaned back in the seat, wondering why that suddenly became a spot that people understood to be dangerous. His mind went briefly to polio, but the woman implied by mentioning the smell that it was a sulfur spring. Didn't the heat and chemistry of such a place kill the virus?

Well, the military required every vaccine known to man, so he and Jett were both protected. From a virus anyway, maybe not from spooks.

After about forty-five minutes, the driver swerved off the road, stopping beside a boulder. The driver turned around in his seat, handing the topo map back to Havoc and tapping a place on the map that was *not* near the spring. "We're here. Do you still want to go to the waters? You must walk from this point. Or would you like me to take you back to Jalal-Abad?"

Havoc could see it was about a mile's hike up the road.

"I'll get out here, thanks." Havoc folded the map. And reached into his pocket for his wallet.

"No," the driver said. "I will not take money for leaving you here. I take no responsibility."

"Okay." Havoc popped open his door and reached for the shoulder strap on his backpack, pulling it along as Havoc climbed from the car. "Thank you."

Havoc would admit that the driver's refusal sent a chill down his back.

10

―――――

HAVOC

Arslanbob, Kyrgyzstan

Sunday, Fifteen Hundred Hours

Havoc whistled as he hiked up the road. The air was crisp-fresh and smelled thickly of evergreens.

He'd taken a chance on the old woman's words. She didn't know anything for sure.

On the way out to the guest house and then heading east toward Jalal-Abad, they hadn't passed anyone on the roadway. If Havoc found Jett, if he didn't find Jett, here he was in unfamiliar territory. No comms. No obvious transport.

The old woman had guessed that the spring was where Jett headed, but she didn't know for sure. This could be a wild goose chase. And then what? He'd be in the middle of nowhere. And judging from the cabby's behavior, it might be hard to catch a ride from this particular location. It might mean a long hike. And he should probably change out of his travel clothes before he headed back on the trail. Especially these businessman's loafers.

He decided that he'd wait until he found the trail, then scramble off in the woods and change. It shouldn't be far now.

So what did he learn at the guest house earlier?

Jett had been at the guest house this morning. She took her pack and was expected back next Friday. She had a headache and a sore neck. There was a possibility that Jett went to soak in a hot spring. But that was conjecture on the old woman's part. Jett didn't tell anyone her plans. Havoc would assume the headache and sore neck would slow her down, but she had a two-hour head start.

If Jett had followed her protocol, she would have mailed her postcard Saturday. That postcard would indicate the direction of her next search grid, but the card wouldn't arrive at the Jalal-Abad headquarters until Monday. No help.

One thing for sure was the body of water that the guest house hostess pointed to on Havoc's map was in Scott's territory.

Had she gone for a soak and arranged to be picked up by the neighbor with the moped and taken back to another point on her search parameter?

Maybe she'd come and gone from her soak already.

In that case, Havoc would have to get back to their Jalal-Abad headquarters, figure out Jett's new coordinates and head back out. Minimally, it would take three days to find Jett. Chances were good that if he couldn't track Jett down at this location, the team might have to wait until Friday to catch up with her.

The powers that be didn't know what was going on with three operators up and missing.

Was Jett in danger?

Havoc lifted and repositioned the straps on his backpack, picking up his pace, reflecting the angst in the pit of his stomach. Maybe Havoc had stared at Jett's photo too long. Maybe his seatmate on the flight into Kyrgyzstan had planted a seed when his bony finger tapped Havoc's sleeve and told Havoc that his heart was strong enough to take risks.

Risk was Havoc's lifestyle. It's what made him feel alive. Havoc got that he didn't do this job and take the risks without years of training and experience. Each mission taught him and grew him in new ways.

Maybe that was true of relationships, too.

That might make sense. That he'd been through the lessons of low-risk dating, like taking a 'Tactical Evasions for Beginners' class for the hundredth time.

Maybe what Havoc needed was to up the challenge. Increase the risk.

As Havoc followed the map, getting closer to where the trailhead leading to the spring was marked, Havoc thought about how he'd gone on searches for many a villain and many an endangered ally, and while he took his work seriously, he had never taken it to heart, not like this.

Jett being endangered felt personal.

Havoc's gaze scanned the wood line. Something was making the hair on the back of his neck prickle. He felt eyes on him. Havoc stopped. Scanned. Wished he was allowed to have a gun in his hand.

Spooked by the stories of the haunted spring? he chided himself.

Well, three hard-core operators *had* disappeared.

Jett might have eyes on him.

If Jett saw him, she might hide. She had no idea that anyone was looking for her.

Havoc didn't want to be screaming out her name. He knew she'd come up through the army to her position, so as he walked, he started singing the best-known cadences that kept the recruits in step as they paraded in boot camp.

After a few minutes with no Jett popping out of the woods,

Havoc decided that the feeling of eyes on him wasn't Jett. He wondered if he should fade into the shadows.

There!

Havoc heard a rustle. Saw movement. Havoc melted into the trees. Pulling out the map, he saw he was still about a hundred yards from the path that wended back toward the spring. If the water was Jett's destination, there would be no reason for her to be back in the foliage, risking viper fangs like what happened to Jett's search buddy, Renée.

The grasses that grew between the trees were tall and thick. There wasn't much else by way of underbrush.

The sound moved closer. Stopped. Stepped forward again.

Havoc was being stalked. He pressed himself against a trunk, hoping to blend. Havoc bent to pick up a stick. He stilled his breath to focus on the direction the noise was coming from.

Looking up at a rock outcropping, Havoc found himself eye to eye with a big black dog. The dog's lip curled as his chest rumbled with his warning.

Scott's K9?

"Digger? Is that you, Digger?" This was an interesting twist. "Are you a good boy? Good boy, Digger." Havoc lifted the back of his hand slowly for the dog to sniff.

Instead, the dog bent his head, snatching up something in his powerful jaw, and started running.

As the dog dashed away, Havoc saw the K9 was dragging gray camo cloth behind him.

It had to be the military K9 that Scott was handling.

Maybe the dog was leading him to Scott? Havoc gave chase.

Wouldn't that be something if he found Scott but couldn't locate Jett?

As they ran, the dog would stop and look around, making sure that Havoc was following. It could be a demon dog wooing Havoc to his demise. Havoc chuckled as he ran.

He was grabbing at the tree trunks, powering himself forward though his speed fell off as he moved through the tight growth and the gnarls of roots. The last thing that he needed was to break his ankle and have to crawl to the road in the hopes of finding help.

There was something decidedly creepy about this place.

With Renée in the hospital with a viper bite, Jett had walked these mountains for over a week by herself.

She was a brave woman, that was for sure.

The dog stood on a rock, looking majestically absurd as a pair of pants dangled from his mouth.

They looked small. Scott was supposed to be about Havoc's size at six feet one and a hundred and eighty pounds. Yeah, those pants would never fit Scott.

Havoc had no idea if those pants had anything to do with the Americans. And even less idea why this dog would be traipsing through the forest dragging around a pair of pants.

"Digger?" Havoc tried to call in a voice that would carry to the dog and no farther. When that didn't work, Havoc pursed his lips to whistle out a soft "come here" tune. "Digger, come." He patted his thigh.

The dog dropped the pants and rumbled at Havoc.

Havoc had been around enough war dogs to recognize the real-world danger this scene imposed. Havoc looked up at the tree to his side and thought if he jumped hard enough, he could reach that branch and do a pull-up.

But that's what dogs liked to do "tree" their prey, right?

Havoc pulled his pack around, reaching into a pocket and pulling out a plastic sleeve of beef jerky that he'd bought at the newspaper stand on the way to find a taxi. Opening the packaging, Havoc pulled off a piece and threw it up to the dog. It bounced off the boulder, and the dog jumped after it.

Havoc waited.

After a moment, the dog rounded the rock, tail wagging, saliva dripping from his lips.

"Are you hungry? Are you hungry, boy?" Havoc waggled the beef. "Come on. Come here, I'll share. Do you want some meat?"

The dog looked back at the boulder where he'd left the pants. Paused. Thought. Then traipsed toward Havoc. It was only in the last few steps that the dog grew cautious again.

Havoc pulled off a piece of jerky and tossed it to the dog. Leaping, the K9 gobbled the morsel mid-air. His gaze locked onto the jerky in Havoc's hand.

This time when Havoc tossed a piece, he brought the dog in a little closer.

A little more.

One more.

Bingo. The K9 was eating out of Havoc's hands. But when Havoc reached for the dog's collar, he shied.

"Hey doggo, I'm a friend, okay?" Havoc held out his hand for this K9 to sniff. While this dog had a distinctly Rottweiler build, there was enough of a variation that it could be mixed with shepherd. Hard to tell. "I wanted to take a look and see what your name is. Is it Digger?" he asked, making his voice high and yippy the way Ty did when he was praising Rory or trying to cajole him into something Rory really didn't want to do. "Are you Digger?" he asked again.

The dog took off at a fast trot. Slowed and looked around to make sure Havoc followed behind.

It felt like an old Lassie rerun.

Havoc headed over to the pants. Picking them off the ground, he shook them out. Women's pants. He looked at the label, size six. Pro-Go fleece-lined tactical. The dog hadn't pierced the fabric with tooth holes. There was no blood. They were dry except for the dog slobber on the thigh and seemed mostly clean even at the ankles. That meant the person wearing them had probably worn gaiters, the apparel that wrapped the shin below the knee and hooked onto the boot, protecting the hiker from everything from burrs and bugs to snake bites. Unless you were a viper with sharp-ass fangs, and your name was Renée.

They hadn't been rained on or dragged through mud.

Yeah, these pants looked fresh. He brought them to his nose and inhaled. It smelled like soap. So they must have been laundered fairly recently.

Havoc glanced down at his own attire. He had dressed for travel in a pair of slacks, the white button-down shirt, and loafers. The same outfit he'd worn since White handed him his bag back at Fort Bragg, told him to suit up, and pointed him toward the shuttle taking them to the airport in North Carolina.

Expecting to pick up Jett and take the cab back, Havoc hadn't bothered to change into his hiking gear. The only reason he had his pack was that he hadn't taken the time to run by headquarters.

Dressed as he was, it wasn't a great way to tramp through the woods, especially since he knew there were vipers out here that already took down one operator.

Sitting on a rock outcropping, Havoc decided the least he should do was change into his boots.

But the dog had other ideas.

The K9 stood there, body trembling. His deep-throated, almost subsonic, growl reminded Havoc, somehow, of his drill sergeant who didn't care one iota if Havoc was naked and covered in suds as he told Havoc to "Drop and give me twenty."

The K9 stomped his foot, issuing orders; follow me now.

Havoc slung the pants over his shoulder and followed the dog. "Okay, buddy, why don't you take me to what you want to show me."

11

***

HAVOC
Arslanbob, Kyrgyzstan

Sunday, Fifteen Twenty Hours

The roar of water filled Havoc's ears a long distance before he reached his goal destination.

On his map, this water feature looked like a pond fed by a natural spring. This map didn't document a source of water that would flow either into or out of the spring. It sounded like a waterfall. Of course, that could be runoff since there had been a major storm in the area with a deluge of rain, according to White's weather report.

Granted, this topo map was based on old USSR surveys done many decades ago.

But that sound…yeah, that was definitely a waterfall.

There were many in this area. Two were listed as famous in the Kyrgyzstan tourism book that Havoc had studied on the flight from New York to Amsterdam. But they were back toward the

Walnut Forest, a good forty-five-minute car ride from where he would hit the trailhead.

Havoc thought he'd be led by the nose to the site. But any rotten eggy smell was outcompeted by the bright evergreen scent of the forest. They had to be getting closer.

The K9 never got more than a couple of yards ahead of him. He kept looking back as if to say, "faster!"

But Havoc's training specified that in terrain like this, slow was fast, and fast was slow. That was a SEAL mantra that Echo heard a lot of since their commander, T-Rex Landry, was a master chief coming out of the navy. One of the strengths of Delta Force was that they recruited from all branches of the military. Each man on the team brought the culture and best practices from their earlier days to their unit. All of that knowledge was dumped into the pot. They learned from each other, and they succeeded together.

"Listen, doggo, you can turn and give me the stink eye all day. I'm not running after you."

On his right, Havoc could now see a creek had cut a path down the hill. The rush and woosh of water against rocks grew louder.

His body picked up the pace to a slow jog. Something in his gut screamed, "Get there, now!"

The K9 leaped onto a rock and hung his head off, turned to catch Havoc's gaze, offered up a stress yawn, and laid there panting.

"What have you got there, boy?" Havoc pulled himself up the boulder and slid forward to look over at what the dog was watching.

There in the water, a woman was face down beside the waterfall. She looked as though her body had been caught on an outcropping of rocks. Her long black hair fanned out around her.

Her body floated over the churning velocity as the water came over the lip and pounded the rocks below.

Havoc was in motion, spinning and flipping himself off the boulder. He raced for the water. Without breaking pace, he shucked his backpack. Toed off his loafers. Dug in his pockets to empty them of equipment.

Throwing his arms over his head, Havoc performed a surface dive so he could keep his eyes on his target. He hit the water, ready for the teeth jarring cold of mountain water.

Diving into temperatures that were just shy of a hot tub was a shock to his system.

He swam the few strokes, pulling hard to get to her faster.

The weight of his pants and the press of the current meant he had to dig deep. As he approached the floating body, Havoc let one leg drop down to see if he could stand. Nothing solid was under his toes. He grabbed at the rocks and hand-over-handed his way to her.

"Jett! Jett!" Havoc yelled his angst. Plunging forward, Havoc sent up a silent prayer that the K9 had gotten Havoc here in time to save her life.

12

JETT

The Hot Springs, Chatkal Mountain Range, Kyrgyzstan

Sunday, Fifteen Twenty Hours

Jett was in heaven. The water temperature was perfectly relaxing. It reminded her of the floating tanks that the AWG provided for their operators. She'd enter her pod with its noise cancellation acoustics, its complete blackout lighting, and an Epsom salt salinity that made floating effortless in the body-temperature waters.

With the boulder walls rising up around her on three sides, casting shadows over the water here near the rock that Jett had claimed as a resting spot, Jett was shielded from the bright rays of the afternoon sun. The buoyancy of the salinity in the floating pods was replaced by a froth of water as it gushed over the side of the rocks—a gift of the terrible storm up in the mountains a few days ago.

The cold water from the higher elevations churned with the

geothermal heat of the spring to near perfection. The roaring waterfall cut off all other sounds.

A benefit and a concern.

Knowing that this area wasn't frequented for fear of zombies or something, Jett felt that she would be able to enjoy this experience without worrying about local randy men in need of a kidnapped wife.

On the other hand, if Jett got into trouble in these waters, that was kind of it.

Of course, that had been true of her time in the mountains since Renée was whisked away to get her viper bite treated.

Jett didn't mind risk. After all, she'd grown up on movie sets, her mother being an action stunt double, her father being a pyrotechnician. The family business was all about blowing themselves up or throwing themselves from the tops of skyscrapers, sometimes multiple times a day.

Jett knew that impossible feats could be accomplished if someone goes into a situation with eyes open, a trained body, and a calculating mind.

Today, all she needed to accomplish was to heal her body from her efforts over the last week.

Jett laid out her sleeping bag in the sunshine. She left a solar charger filling her phone so Jett could read her downloaded books. Comfortable amongst the company of the trees that she loved so much; it would be a picture-perfect day of rest.

Jett gave the dangers of this particular environment about a three on a danger scale of ten. When she stripped herself down to naked, leaving her clothes lying on the rocks beside her pack, Jett decided to bring her knife down to the water's edge with her. She looped the lanyard around her wrist and tightened the toggle just enough that she could manipulate the hilt but wouldn't risk losing her only weapon in the deep water.

Sliding into the pool, Jett had tried various ways to get her neck and shoulders under the water, but the agitation of the falls meant that she couldn't simply float.

Not wanting to use her energy reserves, Jett searched for a solution. Eventually, she'd found her way to an outcropping of rocks near the falls. One rock just beneath the surface, was perfect for Jett to rest her chest and torso. Her wide-stretched arms rested on that rock and helped keep Jett stable. In this configuration, Jett could rest her forehead on the rock that emerged from the water like a shelf. This kept her face down, with a couple of inches between her mouth and nose and the water's surface, easy breathing. Almost zero effort to float here.

With her black hair fanning out and tickling along her back, Jett let herself relax. Let the stress wash away. Let the heat melt the knots and tension in her shoulders.

Jett breathed deeply. The scent filling her nostrils was mostly evergreen, the smell of wild waters with no man-introduced additives and sulfur. Yeah, the definite stench of rotten egg was there but was mostly ignorable.

She let her eyes close, let her worries drift away.

This was near bliss.

And there she stayed, buoyed by the water, daydreaming about eating a giant ice cream sundae with her friends at the Maryland shore. Laughing and being enfolded in the luxury of indoor plumbing, temperature control, and the promise of slipping between clean, soft sheets at night when she would go to sleep in her own bed in her own apartment.

Suddenly, Jett popped her eyes open.

Something wrapped her ankle, yanking her away from the falls.

Jett's brain yelled, "Boa constrictor!" And though that didn't make any rational sense, she didn't have another explanation. As a force rolled her, she blinked furiously, trying to clear her vision of water droplets and the sudden blinding rays of sun.

Her knife, positioned for a strike, was clenched tightly in Jett's fist. The blade laid along the length of her forearm, the edge pointing away from Jett's body. In this configuration, Jett could drive a non-lethal punch or take more dire strikes like slashing into ligaments or arteries. She could lift the knife overhead and plunge the blade behind a collarbone to pierce the heart.

This was the knife hold optimizing options.

And in a fight, that's what Jett was looking for—degrees of violence to match the situation and keep herself safe.

Dragged away from her rock, into waters too deep to find the bottom, Jett took a risk and slid deeper into the water instead of up to the surface. She thought she could get to land with a few hard breaststrokes. There, she could get a better sense of what was going on.

While the moment from her getting grabbed to the moments when she sank deep into the pool's depths was mere seconds, her brain did what brains often do under such circumstances; it defied physics. Time slowed to a snail's crawl.

Jett pressed flat palms upward, thrusting herself deeper beneath the surface. But she hadn't had time to take in a breath, and her air supply was low. She'd need to come up or risk drowning. In Ranger school, that had happened to a friend. Having to hold one's breath as they swam an Olympic-sized pool, and many a would-be Ranger came close to blacking out. Jett wasn't willing to push those boundaries. At the Ranger pool, there were people watching, ready to jump in. Right now, there was no one and nothing to help her in this attack except herself.

Something had her by the hair and was dragging her upward. Jett's foot kicked into a rock providentially positioned close enough to help.

She'd use it. She'd use anything that might help her get free.

A backward stroke got her feet onto the stone, her legs bent low. Jett shoved into her toes with all the power she could muster, springing from the water, her arm arcing through the air to bring her blade down on her adversary.

Blond hair, tan skin came into Jett's awareness.

A hand trapped her wrist, blocking her knife strike.

A man.

His mouth was open, yelling. Jett couldn't hear a word he was saying for the roar of the waterfall. But that grip around her arm was steel. It wasn't the clasp of a tourist who was bumping into her.

"Russian" was the word that bubbled up. The Russians figured out she was here. They were going to capture her and take her in for questioning. And that might just mean a black hole site that she could never escape. "Spy, why exactly was the United States government here in Kyrgyzstan roaming the mountains?" They'd want to know.

She didn't want to kill anyone. She simply wanted to get away.

How many of them were there? How soon would they join in the fight? One on one, that's where Jett needed to work. Just like at the kidnapping scene Friday evening. She was willing to go at it one at a time, not ganged up upon. Of course, on Friday, once Jett had scrambled her way up on the boulder, and the roving band of men couldn't reach her. Add in the runaway horse and the dimming daylight, and they walked away.

It was an easy end to a weird situation.

Could Jett get herself out of this man's reach the same way?

This man, then the next. She'd fight herself free.

Jett scrambled her legs, pulling herself around onto the man's back. She locked her thighs tightly around his hips, crossing her ankles, using her glute and thigh strength to squeeze tight. He could do little to hurt her if she could stay behind him.

Grinding her heels into his scrotal sack might be enough pain to distract him from strategizing the fight. Sadly, she didn't have the option to give him a swift kick since the water wouldn't allow for the speed needed to get him doubled over and vomiting.

Her free arm wrapped his neck, pressing the hard bone of her forearm against his carotid. This was typically a two-handed move. At the very least, she could reach over her shoulder and grab her own clothing and use that to help ratchet down on the artery, stopping the flow of blood and thus oxygen to his brain and letting him go night-night.

But Jett was fighting naked and water slick.

With the wrist of her blade hand still trapped in the man's steely grip, Jett knew that she was fighting a trained adversary. Someone expert enough to deflect a knife attack without warning —that was a military man. This blond hair in a country of black-haired people, he *must* be Russian or Russian adjacent.

A picture flashed into Jett's mind of dragging his unconscious body from the water, tying him up, and asking him a few pointed questions before she disappeared into the foliage, over the rocks, and away.

The man reached up to break the hold around his neck.

Jett tucked her chin, clenched her abs, and kicked into his scrotum as hard as she could.

Since Jett was wrapped around the man like an anaconda, he was the one keeping them afloat. He was trying to kick them toward the shore. There he'd have the upper hand. He was obviously huge. Built like an action hero.

But for the bad guy team.

Action anti-hero.

Jett's mind was pinging around, searching for solutions. She was grasping at anything that looked like a strategic move, and all she could think was, *don't let him get you to shore.*

They dipped below the water. Jett had to tip her head back to suck in a gasp of air. The man tucked his chin into the crook of Jett's elbow, breaking the pressure on that artery. Only a person trained in hand to hand would know to do that.

With a powerful kick, he came up and inhaled a gulp of air before sinking again. Sliding his fingers under Jett's pinky, the weakest finger, he curled it back until she was forced to release her grasp.

Jett felt for the nearby rock. Finding it with her toes, she got her feet solidly positioned as she curled herself around until she was facing the guy belly to belly. Springing up, Jett twisted his wrist, freeing herself by torque and velocity, physics in action.

The man got his feet onto the rock as well. He pulled in, then did a backward dive to get away from her *and* keep his eyes on her.

If he got to shore, he won.

Eventually, she'd have to climb from the waters to the land. There was no way to do that and win the battle. There were certain positions that a fighter never allowed. Facedown, knees bent, was one of them. Another was this scenario, trapped in water.

Jett could see he was screaming at her, but she could only make out the fact that there were sounds. She couldn't pull the garbled words apart to understand them. Or even to know what language he was speaking. But the look in his eye, the look of sheer focus, and commitment to outcome told Jett everything she needed to know.

The only thing that gave Jett the tiniest of pauses as she bunched into her next assault was that this man was wearing a button-down shirt. In the woods. In a place that was considered taboo.

In the end, it didn't matter that he was dressed and in the water. He had grabbed Jett first. Dragged her. Spun her. None of that was normal or acceptable. And she'd kill him before she allowed him to take her to prison.

Jett leaped from the water, her knife strike aimed for the man's abdomen.

She was going to gut him before he gained control.

13

HAVOC

The Hot Springs, Chatkal Mountain Range, Kyrgyzstan

Sunday, Fifteen Thirty-Two Hours

The blade glinted as it arced toward his abdomen. Havoc's hand shot out to grab hold again. Jett was a wild cat. Lethal and unpredictable.

Havoc shouted though he couldn't even hear his own voice over the rush of the waterfall.

He tried to shake the knife from her hand, but it was locked in her vice-like grip.

His mind focused on not drowning, not hurting Jett, and not getting gutted like a freshly caught fish. Havoc realized that Jett had no idea who he was or why he was there. She surely didn't know that he'd thought she was drowning and had been trying to save her life.

Now, it was *his* life that was at risk.

Jett was naked. This was problematic because it gave him no way to grip her clothing instead of her skin. He was leaving bruises. He held her tight, curving his nails into her flesh to keep from sliding off her water-slick limbs.

Wrapping his free hand into her hair, he dragged her up against him. Havoc wrapped his legs around her thighs to keep her from grinding on his balls. He'd need an ice pack when this was all said and done.

But holding her arms, wrapping her legs, they had no way to stay afloat.

He was about to release her and dive deep so he could make his way to shore and wait her out when the shepweiler arrived at Havoc's ear.

The K9 bit into the starched white collar of Havoc's travel clothes and was swimming for shore.

Jett fought harder the closer they got.

By the time Havoc could get his feet underneath him, she was red-faced and spitting.

Havoc had to lock out her wrist joint as he pressed her other arm against her torso and wrapped her tightly into his free arm, lifting her off her feet as he stepped onto the shore.

The K9 shook the water from his coat, barking and circling, his tail wagging.

The dog nearly tripped Havoc as he tried to get them far enough away from the waterfall that he could make himself heard.

Jett fought for her life.

Finally, Havoc flipped her onto the soft ground. He maintained careful control of her knife-hand.

As Jett landed on her back, Havoc dropped his full weight on top of her. He pressed his knee between Jett's thighs, forcing a space for him between her legs.

And she fought harder still. Her teeth chomping at him.

Havoc realized that being naked and alone out here, Jett probably thought this was a rape scene.

Havoc tucked his chin and got his lips to her ear, horrified that he might have made a woman feel that way. "Ma'am, my name is Major Havoc. I was sent by Johnna White to find you."

The K9 was barking and jumping around them, adding to the chaos.

Jett stilled momentarily.

"Ma'am, my name is Major Havoc, U.S. military. I was sent by your government to find you."

Her grip released. She tipped her head back. Eyes squeezed tightly closed, a guttural noise clawed its way out of her throat.

Havoc held, not sure that she'd heard him. It might be that she was playing possum, waiting for a chance to dig her blade between his ribs. Havoc didn't release his hold.

"Ma'am, my name is Major Havoc. I was sent by the United States government to find you," he said a third time as the shepweiler slid his furry mug between their heads and lapped at Jett's face.

Twisting her lips away from the K9's tongue, Jett said, "What the heck? Damn it! What the actual heck? Why would you do that to someone? Attack them like that if you're a friendly?"

"I'm sorry! Okay? I apologize, I thought... I was *trying* to save your life." Havoc still wasn't sure that she believed him. Her knife was still tightly gripped and ready to swing. He wasn't about to let her go until they had this resolved.

She squirmed underneath him. "You mean you were trying to give me a freaking heart attack. Who leaps on top of someone like that?" she yelled.

"Someone who thinks that a person is drowning and that they might save their life." His words sounded as pissed as hers. "Can you put the knife down?"

"No, Major, I cannot. Let. Me. Go."

"I will once you just calm down."

Her eye brows shot up to her hairline, eyelids stretched wide.

Havoc had enough sisters in his family and enough women in his life to know that he'd just stepped into a minefield. A man should never ever *ever* tell a woman to "just calm down." It was a death wish. That look of sheer incredulity said this situation went from on-the-way-to-resolving to back into the red zone.

"Oh, no, you didn't. Did you just *freaking* tell me to calm down? *Calm down?*"

Havoc switched his tone to contrition and tried to infuse a bit of gentlemanly warmth. He was lying between the woman's legs. She was naked. He was sopping wet, rendering his clothes all but useless in hiding the fact that his dick was standing at attention, saluting her. Havoc was extremely discomfited by his body's reaction.

Jett was a beautiful, fit, naked—albeit pissed off—woman squirming underneath him. In Havoc's past, such a position, minus the pissed-offedness, was a green light for some fun. His dick really needed to get with the program, gear down to neutral. And since that wasn't happening, the next option was for Havoc to deescalate so he could get himself out of this position. "I startled you. I'm sorry. It was my intention—"

"To be the hero." Okay, the adrenaline was leaving her system.

"When a hero was obviously not what you needed."

She sighed. "Yeah, I imagine what you saw. Bet it was heart-stopping. Then you plunged into the waters. I'd also bet my knife was a surprise."

Havoc found himself grinning down at her. "I'm going to let go of you now. I'd really appreciate it if you didn't gut me. Okay?"

Havoc rolled off her, lying on his back and catching his breath. "I'm sorry for my introduction," he said, looking at the sky so he wasn't looking at her naked body. He'd seen flashes of breast, thigh, and ass that he was sure would be populating his thoughts. Havoc was uncomfortable with that idea since those views had been stolen from her and not offered.

"Not your usual approach?"

"From up on the boulders, it looked like you were floating face down in the spring. I hoped I was in time to save your life."

"That seems like it deserves a thank you," she said, "for the intention anyway. I could have foregone this scene and been all the better for it. I'm not having the greatest of weeks when it comes to men and their ideas."

Havoc wanted to turn his head and look her in the eye so she could see that he was sincere.

Instead, he threw an arm over his eyes. "I'm glad you're not dead."

"In that case," Jett said, "I'm glad I didn't shove a blade into your heart."

"Appreciated." And then, he began to laugh at the absurdity of the situation.

He heard her tinkling laugh join his.

After a moment, both of them stopped.

Silence draped over them as they lay there, exhausted from their fight.

Both drew a breath deep into their lungs, and as if choreographed, they released that breath together.

Jett stirred beside him.

With his eyes covered, Havoc sensed her standing. Havoc hoped she was going to pull her clothes on.

"Well, shit," she said from over by the water's edge.

Havoc popped his eyes open to a view of long toned legs, a heart-shaped ass, and a pissed-off toss of her wet hair.

Jett crouched to pull something from the water, long and olive green. She held it up over her head. A sleeping bag.

She looked up at the sky and called to the powers that be, "Got any other fun things planned for today?"

14

———

HAVOC
The Hot Springs, Chatkal Mountain Range, Kyrgyzstan

Sunday, Fifteen-Forty Hours

As Jett dragged her sleeping bag from the water, Havoc called over to her, "I'll be back to help in a minute." He took off at a trot, heading to the other side of the spring to gather his pack and the supplies he'd dumped on the ground before diving into this whole situation. He found her pants, too.

Havoc brushed the bottoms of his soles to rid himself of the pebbles and grit, then pushed his feet into the absurd loafers. From now on, Havoc would insist that his shoes laced up tight.

Rounding back, he found Jett standing on a boulder, the sleeping bag draping heavily toward the ground as she was twisting the top, water running freely down her arms.

"I'll take care of that." Havoc held out her pants.

Jett slid her focus from the pants to Havoc, to the boulders, and back to the pants. A questioning furrow of her brow.

Havoc was fighting to maintain focal discipline. "Would you please," he cleared his throat, "put some clothes on?"

"Are you a prude?" She exchanged the pants for her sodden sleeping bag.

From her tone, she was teasing.

"Prude?" Havoc chuckled. "Gentlemanly was how I framed it in my own mind." He decided to wring out the bag while he was still wet. "But sure, prude if you prefer." He'd need to get himself changed and get a clothesline stretched for his clothes and the sleeping bag.

Jett swiveled and headed toward the pile of clothes. "Either way, I wasn't expecting a *gentleman* to grab my naked body today. And for the said gentleman to suddenly be uncomfortable with my nudity, perhaps even accusatory…"

From his peripheral vision, he saw her fighting her wet body into a pair of panties, then she slung on her bra. Yup. She was a volcano ready to erupt.

He'd just give this situation a little space to cool.

"Agreed. You do you. Stay nude as long as you like." And when he said that, his cock gave that thought a standing ovation. His damn wet dress pants did nothing to hide the situation, and Havoc was glad to be wrestling the sleeping bag as a cover.

Havoc squeezed and spun the sleeping bag, trying to wring as much of the water out as he could before he hung it on a line.

Jett swiped at the bottoms of her feet, then balanced on her boot while she lifted a leg and slid it into her pants.

"If you're wondering why your pants were on the other side of the water, the dog had them."

She stood one leg in her pants, the other out as she twisted around and found the K9 lying in the sun, panting, and watching the doings. "Your dog took my pants?"

The puzzlement on her face had him grinning. "Not *my* dog.

The dog. He found me walking down the road. I saw the pants in his mouth, and I followed him to the scene of you drowning."

"I am so thoroughly confused. I'll tell you what…" Jett got her other leg in, then zipped and buttoned the closure. "I'm going to get my shirt and hoody on and go sit down, then you can tell me why you're here."

"Let's work that plan."

Jett walked toward her pack that she had leaned against a tree.

"Are you replacing Renée?" she asked

"Not that simple. Let's go back to the dog. He's not yours, and he's not mine." Havoc draped the sleeping bag on a rock as he moved to his pack. "I don't know what kinds of dogs they have roaming the forests out here. This one has a collar, but he won't let me get close enough to read it. I'm both hoping and not hoping that this is Digger. Do you recognize him?"

"Digger is the K9 that my colleague Scott handles, right?" Jett patted her hands on her thighs. "Digger!"

The dog stomped his foot and looked out toward the rise of the mountain.

"Digger." She smiled and clicked her tongue. "Are you Digger? Where'd Scott go? This is his section of the grid to search, isn't it?" She stepped slowly toward the dog. "Is Scott nearby? Are you Digger?"

The dog shied away from her outstretched arms.

"I know how to fix this." She moved to her pack, where she grabbed an MRE. Waggling it in the air, she said. "A good old American stew. Mmmm. Are you hungry? Do you want some meat?" She turned to Havoc. "I'll heat it up, so he can smell it."

"The stew is one of the tastier ones. Are you sure you want to use it on this dog?"

"I try not to eat them when I'm out here alone. The wolves."

Havoc had served in a lot of places that were mainly desert conditions. There, he'd had a run in a time or two with a ticked-off goat. Once there was a spitting camel, but for the most part, Havoc's deployments were wild animal-free. Even in his times in Africa, the animals seemed dead set on scattering when Echo was moving through.

Jett just tossed out that wolf thing like it was no big deal as long as you didn't eat beef stew. But when Havoc was a young teen, he'd seen a movie about a werewolf terrorizing a small town. And Havoc had decided right there and then that he'd make it his life's mission not to wrestle such a beast.

"You're not curious to see if there's contact information on the collar of a pants-stealing would-be rescuer dog?" She poured water from her camel pack hose into the green MRE heater bag and slid the entrée into the sleeve, shoved it back in the box, then leaned it against her pack to warm.

"To see "Fido' written in Cyrillic lettering?" Havoc had his rope bag out and worked to set up a line to drape the sleeping bag and his wet togs. Even with wringing the things out as best he could, a stiff breeze, and a clothesline, Havoc knew Jett couldn't sleep in her bag that night. Maybe when they got back to the TOC tonight, there would be a dryer.

Havoc was glad she'd be in a comfortable apartment come bedtime instead of shivering in front of a campfire. After all, even a little bit of dampness could suck a person's body heat, putting them at risk of hypothermia. Havoc knew from his own experiences it made for a lousy night and a crappy next day.

Though the day had been unseasonably warm, as the sun sunk lower in the sky, the winds were already pushing frigid air down the slope of the mountain.

Havoc pulled a dry set of clothes out of his own pack that White had put together for him. The team only had a brief moment to lay out the items in their packs, look them over enough that they could identify them if customs asked, and shove them away to head for the airport. That was Friday, and he'd been in go-mode ever since.

Havoc stepped behind the hanging, wet sleeping bag to change. It was partly professional courtesy not to strip down in front of Jett and partly that Havoc didn't want Jett's first impression of his body to be mountain-breeze shrinkage.

And yes, he heard himself clearly think the words "the first impression" as if there was a trajectory where Jett would see him naked in the future. He needed his libido to ignore the beautiful woman and let Havoc focus instead on the unfolding mission.

The two of them needed to get squared away ASAP, get down the trail, and try to figure out how to hitch a ride toward Jalal-Abad, to report in tonight.

He tossed his wet clothes over the line, used a cloth to dry himself, and pulled on his clothes.

So he met her when she was naked, he thought as the pictures of her wrestling in his arms sprang to the foreground. Move the hell on. *She hadn't invited you to that party. You barged in.*

Havoc was still giving himself a talking to about his professionalism when he gathered his socks and boots and rounded the sleeping bag.

There stood Jett.

Oh, man, she was remarkable. Her dark eyes framed in a fringe of long lashes. Jett was so much smaller than she seemed in the water when she was channeling Amazon warrior powers. Jett only came up to his shoulder. And she might weigh a hundred and twenty or so. His weight alone, in that fight, should have given him the advantage. Heck, he was a Delta Force operator. His *training* should have given him the edge. Surprise or no surprise.

Since their first contact, this woman threw him off balance.

She stuck her hand out for a shake. "After playing a round of mortal combat, perhaps I should introduce myself to you. I'm Jett."

"Glad to have found you, Jett. I'm Havoc." When he wrapped her delicate-boned hand in his, he couldn't imagine that just a few minutes ago, this woman was trying to stab a knife through his lungs. Was that why a tingle spread from hand to arm to shoulder until he warmed despite the cool breeze?

"Is that an 'I was looking for you' kind of glad I found you? Or is it a 'hey, I like a challenging meeting' kind of glad I found you?"

"I was sent to track you down. They want you to go with me to Jalal-Abad to the TOC to plan the next mission steps."

"Does that mean they found…*something*?"

"No." Havoc realized he was still holding her handshake. "Next mission steps as in they've lost track of someone. Actually, three someones. Here, let's sit."

Havoc spread a tarp under the tree with a trunk wide enough that they could both lean back against it, their legs stretched long in front of them. "Renée," Havoc said, "is not coming back. My understanding is that she's still recovering from the effects of the venom."

"I'm sorry to hear that. I knew if she wasn't recovered that they'd send someone else next weekend. I wasn't expecting anyone until then."

"Deepak also needed medical interventions and was removed from the mission. I don't know what's wrong with him or the level of concern, just that it wasn't an injury."

"So Scott's on the mountain alone like I was?" She canted her head. A concentration scowl formed between her brows.

"I don't know his story. I'm surprised that your command didn't match you with Scott as a team, so you two weren't out in the backcountry alone on two different grids."

"We're not supposed to know each other. Our experiments are different. They want to make sure that if one of us is questioned, there's nothing to tell about the other reconnaissance attempts."

"I see. Well, Scott hasn't sent his postcards in. He's MIA."

"Oh." She looked over at the dog, who kept his distance and stayed vigilant but was also sunning his belly under a late day's sunray. She reached over and touched the MRE heater bag. "Not yet," she said. "What about Peter and Tink? Are they pulling them in as well?"

"No, actually. They've failed to mail postcards for an even longer period than Scott."

"And someone went to their guest houses to make sure they weren't heading in on Fridays as we're required to do? Perhaps there's an issue with the mail."

"They checked. No one's been there."

"I haven't missed a card, and yet they sent you."

"AWG doesn't want you on the mountain until we have some answers."

Jett scowled in the direction of the road. "Let's give my sleeping bag an hour in this wind to get most of the water weight out, then I'll shove it in a plastic bag, and we can hike down to the road." She reached for the MRE. "Given the way my neighbor was behaving when I asked to come here, I think we're going to be hiking quite a ways before we can convince someone to let us pay them for a ride." She pulled her knife from her belt sheath and sliced the MRE packet open.

"That was my experience, too. The cabby wouldn't put me out in front of the trailhead."

Jett squeezed the stew onto her mess kit bowl. "I'm assuming you talked to the hostess at my guest house. She's a shrewd woman. I thought she'd figured out I was heading this way. Hey there, handsome guy." Jett smiled welcomingly. "Digger! Digger!" she sing-songed.

The dog perked his head up.

"Come on, buddy, come get some dinner." She swirled the

bowl through the air. "Are you hungry?" She put the bowl on her lap.

"Your hostess said she was sorry she'd told you the story. That your head and neck were hurting. How are you doing?"

The dog stood up, looking wary.

"Come on. Come eat," Jett crooned, then looked over her shoulder at Havoc. "I was doing better, then I was attacked."

The dog took a step.

"Come on, buddy," she called. "Come on, Digger. Come eat."

He took another wary step.

Jett picked a piece of meat out of the stew and flicked it toward the dog. It flew from her fingers, arcing down for the dog to snatch it from the air.

Tossing another piece of meat out brought the dog two steps nearer. The K9 was fighting himself to get close and eat or to stay away.

The aroma of beef stew was winning.

The dog was on his belly, crawling forward.

Jett spread her legs and put the bowl between her knees.

The K9 had his face in the bowl, lapping up the gravy greedily.

Jett lifted the dog's right ear as he was facing her. "Military tattoo." She turned her head to the side. "Collar says—Digger." She reached out and massaged Digger's ears until he made low guttural moans in the back of his throat. "In Sharpie, it says in English and Russian. 'Injured/trapped' Oh wow, this was written on the eighth, that was what? Nineteen days, including today. That is so *not* good." She twisted to look Havoc in the eye. "PLEASE HELP is written in all caps."

15

———

The Hot Spring, Chatkal Mountain Range, Kyrgyzstan

Sunday, Fourteen Forty-six Hours

Jett scrubbed her fingers through Digger's fur, making friends. "Almost three weeks. Trapped. Do you think there's any way that he could still be alive?"

"It depends entirely on what 'trapped' means. Does Scott have the same sub-zero sleeping bag as you do?"

"Yes. And when my bag isn't sodden, it's been great as far as temperature regulation. I've not been too hot or too cold this whole mission."

"If Scott is by a water source and can rig some shelter? He should be hungry but fine."

"I hope so. Trapped, though? I saw a movie where the guy got his foot caught in a bear trap. It was old, rusty, and forgotten. Once it clapped over the guy's ankle, he couldn't get it to spring back open. He quickly developed gangrene and died a horrendous death."

"Optimism isn't your go-to, is it?" Havoc asked.

When Digger let out a low chest rumble, Jett buried her face against Digger's side. "You know we're talking about your dad, don't you? I'm not giving up on him, I promise, okay? I'm going to help as best I can. No man left behind."

"My mission is to find you and bring you back to Jalal-Abad to regroup, so we can find the missing AWG members."

"Fancy that," Jett said with complete equilibrium. "Look, someone tried to kidnap me yesterday. I'm really not in the mood for a daily dose of macho shit."

Havoc blinked and shook his head. "What?"

"You heard me."

"No, go back. Someone tried to kidnap you yesterday? Do you know who it was?"

"Who they were? The six of them? No. I don't know who they were, but I know why they were there. They wanted me to do what they wanted me to do. Just like you seem to want me to do what you want me to do because you have 'orders.'" She actually did air quotes. "Are you in my line of command?"

"I'm not making up a mission."

"Right, well, your orders affect you. You aren't forcing me to comply. I won't allow it, and my friend Digger here agrees with me."

As if on cue, Digger lifted his lip to snarl at Havoc.

"This isn't a democracy. We aren't voting. And a K9 doesn't get a vote anyway."

"He outranks you."

"Probably so." Havoc chuckled. "This conversation is degenerating quickly."

"I get that you have your orders. You're welcome to head on back. You'll be going without me. If you decided to help me find Scott, yeah, you're not showing up will spook everyone. They'd think they had not three but five operators missing from this mountain. I'm counterweighing that with Scott's clear and present danger."

Havoc sat stoic.

She scrubbed her hand through the air. "My point is that even if I had been given the order to return to headquarters—which I was not, *you* were—I might ignore those orders knowing that my fellow operator is trapped. Digger is here. The scent cones might be fresh enough for him to track."

"The storms—"

"Were up pretty high in the mountains. And the winds have been okay. I think this is my one opportunity to find Scott and get him to safety." She raised her brows as high as they would go and dipped her chin to make the point that she was recalcitrant and unwavering in her decision.

Havoc read her loud and clear.

"I'm going to try to find Scott. No man left behind."

Havoc put his hand on the sat phone attached to his pack within easy reach in an emergency. Having quick access to a comms unit was a requirement on every Echo mission, but it was particularly warranted in the case of solo missions. A two-minute exchange was all he needed to quell any concerns and get boots headed in their direction to help.

He paused.

"That's fine," Jett said. "Press the button. Let everyone know exactly where we are. Then we'll have plenty of support combing the mountains. The op will be over. And all the little village people, who have no reason to protect me and even less reason to protect you, will point their fingers at us. Look, there are the Americans who have been doing 'science experiments' in the mountains. You can imagine how happy the government would be to scoop us up and direct some very pointed questions our way."

Havoc stilled. Weighed. Reorganized his thoughts—Jett was a headstrong S.O.B. She was aggravating. And she was intriguing.

He liked the roiling energy between them.

Liked that she didn't bend to his wishes.

A conversation with Jett—so far at least—was like a well-balanced meal. Some sweet, a lot spicey. Something wholesome, a little taste of indulgence.

Yeah, he was hungry to get to know her.

Hungry for more.

And those were really inappropriate thoughts, given their circumstances.

Jett leaned forward until they were so close that Havoc could smell the sulfur water in her still-damp hair.

Havoc wanted to reach out and stroke a hand over the silky length, wanted to wrap it around his hand and pull her a little closer. He wanted to taste the sweet red fullness of her lips. Havoc found himself holding his breath.

"We have to stay under the radar," she whispered.

"And off the satellite. Yeah, it was a passing thought. If I had any way at all to send out a message and stay on the target…"

"Choices in the field are often messy." Jett lifted her arms as Digger crawled into the nest she'd made with her crisscrossed legs. "You do what you have to do. I'm going after Scott."

"We're on the same side," Havoc reminded her.

"Not necessarily," Jett countered. "You have your commands, and I have mine. I'm not sure they can happily co-exist."

"I'm not your enemy." He slid back until he was against the tree. "I'm sorry that we met the way we did. I'm afraid it's going to impact our ongoing work." He tugged back the word *relationship*. Pulling his heels in toward his hips, Havoc wrapped his arms around his knees, clasping his hands together. He hoped this position came off as casual. Non-adversarial. "Again, I thought you were drowning and hoped to save you." He paused and canted his head. "What was that?"

"What?" She blinked innocently.

Havoc wiggled a finger at the corner of his mouth. "I thought I saw a laugh trying to wriggle just there."

"I had a sudden flash of the Brothers Grimm *Snow White* story. The prince finds a seemingly dead woman in the woods. What does the man think to do? Leans over and kisses her cold, blue corpse lips."

"My sisters loved that story. I can't say I ever thought of that scene framed the way you said it."

"Am I wrong?"

"Thinking back on how it all played out, Snow White on the funeral bower with flowers. Huh. Unappealing the way you put it."

"Probably surprised the hell out of the guy when she blinked her eyes open."

"You can imagine my reaction when I thought I'd be giving mouth to mouth and CPR, but instead, I'm deflecting knife strikes."

"Keeping you on your toes, soldier."

"Appreciated."

Jett reached over and felt her sleeping bag. "It's not sopping. I feel like we're burning sunlight." She pushed Digger from her lap.

Digger looked very offended with his head tucked low, looking up with sad eyes.

With an indulgent smile as she stood. "Military K9? He acts like a lap dog."

"Smart, though. Fur-face figured out how to entice me into the woods to find you."

"Loafers and dress pants be damned." She dug around in her bag. "I wonder what Digger's trained job is that Scott took him along." Jett shook the bag open then moved to the line. "I'm folding this up and putting it in my black lawn bag."

"It's heavy." Havoc stood to help.

"I'm used to carrying a lot of weight." Since she was standing on her toes to reach, which made her neck pain radiate down her spine, Jett decided to let Havoc do the folding.

"You're packing thirty or so pounds?" Havoc asked. "This will double it."

Jett held the lawn bag open. "No problem. In my last job, I was required to carry a hundred and ten."

"For what? That's got to be nearly your weight."

"Yeah, well, qualifiers are qualifiers. That particular requirement said I had to pack a hundred and ten pounds on my back as we hiked over an hour."

"Brutal." Havoc rolled the sleeping bag as tightly as he could, squeezing out the last few drips of water, then shoved it in her leaf bag. For a moment, he thought of taking the weight in his own sack, exchanging it for his dry sleeping bag to make space. Then, he considered what he knew so far about Jett. She wasn't a lady in distress and obviously didn't want to be perceived that way. Havoc decided on, "I'm glad to take turns with the extra weight. Just let me know. I'm concerned that you've been having trouble with your neck."

"Rocks for pillows. Thanks for the offer."

That went smoother than he'd expected. "So a hundred-and-ten-pound packs. That's too precise of a number for it to have been arbitrary."

"They thought that was the necessary line in the sand. Enough men could do it that they could fill their quotas. At the same time, it was challenging enough that it would keep women from their ranks, preserving the old boys' club."

"And?" Even though Havoc had just met Jett, he couldn't imagine a challenge that she wouldn't accept and conquer.

"They thought wrong."

16

———

Chatkal Mountain Range, Kyrgyzstan

Sunday, Sixteen-Twenty Hours

Digger leaned against Jett's thigh as she walked.

Jett had seen German shepherds trained to walk along close to their handlers. Their heads wrapped around, and they stared up, attentive to any changes in pace or direction. Always ready for their next command.

Jett had also seen the handlers who were tall enough and coordinated enough to teach their K9s to always stay between their legs. If the handler backed, the K9 backed. If the handler squatted, the K9 laid down. They worked as if they were conjoined.

That wasn't the sense that Jett was picking up from Digger.

"I think Digger's pushing me to go north-northwest." She bladed her hand in that direction.

Once she pivoted, Digger eased up.

"Digger, buddy, walk ahead, and I'll follow. Lead!"

"I don't know if Digger speaks English." Havoc was two paces behind Jett. He could easily see over her head.

Jett thought this configuration gave them the most in situational awareness. "How's that?"

"Military war dog. The handlers like to use languages other than English, so the dogs don't get confused if a rando starts commanding their K9."

"Huh. German?"

"Maybe French. Czech. It depends on where the dog was bred and purchased."

Jett tried in Russian, which created no interest. "Do you speak French? Digger, *est-ce que tu parles français*? Come here, *Vien ici*!" She peeked over her shoulder at Havoc. "That's a no, I think." She jogged a couple of steps to catch up with Digger. "No, not French. Well, Digger, my French is from high school, and my German is even worse. Let's try. *Sprichst du Deutsch*?" She grimaced at the sound in her ear. "*Herkommen* - Come!"

Digger paused, one paw in the air. He looked Jett in the eye, tilting his head to the left then the right.

"I'm confusing him."

"Czech?" Havoc speculated.

"I don't speak that. Do you?"

"Not a word. Rory, the K9 that's attached to our team, speaks Rory. His first handler taught him nonsense words and phrases so no one could guess like you're doing now. I didn't pick up any K9 commands that would be useful." Havoc took advantage of their momentary stop, lifting his binoculars and slowly rotating.

She'd stick to English when talking to Digger.

Both operators wore their binoculars looped over their necks. Every fifteen minutes or so, they'd take a mini-break to spin three-sixty, looking for a trapped Scott and anything that might be the something that was the reason they were all out here on the mountain.

"Well, that kind of sucks." Jett started walking again. Again Digger leaned hard into her thigh. Jett raised a questioning brow toward Havoc. "Farther to the north, I think." She bladed her hand to show the direction she thought Digger was choosing.

For all she knew, they were just cruising the mountainside. Heck, they might not be looking for Scott at all. They might be on the path of a long-horned ram.

Wouldn't that just suck?

"So here's what I think happened this morning," Havoc said as if he could read Jett's apprehensions over trusting Digger. "I was on the road hiking toward the trailhead to get to the spring after the hostess at your guest house told me she thought she'd made a mistake in telling you about the healing waters since it's on haunted grounds."

"And then you thought you'd found me floating face down, dead, and that would confirm the presence of devil's spawn."

"If you'd been dead, yeah, I might have hightailed it out of the area pretty fast."

Jett laughed. "To go where? We're in the middle of nowheresville."

"One problem at a time. First and foremost, get away from the spooks and zombies."

"Agreed." Jett found herself grinning. She'd been smiling entirely too much for a possible life or death situation. She felt guilty out here enjoying the banter with Havoc while Scott was suffering.

"I heard rustling as I hiked. I thought an animal was stalking me. Then it disappeared, then I heard it again a while later. It was Digger. I think he saw me, wanted to signal me to come to you, and went to get your pants."

"To what end?"

"Follow along with me. Digger was tasked by Scott to go get help. That's obvious from the collar."

"Right." Jett put her hand on Digger's head, rubbing her thumb back and forth as they hiked together.

"Let's, for the sake of conjecture, stipulate that Digger found you. He wanted you to help. But you weren't paying attention to him since you couldn't hear the barking over the water."

"Okay."

"I bet you had your pack around Scott. And I'd bet even if it's subtle that Scott's scent was on your bag."

"I never met the man. Plausible deniability. And I certainly never met Digger. But my bag could well smell like Scott. He was the one who sorted the equipment into the six boxes. Sat phones, shelf-stable foods, manuals. He put together the collection protocols that were our cover stories and the equipment we'd need to do those experiments. Digger would definitely have smelled Scott on my pack."

"You were floating in the water. Digger can't get you to come out and follow him. My next guess was that he heard me."

"What in the world were you doing that he would have heard you from over by the spring?"

"I thought that if you saw me, you'd hide. I was trying to figure a way to signal that I was a friendly."

"Spill it."

"I was singing army marching cadences from boot camp."

Jett tipped back her head and laughed. Then stood at attention, throwing her shoulders back, tucking her chin, she stomped the ground and stepped off marching. "Left. Right. Left. Right. Left. Right. Hut!"

"Yeah, well. Here's me trying to figure out the Digger thought process. He sees a bag that smells like Scott. He sees you and thinks you belong to Scott. As in, your things smell like Scott. You're floating. Digger needs you out of the water to go get Scott."

"I'm following."

"Digger runs back to the spring and grabs your pants to show me. Hey, come follow me to the woman and get her out of the water so she can go get Scott."

"Did you do that, smart boy?" Jett leaned over to better scrub between Digger's ears. "Were you the smarty pants that figured all that out?"

Digger stuck out just the tip of his pink tongue and looked very pleased with himself.

Jett looked over her shoulder at Havoc. "I'm trusting the smarty boy. He seems to want me to veer in the direction we're hiking."

"No reason not to. I'm willing to go along, for a while anyway."

"If your theory is that Digger brought you my pants to show you that he wanted to lead you to me, then the sleeping bag makes all kinds of sense."

"How's that?" Havoc caught up to her, so they'd be walking side by side.

"Scott picked out the sleeping bag for specs specific to this area. I had laid the sleeping bag out under a tree, thinking that after my soak, I'd just lie down and read for a bit. Let's say Digger gets to my camp. He smells Scott on the sleeping bag, and he tries to bring me the bag to tell me to go get Scott. But I'm in the water, and I don't pay attention. The wet bag gets heavy, he abandons it. He decides that since I'm not answering his barks, not even looking his way, that I too might need help, so he goes to search for another human."

"It must be something that he was trained to do."

They walked in silence for a long while. The sun was getting lower in the sky. Jett knew they'd need to camp soon.

Her first chore would be getting a roaring fire going, getting her sleeping bag hung up and dried out, or sleeping was going to be a cold, damp nightmare.

"I'm curious. I get that two of my teammates had medical issues going on. It is odd that the others didn't check-in. Assuredly, that needs follow-up. But you'd think that they would hire a search and rescue group that wasn't connected to the U.S. government to come in and find us. Like those guys in Iniquus search and rescue. I get that they normally go into natural disasters, but they do smaller searches. I read how last spring they saved a film crew off a Virginia mountain in a freak storm. And I know that universities and big corporations have insurance contracts in place. There was that oil guy and his wife that got kidnapped off his yacht in the Red Sea. Wasn't it an Iniquus force that went after them? This kind of thing seems like their bread and butter. And it would make my cover look more authentic if it were a private entity instead of a—what are you?"

"U.S. military."

"Uh-huh. Okay. You're a secret-someone associated with the military but knows Army marching cadences from boot."

"The K9 on our team, Rory, used to be handled by a SEAL who goes by Trip Wire."

Yes, Jett noticed how Havoc smoothed on by her question. She'd bet the last chocolate bar in her pack that he was a Tier One operator, SEAL Team Six or Delta Force.

"Trip Wire was medically released from the Seals and joined the Iniquus search and rescue team, Cerberus Tactical K9. Because of Rory, our team is in tight communications with Trip."

"He's handling a different dog?"

"Valor. She's strictly search and rescue. Trip Wire and Valor were on the team that found the missing people in Virginia that you mentioned."

"So why do you think they brought in American military when they could have just told the Kyrgyzstan government that the research scientists weren't clocking in, and they'd come to do a search? Honestly, wouldn't that be a better cover? I mean, and this isn't to be ugly or anything, but you're kind of putting me in danger by showing up. If we're found, you could blow the whole op."

"Not my call. And sorry if that's the case."

"Still, do you know why?"

"I can guess. Did you know that the AWG sent a different operator into Slovakia?"

"Yes, she joined up with a group of real-world researchers to get into the back of the Tatra Mountains. Her undergrad background meant she could hook up with the ornithological studies."

"The what now?"

"Bird migration studies. Her mission inspired the AWG to put our studies in place. After our imbed found references to this mountain."

"That's what I was told. Did someone brief you on the Slovakia events?"

"Events?" Jett caught Havoc's gaze. "I guess not." With her momentum broken, Jett stopped to do a sweep with her binoculars.

Havoc lifted his binoculars too. "The AWG scientist disappeared. The group actually had a university contract with Iniquus exactly as you were describing. A Cerberus Tactical K9 team went in to find the missing bus of scientists."

"Was that mission successful?"

"We weren't apprised beyond that one of the scientists might have been marked. And while there was a nice, neat, publicly reported explanation of who kidnapped the scientists, involving a Norwegian oil executive, that fell apart under scrutiny. The patsies were duped."

"Old school mobster speak. Still, my original question hasn't been answered. Why are you here?"

"Honestly, I'm not sure that Iniquus would take the contract."

"Because…" She let her binoculars hang as Jett started off at a quickened pace, heading north.

"My understanding of how they work is they don't go in blind," Havoc fell into step. "It's not like my unit. We show up when and where we're told to. We do what we're asked. We succeed at a specific goal and leave. Go get this document, go take out this terrorist nest. Iniquus wants the whole story. They run on a golden reputation."

"Agreed."

"Uncle Sam has no problem with hanging people out to dry for expediency's sake. So yeah, Iniquus often goes in and works on issues right on the line separating black and white. Things that the government needs—for diplomatic or treaty reasons—for a private entity to handle."

"And take the heat for."

"Probably. In the case of the AWG reconnaissance operator, the Slovakian government told the U.S. to back off because the Slovakian government had their own search and rescue going for the missing scientists. It was being handled. Iniquus ignored that because they were working a private university security contract."

"I see."

"End story, my speculation for why Iniquus isn't here, and you get me, instead, is that if Iniquus is jumping hoops for an entity, they want a lot more data. A clear picture."

"I only bring them up because they're already involved in this issue. Did your commander tell you that their people were shot in a communications attack?"

"Strike Force? Yeah. They did."

"That's weird. So you're here because even though Iniquus is privy to the comms issues—both as the victims of an attack and as they went off to save their contracted scientists—that the government wasn't willing to tell them enough that they'd feel comfortable going after Scott, Peter, and Tink?"

"And Digger."

Jett put her hand on Digger's head. "Of course, we aren't forgetting about you, sweet boy. I just wish you could talk. Do you know what's going on?"

17

———

JETT

Chatkal Mountain Range, Kyrgyzstan

Sunday, Seventeen Hundred Hours

"Sun's over the horizon," Jett stated the obvious. Digger had led them into a denser part of the forest. Much different than the landscape that Jett had been pacing for the last week. "We need to set up camp soon."

"The weather report said the temperatures are going to drop tonight. Bonus, though, tomorrow should be well above average."

Jett stopped to scan.

"How's your neck and back?" Havoc asked.

"Shhh. We do not speak of it."

"Would you like me to take some of the weight? I can certainly carry the sleeping bag."

"If you're sincerely asking. Yeah, that would be appreciated." Jett unhitched her sternal and hip belts and let her bag slide down her arms. She stared at a tree trunk, holding her breath.

Havoc moved up behind her. Instead of gathering the bag with their wet things, he gently put his hands on her shoulders. "Bad?"

She closed her eyes and felt the kindness in his hands as they lay there, warm and gentle. Softly, Havoc swirled his thumbs down the length of her neck. She didn't answer him. In a man's world, men could complain. A woman learned to suck it up, or she got a reputation for being weak and needy. That was Jett's experience anyway.

And Jett liked to play in the men's world. So she'd learned to chomp down on showing weakness.

"That's all the information I needed. Let's make our way to camp." He picked up her bag and slung it on his front, adding her pack weight to his.

"No." Jett stretched her hands out for the pack. "I'm not letting you do that."

"Jett, you don't have to prove to me you're superhuman. If you were one of my brothers, I'd take the pack. I have, on many occasions, taken their packs. And they've taken mine."

Jett pursed her lips and gave him a curt nod.

"It's like that, is it?" He canted his head.

Jett felt immediately contrite. He was helping her. Jett was actually pretty darned grateful. Maybe she could show it just a bit. "Thank you. I appreciate the help." And feeling self-conscious, Jett changed the subject. "There's too much of an incline here to safely camp. Let's see if we can find something flatter, maybe if we went a little more northwest." She pointed off into the distance. "That is if Digger will allow it."

Digger looked around, wondering why his people had stopped.

"You never use a compass." Havoc stepped off the goat path they'd been following for speed's sake and was now side by side with Jett.

"What?"

"A compass?" he repeated. "Do you have one?"

"I have three with me. One in my pack, one integrated with my watch." She extended her arm and wiggled it for Havoc to see. "A third one is in my emergency redundancy packet in my cargo pocket. Four, I have four. The last is on the sat phone. Why?"

"Because you just blade your hand to show the path you're going to take, announce the direction, and go."

"Right." Jett bent when she spotted a pair of sticks that looked like they'd be good walking poles.

"And I'm following along like a dupe."

"Only a dupe if I took you in the wrong direction." Jett sent him a tired smile. "I haven't led you wrong yet, have I?"

"Hard to tell, honestly. It's one thing when the sun gives us a sense of direction. It's another thing here in the near twilight with no sun visible. Is it a trick of some kind?"

Jett laughed. "You know I read an article a while back that men have a better sense of direction than women. And the researchers speculated that men are like birds."

"How's that?"

"Oh, a hypothesis that birds have a magnet in their beaks, helping them to stay on course. Magnetite-based receptors."

"Is that true?"

"Still under study, I think. Birds. Fish. The scientist thought perhaps human males had metal in the tips of their noses, giving males superior ability to navigate a linear path over distances, where women store images to know directions in a known circuit for small game hunting and food gathering. I, for one, don't buy into the theory. I think it's a form of Dunning-Kruger effect."

"That the people who know the least feel like they know everything. The people who actually have expertise on a subject know how much there is yet to learn, so they feel they know less.

Those two concepts taken together means they've inverted reality."

"Nuts how that holds true, right? So I think some men *believe* they know where they're headed, and they just keep wandering around until they get there." She caught Havoc's eye. "I'm jabbering to kill time and poking fun, I guess, to gauge how sensitive you are."

"Conclusion?"

"Still under study." Jett swung her head, hoping that an obvious camping spot would suddenly pop into sight.

"But you seem to know what direction you're heading all the time."

"You have your compass out. You can see for yourself if I'm calling the right directions."

"But *how* do you do it? Teach me your ways, oh Master of the Four Corners."

"I can't. Sorry. I will tell you how I came by this skill. Granted, I can't do minute directional changes. You can't tell me to go thirty-eight degrees and expect me to land on the spot. Though my friends tested this out once, and I wasn't that far off on a short route." Jett picked up the pace to a near jog, starting to feel anxious about the dwindling light.

"Putting this conversation together in my head, I've decided a rogue scientist implanted magnets in your nose as a child."

"Actually, that's not far off. My grandmother lived with my family when I was little. She watched me while my parents were working. I called her Babushka. Babushka never said things like, 'Go up to the corner and turn right.' Instead, she'd say something like, 'Go thirty meters to the crossroads and take the southeastern road for a hundred meters. You'll see the house with blue shutters to the north.' She always gave a distance and a direction."

"She did this when you were little?"

"For everything. 'Put the keys in the bowl on the south of the table. Take my north hand.'"

"That sounds complicated for a little one."

"I don't think that was the case. I mean, I had my babushka there orienting me in the correct direction. When she was little, Babushka was given a compass as a birthday gift. It was probably one of the cheap things you can buy on the camping aisle at a discount store. But she didn't have any toys. Her family was always on the move. So she used it constantly."

"Moved because of her parent's work?"

"Yes, she came from a circus family."

"Funny." Havoc pointed toward something, but he was a good six inches taller than Jett. All Jett saw was thick tree trunks surrounded by a blanket of fern.

"Oh, I'm being serious. They were called 'The Uzbek Family Fliers.' What are you seeing?" Jett asked.

"It looks like an open ground with enough space to be able to light a fire without risking setting the forest ablaze."

They pivoted in the direction he'd pointed. "Circus?" His voice was painted with curiosity.

"Horses. She did acrobatics on bareback horses."

"Like when they flip people up, and they stand on each other's shoulders?"

"That's right."

"And you can do that?"

"My mother could do the gymnastics, running up to the stampeding horse, leaping on its back, basically doing a balance beam act as the horse galloped under her feet. Mom is fearless. She and Babushka taught me some of their skills. I can ride. And yes, I can do some tricks like standing up on the back of a horse while it's running the ring, saddle tricks where I flip on and off, ride hanging upside down from the saddle horn—but not on any horse, mind you. The horses are as well trained, if not better trained, than the people. Good thing I learned those skills. They got me out of a pickle Friday."

"Should I ask?"

"Nah. It's not that interesting."

"I can honestly say I've never met anyone with that in their background."

Digger came around behind them and pressed into Jett's leg. She lost her balance and teetered for a moment. Havoc reached for her hand, and she righted herself.

They walked for a few steps before Havoc seemed to realize what he'd done and released her. Jett was kind of bummed. His hand had been warm and steady. After being alone in the mountains for so long, Jett truly appreciated the luxury of human touch, storytelling, and two people with a shared goal.

One of the things Jett had learned in her previous career, fighting wildfires in Montana, was what it felt like to be the "tip of the spear." When she and her fellow smokejumpers parachuted from the plane, they dropped into the backcountry. Way back in the backcountry, there was no help. Sometimes she worked shoulder to shoulder with her teammates. Sometimes she was off working a section by herself. A hundred and ten pounds on her back, swinging a pickaxe, the furnace-like heat of the fire eating its way through the dry vegetation getting closer and closer.

In that smoke and heat, even a rescue helicopter couldn't get in.

Jett was basically on her own with her pack supplies. Whether she lived or died was all on her.

It was an eerie feeling.

Jett often thought about the level of courage it would have taken pioneers to set out on foot or horse or even bicycle to get themselves out West. Once there, they'd find no one and nothing to ease the burden. Their homes, their lives, their safety.

Jett thought she had the personality to have been a good pioneer.

She liked the challenge.

She enjoyed her job in reconnaissance for the AWG.

But she'd admit that it wasn't bad to have a bit of eye candy, a kind voice, and a helping hand working the goal with her.

"Is your babushka still alive?" Havoc pulled Jett's attention back to their conversation.

"A car accident a few years ago took her from us. A shame. She was a very cool lady."

"She'd have to be."

"How's that?"

"Apples not falling far from the trees and all that."

Jett ducked her head as she grinned. "Aww, that was almost like a compliment."

This felt flirtatious and fun. A little bit like a first date with all the get-to-know-you questions.

But that's not what this was at all.

This was two people going rogue with the hopes of saving a fellow warrior's life.

This was, in fact, life-or-death.

18

JETT

Chatkal Mountain Range, Kyrgyzstan

Sunday, Seventeen-Fifteen Hours

A long silence rested between them as they stepped onto what Jett thought was a game trail. And while Jett was good with racing up and down mountains, she wasn't a goat. "Watch the rocks. They've proven to be treacherous in this area. They roll if you catch your boot on them. And there are a lot of seams in the outcroppings. I've caught my heels a few times, and it's tripped me up. Face planting isn't a lot of fun with a pack on, and now you have the two. Thank you again."

"You're welcome, again. I'm thinking about my own grandmother," Havoc said. "Gran said left and right. She liked to sit and read books with her cat purring in her lap. Traditional. Though, I guess there are different traditions, so I should define that. She liked her house and her garden. She raised her kids, doted on her grandkids. Volunteered at the church."

Jett nodded.

"I guess circus is a family tradition, too. Did your grand-mother not travel with her family after she retired from their act? Is she the one who taught you to speak Russian?"

"Yes to the Russian. Babushka lived an extraordinary life. I can't say she followed anyone's traditions. She ran away from the circus when she was fifteen."

"Isn't it supposed to be that people run away to join the circus?"

"According to—" Jett gasped.

"Your neck?"

"Yeah. I don't think it's encephalitis. I was wearing DEET, and my clothes are all treated with Permethrin to keep the ticks off."

"Encephalitis? You think your brain is swelling?"

"Just make sure you coat yourself in tick spray. They're pretty bad out here."

"We're almost there. Just past that rock." Havoc pointed ahead of them. "Testing your babushka's theory that she could teach you distances as well as cardinal directions, how far is the rock?"

"Forty-two meters," Jett said without hesitating. "Thirty-five paces."

Havoc pulled a laser device from his thigh pocket, pointed it at the rock, and looked at the read-out. "Nope. Sorry."

Jett grabbed at his wrist. "Let me see."

He held up the read-out, and it was only forty point six meters.

"Weird. I'm rusty, I guess."

They were silent until they reached the boulder.

"Thirty-five paces, exactly," Jett said as she crawled onto the sun-warmed surface of the flat boulder. She rolled over and closed her eyes. "It's so relaxing to feel the heat radiating into my sore back."

She heard a thunk, then another as Havoc released the packs and set them down.

"I'm happy to rub your neck for you if you think that might help."

"You would? Okay. Thank you." Without opening her lids, Jett rolled back to her stomach. "You know what you're doing, right? This is trained and not something you picked up on the dating circuit?"

She could feel Havoc getting into place at her side.

"If you feel I'm crossing a line, just let me know."

"Promise." Actually, Jett thought a little line crossing might not be bad. Jett would admit that Havoc sparked her curiosity. She might be down for it if this weren't a 'fix the crick in your neck' massage and actually was Havoc testing the waters to see where things might go.

Thinking about where she'd like his hands to go, Jett wiggled to reset her system to "mission ready" instead of personal desire.

She was a young, healthy woman. And she'd been climbing these mountains for months without any intimate touch. It made sense to her that her hormones were in a bit of an uproar. They'd settle down once she caught her balance.

"We're trained in this as part of our medical stuff." Havoc rubbed his palms against each other to warm them through friction. "Like you, my team is often out where there's no help to be had. We take care of each other. A brother who can't turn his head because his neck hurts is a brother who can't turn his head to see the enemy coming."

"Got it. Thank you."

Yeah, he was good at this. He rested his hands on Jett's shoulders. Just the weight of his warmed hands felt so good. After a moment, he gently pressed and released.

Havoc wasn't going to be one of those guys who grabbed hold of her neck or shoulders and squeezed as hard as they could. It was a terrible thing to do to muscles. You have to ease in slowly, let the muscle trust it won't be further damaged, let the muscle relax. Just…mmm…relax.

Yes. Very good at this. Jett bent her elbow and tucked her face into the crook, so he didn't see that she might just be drooling a little at the corner of her mouth.

"I'm stuck on your babushka running away from the circus."

"She and her best friends. Babushka rode horses. Her friends were those people who dance while holding onto a rope."

"Where were they from?"

"The rope girls? I don't know. Babushka was from Uzbekistan."

"How old were they?"

"Fifteen to eighteen. They were touring in the United States, and Babushka said she was surprised by the people smiling and laughing. Not just at the circus, but walking around the streets, they smiled. Where she came from, people were pretty miserable, trying to drown their depression and anxiety with vodka. A lot of domestic abuse. It was a hard life for women at home. She said in the circus, things weren't so bad. But liking the warmth of the smiles in America, the friends decided to jump off the circus train when it slowed at a railroad crossing, and they ran."

"Uzbekistan was part of the USSR back then. Seems to me there would be some political blowback."

"Exactly," Jett mumbled.

"When the girls defected, did it make problems back home in Uzbekistan?" Havoc asked.

Jett wondered why Havoc kept bringing up her grandmother while he had his hands on her. Either he was really interested in her babushka's circus story, or maybe he was trying to keep conjuring old-lady images to keep things platonic.

"I've read about athletes defecting while they're traveling for international competitions," Havoc added. "To dissuade defections, authoritarian regimes sometimes have pointed conversations about the health and safety of their families left at home."

"Yeah."

"There was that Olympian at this year's games," Havoc said as he kneaded her shoulders, melting the pain. "The sprinter who now has asylum in Poland."

"I read about."

"When the girls escaped from the circus, were they granted asylum? America would do that for folks escaping communism."

"Yes, Babushka was granted political asylum. She wasn't worried about her family. Their close family was all in the circus. The circus contracts were years long. By the time my family was repatriated, my babushka's defection would be too far in the past. Hey, Havoc?"

"Mmmhmmm?"

"Can I take a raincheck on this massage until later?"

"Am I hurting you?"

"I'm worried about losing daylight. I need to get a fire going to dry my sleeping bag. I want to set up camp while I can still see. And to be honest, I'm about starved."

"Do you need help getting up?"

"I… Hmmm." Jett pushed back into a child's pose to see if lying down had locked up her spine. She seemed okay. Jett pressed into her hands and squirmed backward off the boulder.

"Good?"

"Yes, thank you." She stood, tipping her head this way and that. "Wow, you have the magic touch. I'm a good fifty percent better."

"Glad it helped," he said with a grin. "Now, aren't you glad you didn't gut me at the spring earlier?"

"I think we both can let that scene go, don't you?"

"I don't know. When you live through something with that level of emotion, you have to replace those memories with better ones to move forward. Time will tell."

Jett was left wondering just what kind of "better" memories Havoc might be anticipating.

19

———

Chatkal Mountain Range, Kyrgyzstan

Sunday, Seventeen-Fifty Hours

Jett was off to collect firewood.

Havoc had offered to do it, but Jett said she preferred he put his height to good use and string a line for her sleeping bag.

Pulling the sodden cloth from the black plastic bag, yeah, there was no way this was going to dry out in time for her to sleep in it.

He'd let her come to that conclusion.

When she did, Havoc intended to invite Jett to sleep in his bag with him. Heck, he couldn't count the number of times he and his buddies would end up shivering together under their woobies—Army-issued poncho liners. You do what you have to survive. Tonight was supposed to be frigid with the possibility of snow.

If they were going to make progress finding Scott tomorrow, Jett needed a good night's sleep. She was already a hurting puppy.

With the sleeping bag draped, their tents pitched, and three

MREs heating, Havoc took up his binoculars and crawled up on one of the boulders serving as a windbreak from the draft sliding down the mountain.

Havoc methodically searched the area down toward the valley floor. He was looking for any signs that a human had passed this way. He searched for anything that might have been left as a trail marker or a signal. After finishing one section, he moved to the next, then the next, and …wait. Was that movement?

Havoc closed his eyes and let his vision rest for a moment, then he lifted the lenses again. Hmmm. Maybe what caught his eye was the wind pushing against the evergreen branches.

He sat and bent his legs up to create an arm support with his knees, then trained the binoculars where he thought he'd seen something. If not a branch swaying, it could be any of the animals White had warned them about with her encrypted file reports. Bears and wolves were around this area, but also long-horned sheep. Heck, he'd found Digger meandering around the woods. Someone's pet could be out here chasing chipmunks.

There, he saw it again, movement.

Havoc rolled from the rock and slid toward his tent to dig the thermal monocular from his pack. If anything unfriendly was out there, Havoc didn't want to call attention to their camp.

Luckily, Digger had opted to escort Jett into the tree line in the opposite direction as she hunted for dry campfire fuel. One less concern about bringing unwanted interest to their camp.

Back on the boulder, lying flat on his stomach, Havoc focused down amongst the leaves. With a range of six hundred meters, if there was something mammal in those trees, he'd be able to pick it out. And sure enough, amongst the blue and green spectrums, there was a blob of red and orange. A huge-ass blob of red and orange. That wasn't Scott, too big for a human.

"Do you see something?" Jett whispered from behind him. There was a thwack as she dropped her tarp of wood.

"Don't know. It's not moving. But it's showing up red in my thermal vision." Havoc rolled to see Jett drop a separate pile of tinder next to the larger pieces. She'd collected enough that they'd keep the blaze going long enough for them to tuck in.

"You set up my tent." Jett sent him a smile that felt genuine and warm to Havoc. "Thank you."

"I positioned them both on my groundcover since you were busy using yours."

"Yup, that works." She unzipped the flap and dug a fire-starting kit from the front pocket of her pack. Moments later, Jett had flames licking waist high.

"You're pretty good at that," Havoc said.

"Imagine that." She reached up and felt her sleeping bag and scowled. "Digger, I swear if you weren't so darned cute, I would be furious with you."

Digger popped his brows up and stuck out just the tip of his pink tongue.

"You know you'll have to sleep with me in my tent," Jett told Digger. "It's going to be at least a one-dog night." She looked off at the tree line. "I may need to find more wood."

"Hey, Jett, can I interrupt your planning for a minute?"

"Mmmm"

"Can you take a look at that heat signature for me?"

She brushed off her hands, sent a glance to the fire, then Digger, then did a scan of the area before she reached for Havoc's hand to climb the boulder.

Havoc held his monocular out to her. "Thermal," he said.

"Okay."

Blading his hand in the direction of the big red blob, Jett nodded and held the device to her dominant eye. "Huh," was all she said as she handed it back.

"Bear?" he asked.

"Way too big." She wiggled her fingers toward the binoculars hanging from the chord around Havoc's neck.

He pulled off his ball cap, scooped the strap over his head, and held them out for her.

"Thanks." Jett's fingers brushed over his hands, taking the binoculars from him. A buzz went up Havoc's arm where she touched him, and he both liked it and told himself he was acting like a high school freshman with a first crush.

Crush? Was that what this was? He thought he'd long outgrown such nervous excitement just to be near someone. While Havoc was thinking about the effect Jett was having on his internal circuitry, Jett was all business focusing the binoculars.

"Uh, okay. What we have here is a brown horse." She handed the binoculars back to him, and Havoc lifted them to his eyes.

He didn't see what she did. All Havoc saw was brown tree trunks. Kind of embarrassing in that he was the Echo sniper. Most of what he did in that role was to lie out in his ghillie suit, eyeball glued to the lens, watching the bad guys, and calling out movements for his partner to note. His visual dexterity was his key contribution to Echo.

"I threw rocks at a mare last night," Jett said. "She was about that coloration. The pebbles spooked her, and she ran. I wonder if that's her. It's an odd place for a horse to be standing. And you're right, it's not moving. I think I want to go down and take a look. If the horse is tied up and someone is camping down there, I want to know." She turned stiffly toward her fire. "Though, maybe I should have assessed before I lit the fire."

"You threw rocks at a horse?"

"Long story. I'll be back." She scooted onto her belly and slid from the boulder.

"You're a hundred percent it's not a bear."

"I'll tell you what. I'll take a can of bear spray with me. I'll put my hurricane whistle between my lips. If I blow it—"

"I'll know to run in the other direction."

Jett stopped and caught his eye, then burst out laughing when he grinned at her.

Dragging the can of bear spray from the side pocket of her pack, she poked that into the cargo pocket on her left leg. Pulling a rope out and draping it over her neck, Jett looked toward the hot spot. "If a bear does maul me," she whisper-called over her shoulder, "don't be sad. I've led a good life."

20

Jett

Chatkal Mountain Range, Kyrgyzstan

Sunday, Eighteen Hundred Hours

They hadn't put a rope on Digger. He seemed to have it in his mind that he was the one in charge. He was leading the two where he wanted them to go. Now, Digger was lying contentedly in front of the fire, with droopy eyes.

"I bet he's hungry." Jett smiled toward Havoc. "Is one of the MREs for Digger?"

"I thought it best. With any luck, Digger's our guide to Scott. We don't want him to go out hunting for his supper tonight."

"Yeah, that would be bad." Jett adjusted the rope she had draped over her shoulders. "Speaking of bad, it doesn't seem that you've been around many horses."

"That's very true."

"You should wait here then. Horses read body language pretty astutely. I don't want

to rile the horse."

Havoc had looked bemused as she started down the slope.

Now that she was closer, the horse was aware of her.

Jett stopped and rolled her shoulders. She imagined roots growing into the earth beneath her feet. Her babushka had taught her to ground herself and release her stress before she approached a horse. When Jett approached, her countenance was a calm authority, slow, smooth, and confident.

Jett angled herself, so she was walking toward the horse's shoulder. She wanted the horse to be able to see her easily. Approaching at a blind spot, or sneaking up on a horse, were both recipes for a horse to race for safety.

Pausing to recall the right tune, Jett began to sing one of her babushka's "catch a horse songs." They weren't written for catching a horse per se, but they were the folk songs from when her grandmother grew up in the circus. They would sing to the horses as they groomed and cared for the herd. It calmed the singer, and the singer's calm, in turn, helped to soothe the horse.

Jett knew that the horse was paying attention to her by the direction of his ears. Side-stepping and snorting, the horse angled his head to protect his vulnerable neck from a possible enemy. The horse nervously stretched his eyes wide.

Even in the dim light, Jett could see how dire the situation was for the horse. The lead, encircling his neck, was caught between two rocks. All of the vegetation within reach had been munched down to the soil. The back legs had long rips filled with coagulated blood. The skin under the rope was raw and angry from where the horse tried to free itself from the rocks.

The horse danced his feet, pawing his front hoof.

"You're okay," she hummed in Russian. "It's okay. Calm. Calm."

His head came up—was he asserting his dominance or getting ready to bolt? If he tried to bolt, he'd hurt himself further. As a prey animal, a horse's primary protection was to run. Hooves were also one of a horse's weapons. Getting kicked was dangerous.

It wasn't worth a kick to the gut to free this beast. Not this far out in the middle of nowhere.

Again, Jett made soothing sounds, clucks, and shushing noises and held her hands open and up in front of her. She took a step forward.

"Poor guy, let me help you get free. Think of the cool water you can drink. That will help, won't it?"

The horse responded with flaring nostrils, a snort, and a foot stomp.

Jett stopped where she was, singing, "Your lip is tight, and your tail is tucked. If I'm not careful, this rescue is going to go badly for both of us. Talk about a mission that's FUBAR."

The horse looked her right in the eye.

"Sorry. Too crude?" She put a smile into her eyes. "Sweet boy, I'm here to help you feel better. Do you miss your herd? You're traumatized, poor thing. Let's see how we get along, okay?"

A wolf howl went up miles away and was soon answered by the pack.

Jett looked up at the half-moon rising higher over the horizon.

While Jett wanted to save this animal from a painful death by dehydration, she was also worried that a tethered horse would entice the wolves down toward her camp. There was a hierarchy at play. Jett's safety trumped saving the horse. But saving the horse could also bring Jett, Havoc, and Digger a bit more security.

"It's okay. The wolves are far, far away. That came from miles away. A big guy like you trying to crash around the woods in the dark, the wolves are much better at seeing at night and much more agile amongst the trees. You need to get home. I bet you want your nice warm stable with some fresh hay. Let me help you. Okay? Food and water, that would help, wouldn't it?" Jett thought that the little trickle of a creek wasn't all that far, just down the slope about a hundred yards. It had probably formed thanks to that huge storm the other night. "Can you calm? Will you let me help you?"

The horse shied, moving to the far side of the boulder his lead rope was caught on. Jett followed him around, one eye on the horse one on the rope.

She pulled her knife from its sheath. If the horse would stand still, she could simply slice the trapped piece of rope free.

There was a ting as the horse's back hoof kicked at a sizeable stone, rolling it down the hillside.

There in the cavity left behind, lifted a viper's triangle head. It held steady as if surprised that its nice sun-warmed rock was suddenly gone, exposing its cold-blooded body to the shock of night air.

Jett froze.

This was how Renée was bitten. A missed step, a rolling rock, a frightened viper that whipped out for a strike.

The horse, now aware of the threat, tried to rear, tried to pull the rope free.

If he stepped on the viper's head, it might crush.

But then again, Jett had once found a copperhead in the street. Its body had pressed flat under the weight of a passing car. But it was still alive and struggling to glide off the burning hot asphalt. Jett hated to see the suffering of the slow, torturous death. Jett had signaled an SUV to please run over the snake to euthanize it. And the SUV guy tried. As big and heavy as his vehicle had been, as on mark as he'd been driving over the head, it took three tries.

That memory flashed into her mind.

If the horse didn't crush the head, surely the snake would sink its fangs. Then it would be the horse that Jett had to euthanize, and that thought was horrific.

Jett planted one hand on the rock and grabbed at the horse's rope with the other hand. "Please don't kick me." She sawed furiously at the line.

She held her breath until the last strand severed.

As the horse reared and whinnied, Jett threw her arm protectively over her head.

The snake coiled and sprang at the hooves as they landed mere inches away.

Jett thought the horse didn't fully realize it was free and could run away.

It reared again, its hooves pawing at the air, terror shrieks filled the night sky.

From behind Jett came a streak of black fur.

Digger leaped into the scene of flailing hooves with a vicious growl, frothing saliva.

As the viper sprang toward the horse's legs, Digger's teeth sank into the snake just below its head. With his powerful neck, Digger shook the snake, backing away from the horse and Jett.

The horse spun and dove into the forest.

Jett, without a thought in her head, other than that Digger was a teammate, reached out and grabbed the snake's tail. "Drop it, Digger," she screamed.

And to Jett's surprise, Digger caught her eye, and as if choreographed, Digger opened his mouth. Jett lassoed the snake over her head and sent it flying into the tree line.

Havoc came sprinting up to her. "Jett, are you okay? What happened?"

She bent, supporting herself with her hands on her knees, her chest heaving as her body responded to the dangers. When she had enough air to answer Havoc, she said. "Vipers in the area. You'll want to check your boots in the morning."

21

Chatkal Mountain Range, Kyrgyzstan

Sunday, Eighteen-Seventeen Hours

When Jett had stood, Havoc grabbed her into a hug. "Why would you do that?" His voice was exasperated.

"Crazy, I guess." She spun, so his arm draped over her shoulder, and she pointed back to their camp. "Honestly, something like that happened to me before when I was a smokejumper."

"Like parachuting into the wilds to put out forest fires? So much is making sense now."

"Like I know how to start a campfire?" Jett chuckled. "Thank you for a warm arm. Whew! It's suddenly got really chilly." She shivered and leaned into him.

"You're welcome. And I was thinking more about the hundred-and-ten-pound pack and run with the old-boy posturing than lighting a fire. What was the story from before?"

"There was a wounded fawn that was bleating somewhere in the forest. Though the call was close, it was on the other side of the fire line. It signaled in predators, tired and hungry from racing away from the flames. When the brown horse heard the wolves communicating, it might start screaming. Like with the fawn, I thought the horse's terror would let the wolves know that an animal was in jeopardy and call the pack down this way. Honestly, I already had a life-or-death fight today, and that's my quota."

"Mine, too. Digger would probably give us a heads up that the pack was circling us." Havoc curved down to scrub a hand between Digger's ears. "With our weapons limited to bear spray and knives, things might not go so well."

"Low profile is the best weapon."

"I agree. Freeing the horse was necessary. Come eat."

She huddled on a rock in front of the fire while Havoc handed her an MRE then grabbed one for himself. "What happened that the horse was down there like that?" Havoc started opening the various packets and setting up his dinner.

"It must have been there for a while. It's clearly exhausted from pulling and raw from the rope."

"Did you take the rope off?"

"I debated that when the horse was still tied, before it exposed the snake. The line had colored ribbons on it. That might be a way of identifying different horses. I cut the rope out of the rock. Hopefully, it's short enough now that he'll eat, drink, rest, then go find his people." Jett squirted some peanut butter on a cracker and ate it without tasting it. "Though, that might be hard to do. Some nomadic families move with their herds. They may be well away."

"Is there a reason you think that?" Havoc shoveled up a spoon of what looked like chicken stew.

"Uhm. There's a breed of horse called the Kyrgyz horse. It's got great stamina and is adapted to living in the mountains. A friend of mine rode one on the United States *kook-boro* team.

Mmm, that's not what they call that sport here in Kyrgyzstan. It's something else."

"A game on horseback? A race?"

"Team sport like polo only not. There's a fresh goat carcass on the ground. Each team tries to lean off their horse and pick up the dead goat. Then the team works to protect the person with the goat as they move to their goal. The goal isn't like a polo goal. It's more like a gigantic vat where they throw the carcass in and get the point. The other team has to dismount and go into the vat to get the dead goat. They throw it out, and the game is back in play. Whichever team gets the dead goat into the goal vat the most times wins."

Havoc held his spoon mid-way to his mouth. "This is a joke, right?"

"Nope." She squeezed the last of her peanut butter onto her second cracker. "True story. And that game is no joke. My friend is a titled MMA fighter, and he said he'd never done anything in his life as challenging and exhausting."

"How much do you think a dead goat weighs?"

Jett shrugged. "I dunno, maybe about as much as Digger there?"

Digger shoved into his front paws, lifting his torso and pulling his head back as if to say, "Uh-uh, you leave me out of the dead goat games." Jett and Havoc were doubled over laughing at him.

Digger laid back down.

"So my friend, actually he's not my friend. He's my friend Stella's boyfriend, Brady. Brady thought he was signing up for a different horse sport called *Er Enish*. That one is sort of like wrestling but on horseback."

"That makes sense with his MMA background. And I suppose, historically, that would make sense, too. These are descendants of Kubla Kahn. I read about how they'd drink horse blood when they had nothing to eat and how they'd ride into battle against the nomadic peoples. I could see the importance of being able to wrestle someone down from their horse. Steal the horse, put your adversary on lower ground where it's easier to kill them."

"But you can't imagine a reason for goat polo?" She opened her packet of chicken and noodles, deciding not to bother putting them on her mess plate.

"In the evenings, after a long day, my team and I like to play volleyball. It's a tradition that goes way back."

"To inception? So you *are* Delta Force."

"I didn't say that."

She pointed her spoon at him, then dug a bite from the packet. "You didn't deny it either."

"Volleyball is a lot of fun. And we're all aggressive as hell, but it serves a purpose. Cohesion, jumping strength, teamwork. Something lighthearted compared to our training exercises. Yeah, I'm guessing the dead goat polo is a Kubla Khan version of volleyball. And the wrestling on horseback is just training for battle."

"If you say so," she said out of the side of her mouth so she could speak before she swallowed. "So tell the truth, what group are you with?"

"Echo."

"Okay, Echo. With what institution?"

"The U.S. military."

"Pulling teeth." She shoveled another spoonful of noodles into her mouth, not even tasting them, just glad to have the calories. "I'm assuming a Tier One operator or someone who's an asshole."

"Not always mutually exclusive."

Jett sent him a grin.

"Your name Jett. Is that a nickname?"

"My name is Rosetta Jetteau Vargas."

"Jetteau – that sounds like the French word for water jet?"

"Exactly. My parents were working on a film in Belgium when I was born. And my father really liked the sound of the word. Mom liked the idea of calling me Jett, so there you have it."

"Movies?"

"Mom was a stunt double. Dad was a pyrotechnician. He made things go *boom*, safely. Now that they are older and retired, they sometimes consult."

"You hear about that kind of job, but I've never met anyone that does that."

Jett scraped out the last of her noodles, then held out the bag to see if Digger wanted to lick it clean. "Where did you grow up?"

Digger belly crawled over and sniffed.

"New York outside of Rochester."

"What did your parents do?"

"My father is a third-generation mason. The family has a brick and pavement company. Mom was a stay-at-home mother. She did the books at night, sitting at the kitchen table. Very traditional. Catholic. I was an acolyte at my church."

"Why did you say that?" She wiggled her finger at the bar of chocolate on Havoc's plate. "I'll trade you the chocolate bar for my candy."

Havoc handed her the chocolate with a smile.

When Jett stretched out the purple bag of candies to him, Havoc held up a hand. "I'm good. Why don't you hold on to those for tomorrow?"

Jett ripped open the packaging, desperate for the infusion of chocolate. At that point, *any* chocolate would do. "Grew up Catholic, not practicing Catholic?"

"Exactly. It's more of a traditional touchstone for me. My parents were hardcore."

"Yeah? Lots of kids?"

Havoc swiped a finger under his nose, and Jett scrubbed a napkin to clean herself. "Thank you."

"Six. I was number two in that crowd."

"Are you allowed to tell me your real name?"

"No, sorry. Not until I'm off the clock."

Jett thought it was a weird dynamic that she was starting to feel 'linked to' rather than 'allied with' Havoc. A real connection. A lot of curiosity. And a fair share of sexual tension. And yet, what did she really know of the man? Not even his first name. *Put on the brakes, girl!* "So you'll tell me after this whole thing is done? You know it makes me think that you don't like your name. Ebenezer? Winston?"

Havoc startled, then concern drew his brows together. "You don't like Winston?"

"You can't say it without sounding whiny. I'm sure I must have a Winston in my past somewhere that settled that impression in my mind. I'm picturing a runny nose that he wipes off with his hand then touches things."

"Vivid imagery." He chuckled.

"One of two things are going to happen with either the name Ebenezer or Winston. A. You're going to get the shit kicked out of you by the other boys. Or B. You're going to learn to fight so well that you might become a special forces operator." Jett looked for a body language tell.

"I think you need something like a Barney or an Egbert for that." Havoc got down on the ground when Digger rolled onto his back and looked over to see if there were any takers for giving a belly rub.

"Egbert?" She paused. "That doesn't seem to fit you. Round and white, Humpty Dumpty-ish."

"That was a funny look that crossed your face."

"Yeah, I was just thinking back to an interaction I had in the mountains. Not an interaction. I was hiding behind some boulders. But this guy was describing me to his friends. His friends thought my skin color looked sickly white."

"Are these the guys who tried to kidnap you?" Havoc's posture instantly changed; he seemed to swell in size, and the look on his face hardened. Intimidating as hell if you weren't used to men morphing like something out of a sci-fi flick in front of your face—going from good old boy to stalking panther in the blink of an eye.

"They were, but not because of this case. Just some horrific, misogynistic custom they have going on in this country. A cautionary tale to the whole idea of 'Chesterton's Fence.'"

Havoc relaxed his shoulders a little and turned part of his attention to rubbing Digger's belly. "I don't know that one."

"The basic idea is that you shouldn't tear down Chesterton's fence until you know why he built it in the first place."

Havoc held up a finger and seemed to run that around in his mind for a bit. "An interesting concept. It has its applications. But if you spent your life hunting down the whys and wherefores of the existence of every fence that Chesterton built, you might not get much done."

"It comes out of an early twentieth-century book by Chesterton."

"So not a farmer with a strangely placed fence."

"This author was talking about a reformer who sees a need to reform. Or sees a fence and sees a need to pull it down. Good intentions can lead to bad consequences. And that's what my guest house hostess, Tetushka, the one you met this morning—I think I already told you, I call her Tetushka…"

"'Auntie' in Russian, that's nice."

"Isn't it? She's been great. As a matter of fact, she showed me on my map three spots that were filled with ghouls where no one should go. The first was the sulfur spring. I really want to check out the other two. Mystery Solving 101."

"Ha!" Havoc laughed. "That was what I thought when Tetushka told me about the haunted spring. Go on, what does Tetushka have to do with Chesterton's fence thoughts?"

"USSR era policy took a weird alternative route: instead of protecting women, it made their lives living hell. The intentions were admirable."

"In the USSR policy?"

"Yep. They attempted to give males and females a more egalitarian education. But…here we end up with social constructs that encourage my taxi driver to bring his friends up into the mountains to kidnap me and make me his wife."

"What? It's a tradition in Kyrgyzstan for taxi drivers to kidnap a woman for his wife?"

"Men in general. But yeah." Jett shoved her wrappings into the waste bag and sealed it tight.

"I…" Havoc shook his head. "What?"

"That was my reaction." She stood and gathered Havoc's trash as well. "You cooked. I'll clean."

"I've been heading into socio-political dynamics that I can't fully appreciate by simply showing up. I roll up on a situation that I don't understand. 'Ah, I think this might be a Chestnut fence.'"

"Chesterton's." She went and sat on the tarp with Digger and Havoc.

"Thank you. Typically, when I roll up on a situation that I don't understand, I let the person who knows the dynamic best set the pace. I don't want to go in and do something that will upset the status quo because I don't grasp the nuances." Without asking, Havoc slid into place behind Jett, his legs on either side of her. "I'm going to work on your neck the way I promised earlier."

"So much gratitude. Thank you." Jett swept her hair to the front out of Havoc's way and combed her fingers through the length. She lifted in and sniffed. "I'm going to smell like sulfur until I can get to a shower."

"Dangerous stuff that. Do you think the ghouls will think you're one of their own?"

"In that case," Jett said sleepily, "I'll be fine. You're the one that will be the outsider." She exhaled stress. "So, is that how you're handling this mission now?"

"You lost me," Havoc said, warming her neck with calloused hands.

"You rolled up on this AWG situation."

"And I'm stepping back a bit until I get my sea legs. Yes. You're in charge since you've been on this for months, and I just stepped off the plane a few hours ago."

"Crazy how things can change so quickly, huh? Sea legs… You're Navy. You're a SEAL."

He slid his thumbs down either side of her spine, and Jett felt her muscles melt under his ministrations. "I started in the Army, and I remain in the Army. Back to the cabby looking for a wife. They kidnap their wives…surely, they wouldn't kidnap foreigners. Right? Is that legal?"

"I'm told that tradition trumps religion which trumps law. So if it were illegal, it's pretty far down the 'We-give-a-shit' list. The police turn their back. But to your point, they thought I was local. I'm an Uzbek-Costa Rican mutt. I guess my eye shape and my hair made him think I was from the country. I didn't speak to him."

"Hmm, maybe. You're fair-skinned compared to the people I've seen on this trip." Havoc gently kneaded her shoulders, making Jett groan under her breath as his thumb found a knot and pressed against it with his thumb.

"They did mention that my skin looked like curdled milk."

"Huh."

"What, 'huh?'" Jett turned slightly to catch his gaze.

"Once seen, cannot be unseen."

"Thanks."

"Yep."

Silence fell companionably between them.

After a long moment, Jett added, "You know there's another horse game they play here with the same idea of just taking what woman you want. It's called *Kyz kuu*."

"Translation?"

"Girl-chasing. A marriage, if you will, between horse racing and a middle-school kissing game. A guy on a horse waits at the starting line. Are you picturing this? The girl gets on her horse and gallops past the guy. They race for the finish line. So the girl, in essence, has a head start."

"Because she has momentum, and the guy is starting out cold."

"Exactly. She goes roaring past him. If he catches her before they cross the finish line, he tries to kiss her. That's a win."

"For the guy, maybe," Havoc said, pressing his thumbs up under the ridge of Jett's skull that had been a dull ache for days now.

She could kiss this man for the relief he was bringing her.

"What happens if the girl beats him to the finish line? He loses?"

"Beats is the right verb. If she gets there first, she can whip the guy, and that's her victory."

"Sounds a little like our meeting."

"I didn't whip you, and you didn't kiss me."

"And yet, I look at it as a win-win, surviving and all. I'd love to see a guy on horseback attempt to give you an unwanted kiss. After what happened at the waterfall, I'd bet on you. I'd be rich." He stood up and reached for her hand to get Jett up too. "Time for bed. We have a big day hunting for Scott tomorrow."

"Would you split the winnings with me?" Jett went over and felt the sleeping bag.

"Whatever split you deemed to be correct. Still damp?"

"Sadly, yes." Jett sent a demoralized glance toward her tent.

Havoc picked up his binoculars. "I'm going up on that boulder to take a last look. Maybe I can spot the flicker of a campfire. While I'm gone, I'd like you to consider an invitation. The weather report that I read before coming out to find you this morning said possible snow tonight. The rating on my sleeping bag is subzero, and it's extra wide. We could both fit in it. With Digger sleeping at our feet, we could keep the body heat in one tent. Though three in my tent will be tight. We can store the supplies in the other."

Jett didn't answer. Standing toe to toe, she tipped her head back, and their gazes held. Havoc gently brushed the side of her face. "Just an offer, I'll be back."

22

Chatkal Mountain Range, Kyrgyzstan

Sunday, Eighteen-Fifty Hours

Walking back to the campsite, a grin spread across Havoc's face.

A pink glow stick lit Havoc's tent. He could see the shadows of Jett spreading his sleeping bag.

Havoc was out of his element with Jett.

Once a call went up, Havoc was mission ready. Mission focused.

He'd fought knife battles in rivers before. He'd hiked mountains with hundred-pound packs looking for persons of interest, precious cargo, intel—all of it.

Havoc couldn't count the number of missions that had him doing HALO jumps—sucking a lungful of bottled oxygen before popping out of an airplane at high altitude and waiting until the last possible moment to pull his toggle and release a chute. He'd landed in some of the bleakest, most volatile places in the world.

Hell, he'd spent a week surviving on worms in a jungle as he marched a warlord to his trial. He didn't love that particular week shin-deep in mud, swarmed by mosquitos.

And yet, he *did* love it.

Havoc thrived with the physical and mental challenges of his job. He couldn't wait for his next mission assignment.

But he'd never been on a mission like this.

Not even remotely like this.

The picture of Jett bent over at the water's edge with her heart-shaped ass sifted back into his awareness, and his body instantly responded.

Havoc was usually good about filing things away. But not this time.

He needed to keep his head on straight.

Wipe the shit-eating grin from his face.

And remember that Scott's life was on the line.

Peter and Tink could also be in dire straits.

Hell, even the *world order* was at risk.

And yet, he grinned, knowing that Jett was going to trust him, a stranger, and sleep tucked tight in a single sleeping bag.

That meant something, right?

When he thought that, his dick jumped to attention.

Yeah, that couldn't happen tonight. Maybe if he slept facing away from her, she could find a comfortable way to tuck in without getting stabbed in the back by his curious cock.

Maybe she'd just fall straight to sleep and would never know.

Havoc caught himself on this walk to his tent, with the glowing pink light, thinking more in lines of personal life, not work. And for that, he rebuked himself.

Havoc's being here wasn't a job. It was a calling to go out and accomplish the things, save or take the lives, grab up the 'precious' whatever that Uncle Sam was looking for next.

Being with Jett wasn't work, either.

It was easy. Smooth. Even amongst the tumult of the day. It still felt that way to him.

Havoc liked to listen to her ideas, to laugh with her. Look at her. It was a kind of magic, really, that when she was next to him and touching him that everything seemed…good.

But maybe what was going on in his mind wasn't what Jett was experiencing.

He'd have to ask more questions, let her set boundaries.

Then he remembered the knife in her hand as she was ready to stab the shit out of him at the waterfall. Jett was a fully actualized woman. He felt sure she'd let him know if he put his toe over some line. But he never wanted it to come to that. Once crossed, it was hard to regain trust. Yeah, he'd ask more questions to make sure that they were feeling the same thing, and if they didn't, then he could back the hell off.

He wasn't sure how he'd make himself do that.

He should back the hell off either way. *Mission focused.*

Man, she was smart. Brave. Capable. Kind. This job hadn't broken her ability to have empathy and be thoughtful.

As his mind moved through this internal conversation, he thought of the old man with his fingers tapping Havoc's sleeve on the plane. "A heart is the strongest muscle." And, "Tell her you love her."

He didn't love her; they'd just met.

But he was falling under her spell.

And, honestly, that was just fine with him.

But when the mission ended, he'd probably never see her again,

Wasn't *that* a hell of a thought?

23

Havoc

Chatkal Mountain Range, Kyrgyzstan

Sunday, Eighteen Forty-Two Hours

Havoc slid into their camp on silent feet.

The wolf pack seemed to have finished their eerie serenade. Havoc imagined what it would be like to try to sleep alone on this mountain listening to that as Jett had. It must have made for some uncomfortable nights. And he wondered if that's why Jett's neck was knotted tight.

Jett had banked the fire, and there was a mess kettle with hot water. He assumed it was for him to wash up.

She'd left the windows and door unzipped on their supply tent to allow airflow through the netting.

With his headlight switched to red to preserve his night vision, Havoc unzipped the door to her tent and stopped to observe.

Jett had laid her sleeping bag out flat in the little pup tent. Her clothes spread out to air. Jett had pulled the dried clothes from the line and neatly folded them, placing them on top of his sack. They were the clothes Havoc was wearing when he dove into the water-fall pool to save her from drowning—a hero in search of a damsel in distress.

There was no such damsel around, that was for sure.

Moving them to the side, Havoc tugged at the draw string to open his bag.

At home, he slept commando. On missions, he slept in briefs with his clothes laid out beside him, ready to jump.

Neither was going to work tonight.

Snagging his Dopp kit, Havoc pulled a silk base layer, pants, and shirt. They'd have to do.

After a trek into the tree line to relieve himself, Havoc cleaned up from the day, changed, and stood outside his tent. "Jett, I'm coming in."

He squatted and sat just inside the door to pull off his boots. He remembered what Jett said about checking them for snakes in the morning. Fun times.

Digger lay twisted and belly up at the foot of the tent. He peeped through a half-lifted lid then shut his eyes, uninterested in Havoc's doings.

Havoc crawled over him.

The tent was a good size for one. Tight for three.

Jett rolled over, her face soft and sleepy. Her eyes blinked open.

Without thinking, Havoc reached over and traced a finger over her forehead, moving the silken strands of her jet-black hair out of her eyes. A gentle smile wiggled the corners of his lips, and she smiled back.

Their gazes held.

"Everything okay?" she asked.

"I didn't see any signs of campfires. Looks like Digger's content."

"He snores and passes gas."

"Sounds like one of the team."

She wrinkled her brow and pursed her lips to make a stink face. "You're going to snore and pass gas, too?"

"Kick me if I do. I'll go sleep in the other tent."

"No, you won't. It's freezing, and you'd go hypothermic. I am not dragging your body down the mountain. No dying. Do you hear me, soldier?" Without waiting for a response, she added. "Come crawl in. I opened a chemical heater, and it's pretty comfortable."

She was pressed into the seam of the bag. And Havoc was again surprised by how little she was. How big he was in comparison. And yet, she damned near killed him today. That was some fierce training she had. A warrior's mindset.

"Not to embarrass you, but I'm just going to say this out loud. I have a…male body."

She tipped back her head and laughed.

"That dropped my testosterone about fifty points." Havoc pitched his voice to sound wounded.

"Sorry, I just know what you're getting at. A healthy male. Morning wood. Am I right?"

"I don't want you to be uncomfortable. I thought if it was said…"

She was thinking about my morning wood?

"I'm a big girl. I know how bodies work."

"But that kicking you were planning for snores, please use it at any point if you need me to adjust."

"Thank you."

He slid deeper into the bag and zipped it closed. "Amazing country," he said, hoping that a change of conversation would move his thoughts someplace other than his dick. "What have you seen out here?"

"A lot of beautiful vistas," she whispered. "Amazing wildlife. Nothing of help to Uncle Sam."

Havoc lowered his voice to match hers. "Any guesses?"

"Just those haunted places that Tetushka circled on the map for me. The places that the locals will not go. One of the locations is in Scott's area, and the other is over at the edge of Scott's grid and Peter and Tinka's grid. Both should get eyes on them even if it's just to rule them out."

"You were ruling out the haunted spring?"

"One stone, two birds. Yeah, I checked that box. But I found a city slicker in loafers and a beautiful doggo."

"And a horse."

"That wasn't at the spring, but yeah, not a bad day treasure hunting."

"I'm a treasure?" Havoc asked with a chuckle.

"Or fool's gold. The jury's out."

Havoc wasn't sure what to say to that, so he stayed silent.

"I apologize. That wasn't at all the truth. Though your approach was startling, I am very grateful that you dove for me when you thought I was at risk. I'm grateful that you decided to continue with me while I try to find Scott. Yeah, I'm grateful to have a companion. It's easy to get weirded out in the backcountry alone with no comms. In the week I was on the mountain alone, I only saw six people, and that was on my way down. It's eerie to know you're it. There is no help."

"Those were the six kidnappers?"

"Yep."

"There is the satellite phone in an emergency."

"You know that depends. Weather. Tree canopy. A body that is capable of retrieving the phone and pressing the buttons."

"The planets have to align."

She laughed. "Exactly."

The wolves took up their call and response.

A shiver ran through Jett, and Havoc pulled her back, so she was leaning onto his chest. He rubbed her arms to warm her. "Does that happen often?"

"Every night. The sound seems closer tonight. But I'm quite a distance from Friday's grid. So they might not be moving toward me. I might be moving toward their territory."

"Hard to sleep with that going on."

"It is indeed." Jett spun so she could look Havoc in the eye. "I wonder what happened to Scott that he couldn't call for help."

Havoc scraped his teeth over his lip. "I'm trying to keep my imagination in check. Being out here, seeing the terrain and the dangers, the rocks and wildlife. I can see how things could go very badly, very quickly, and with no immediate support? We just need to hold onto hope."

Jett whispered, "And cross our fingers that we're in time."

24

———

JETT

    Chatkal Mountain Range, Kyrgyzstan

Monday, Zero Seven Hundred Hours

Up, fed, dressed, packed up, Havoc looked down at Digger. "Ready, boy?"

Digger sat, waiting for a command. Havoc held out a notebook where Scott had handwritten scientific data as part of Jett's cover story.

They had no idea if Digger had been scent trained. They were guessing at this point about how to best signal to Digger what needed to happen.

Wafting the notebook under Digger's nose, Havoc said, "Where's Scott? Where's your dad? Go get Scott."

Digger's nose was up in the air. His nostrils pulled the scents in as he oscillated his head. Then, without looking back, he took off.

"He's heading north by northwest. That's the same direction as yesterday."

"He might have a girlfriend in the wolf pack," Havoc said.

Jett sent him a stink face and trudged behind Digger.

Throughout the morning, they were mostly silent as they focused on scanning the vista.

Now, they were well into the day. The sun was brightly overhead. Jett kept turning around and looking behind them.

"What's up?" Havoc asked as she came to a complete stop.

"I thought…well, son of a gun."

Out of the woods came the horse from last night. He walked right over to Jett to nuzzle her.

"He thinks you're his mama," Havoc said.

"That's not good. Go home! Go home, horsey!" She clapped her hands then threw her arms in the air.

The horse looked contented and had zero interest in going off somewhere else.

"In ancient times, if you saved a man's life, that life was dedicated to you. Seems this horse might have been raised in that philosophy."

"Keep going." Jett pointed toward Digger. "I'm not coddling this horse. He belongs to someone, and the more we interact, the harder it will be for him to head in the right direction."

"He's an orphan."

"Yeah, well. I'm also on the hunt for my colleague."

"There are reasons why a horse might be helpful."

"No, there are reasons why a known and trained horse might be helpful. We know nothing about this horse."

"Still—" Havoc started, then his hand shot out to stop Jett. "Wait. Shh. Do you hear that?" Havoc dropped his chin and focused on the sounds.

"I don't hear anything. What are you—"

"Shhh. Listen."

Jett shook her head then whispered, "What do you think you're hearing?"

"Heavy metal?"

"Scott, there you are. What the hell are you doing?" Jett called out when she saw a man lying on the rock reading from his phone.

When Scott looked up to see Jett, Havoc, and Digger, he rubbed his eyes and stared harder as if in disbelief.

"Scott," Jett called as they approached. His setup was improbable, balanced the way it was here on the slope where they were. "What happened to you?"

Scott collapsed his head onto his arms and started crying. Big, hysterical sobs.

Digger ran in and licked Scott's face.

Scott reached around Digger's neck. "I love you. I love you. Thank you. God bless you. When you didn't come back last night, it was bad. But you were doing it. You were finding help. Bless you. God bless you."

Jett was crying along with Scott.

Havoc was glassy-eyed, too, as they made their way over the lip of rock to see what had happened.

Scott was lying on his stomach, piked at his hips. One leg stretched along the flat surface. The other leg wasn't visible.

Jett laid down beside Scott, so he didn't use up any energy trying to see and communicate with them.

Havoc circled around to assess the situation. "Yeah, man, looks like your leg is wedged in here but good. How the heck did this happen?"

"Let's get him fed and hydrated first," Jett said. "Then we can hear the story."

"I've been doing okay with the hydration." Scott's eyes

burned with excitement at the mention of eating. "Some food, though, would be awesome."

Jet pulled out some of her MREs. "What do you want? Sweet, we can do breakfast. Or we can do like a South American kind of thing. Chicken noodles with vegetable sauce?"

"That one sounds good. Anything really. I've spent a few days eating dog kibble, so you know I'm not particularly picky. Do you have enough to feed something to Digger?"

"He's already had two," Havoc said. "Any more, and he might have intestinal issues. He's probably been hunting if you haven't been feeding him. He seems to be a healthy weight. And he was 'normal dog' hungry when we fed him, not 'dog starving to death' hungry."

Digger lay at what looked like a practiced angle as Scott scrubbed his fur. "I was hoping Digger was feeding himself. Not that I wanted my best bud to go hungry, but when you have a hankering for dog kibble, it's a rare person who can bring themselves to share." Scott got teary. "I hoped… I know I've been losing weight, but Digger seems to be gaining weight. As long as he was doing okay, I figured I could be a little selfish with the kibble."

Digger reached in and lapped at Scott's face.

"I'm going to heat this up for you." Jett moved Scott's cup closer and filled it from her water bladder. "I'd like you to be drinking. I just filled my camel bladder. It's been filtered and treated with iodine tablets, so it'll taste appropriately bad." She stabbed her knife into the MRE packet, pulled out the contents, and spread them on a flat part of the boulder. Tearing open the green heater bag, Jett slid the main meal component into the bag. "Five minutes, and you'll be chowing down. Let's get that one in you and see how you're doing, digest a bit before I give you another, okay?"

Jett turned. "What are you seeing, Havoc?"

"The guy's got his leg stuck between two rocks," Havoc said. It was the way they trained to deal with issues. No emotion. No handwringing. You arrive, you assess, you work the problem. Keep everyone calm, crack a few jokes. It helped the mind find creative solutions.

"Brilliant assessment," Jett said as she pinched the skin on the back of Scott's hand to check his hydration levels.

"Thank you," Havoc called back.

"Scott, you're not as dehydrated as I'd feared, but I'd like you to sip at the water. No glugging, okay?"

"How did you get into this position?" Havoc asked as he pulled on his headlamp and pulled out a penlight from his pack.

"I was on my own for a couple of days because Deepak was having chest pains. I'd abandoned our gear and got him down the mountain. Do you have an update on him?"

"Sorry," Havoc said. "I was told he had a medical issue, and that's it."

"That's it until I see him. Then I'm gonna kill him, leaving me on the damned mountain like this."

Jett lifted his hand to check his pulse. "Let's leave the homicidal intent off to the side while I get your baseline pulse, and then you can go back to steaming mad."

"I was setting up the camp, trying to figure out what equipment I needed to hike out and what equipment to bury under some rocks. I couldn't carry all of Deepak's stuff and mine, too. What if I were to twist my ankle or something?"

"Exactly," Jett said. "Your pulse is a little fast. Understandable. I'll check again after you've had more water. Drink."

Scott took a sip. "I looked up the night of my predicament, and there's a flash of red. Okay, now my frame of mind." He paused and looked at Jett. "Is Havoc read in? Can I talk about this?"

"You're fine. Drink."

"My thought process is that the Zorics are taking advantage of the rocky area." He sipped some water. "That they might have their set up in a cave. That would prevent the satellites and drones from finding heat signatures, lights, or electrical activity on the surface. We believe the Zorics only turn on their apparatus for a test assault, then everything is immediately shut down and goes dark."

"Right," Jett said.

"I was bent back looking at the stars, thinking that it was amazing. One of those night skies so chockful of stars that it was impossible to find constellations. Then a flash of red surprised me. I thought it could be a flare in the distance. Down on the little plateau, I couldn't see the trajectory. If I knew where it was heading, I could figure where it came from."

"Drink."

"The origin of the flare probably needed investigating." Scott picked up the cup and emptied it into his mouth, holding it out to Jett for more. "I was doing my best mountain goat impression. And obviously, I don't qualify. My heel caught in a crevice. As I grabbed at rocks to catch my balance, my foot turned and slid down too. And as it turns out, my foot is caught in there. Now the good part is it's a pretty deep hole, so for bathrooming purposes, I'm all set to go with some painful shifts. I can keep my area pretty clean. The bad part? Everything else."

"When did this happen?"

Scott reached out to a little bowl that had been scooped out like a bird's nest full of eggs. He picked up the pebbles and counted them out. "Twenty days ago."

"I was hoping that the date you wrote on the collar was a mistake," Jett said. "Holy shit."

"Yeah, that's what I've been saying this whole time. But I figured sooner or later, someone would show up. Barring that, I figured I could pull myself free if I starved myself down to being skeletal enough. Might take a few months."

"Yeah, but then how would you get down the mountain?" Jett asked.

Scott pointed to a plastic bag that was out of his reach. "That's a First Strike ration pack." First Strikes were a grab-and-go. While an MRE covered a single meal, the First Strike packs contained a full day's rations, about three thousand calories spread over three meals and snacks. "I figured once I was bone thin and could pull my way free. Eat enough food to get my body ambulatory and wend my way down to the road. We're a day's hike from help."

Jett sent him a look of disbelief.

"Don't look at me that way. It's a solid plan."

"Starvation was your strategy?" Jett shook her head.

"It wasn't really the plan I would like to work, but the food I had was the food I had. I tried to be strategic about my circumstances. Massive weight loss. Hopefully, not starvation. I took my inspiration from that story about the truck that was too tall for the tunnel that got stuck. All of the engineers couldn't figure out how to get it free, wedged in the way it was. But it was blocking the mountain passage. Finally, this little kid suggests they just deflate the tires. And everyone smacked themselves in the head. They deflated the tires, and the truck rolled on out."

Jett handed him a pouch with a banana nut ranger bar. "Here, start with this. Do you want me to make you some tropical punch?"

Scott was shoving this bar in his mouth, and Jett snatched it back. "You're going to vomit everything up. Go slow. Here, I'll help mete it out."

He chewed and swallowed and said, "I could go for some punch."

"Go on," Jett said. "You were explaining your strategy."

"I tried to judge how best to make that work. Three thousand calories per pack were enough for a big guy on the move, the fewer calories I took in, the sooner I might be able to get free, but I didn't want to be so weak that I couldn't hike myself out. That's why I shoved that last bit out of the way. This is me trying to deflate myself."

"But your boot is stuck," Havoc pointed out. "And your boot is tied tightly around your ankle. You're not angling your ankle to pull free of that no matter how skinny and delicate your foot became."

"Shhh. I don't need your negativity." He accepted another piece of ranger bar from Jett. "I thought if my thighs were a few inches smaller and my arm could snake in, I could reach scissors or knife close enough to undo the laces. At one point, I thought I might be able to twist and turn to abrade the shoelaces, but that didn't work. The rocks are pretty sharp down there. I'd be willing to risk a gash and an open wound if I truly believed it would work. But from how things felt, it was a bad choice. It's been pretty awful out here to begin with. Feverish with blood poisoning didn't seem that appealing. I was working my plan. I had my solar battery charger out. I've been listening to books on tape, listening to my music playlists. I played them on loud while the sun shone. I figured if anyone was in the area, they'd find me."

"That worked," Havoc said. "Good job."

"And I let the battery wear down at night blaring the music."

"Any particular reason for heavy metal?" Havoc asked, elbowing Digger, who had moved down to sniff around where Havoc was conducting his assessment.

"Scare away the wolves and brown bears." Scott ate the last of the bar and watched Jett put peanut butter and apple jelly on a wheat snack bread.

"What?" Havoc came up on his elbow.

"Seems like a nasty way to go, stuck here as I am like a Scott-sandwich at a picnic."

"Scott, I'm handing this to you. But slow," Jett said. "We don't want you vomiting it all back up."

"Wasted calories, and that would be a huge mess," Scott said.

"We don't want to add to your discomfort," Jett countered. She took back the sandwich and broke off a piece for him.

"I agree with my tactical brain. But I'm fighting my hands that want to grab at you and all the food. The starvation diet has been going on for almost three weeks. You might want to pull yourself back a tad if you're denying me food."

"Not denying. Postponing."

"Still, for your safety. My survival pedal is pushing down pretty hard."

Jett scooted back out of his arm's reach and pulled the food along with her. While Scott's tone had been light and teasing, the gleam in his eye told Jett that he was being honest. A brain that senses its body is in danger can do some pretty unexpected and hellish things to stay alive.

"A wolf would have chewed off its leg to get free from a trap." When Havoc said that, Jett assumed Havoc was trying to distract Scott. Jett was sure that Havoc had picked up the same cues that she had.

"Yeah, the sad truth was I couldn't get my mouth around there, or I might have tried. I was still hoping to become a skeleton and just untie my shoe. I mean, there are worse things than to have to eat a cheesecake or twenty to get the weight back on. I just tried to keep myself distracted. All I had was my phone, my chores, and reading my Kyrgyzstan tourist book."

Jett handed him the rest of the peanut butter and jelly cracker. "What were your chores?" Jett asked crab walking down the hill to conference with Havoc.

"Let's see, every night, I would set the mess kit pot under the rain poncho dew funnel. Between that and licking my tent in the morning, I stayed okay hydrated. Then I move all of my things out of my tent, put the tent over me, and put all my things back in there to keep them safe."

"Pro bonus, you have a good tan going, lots of Vitamin D," Jett said as her gaze locked with Havoc, and he slowly shook his head to indicate he hadn't come up with a strategy.

"You take the wins where you can find them," Scott said, his agitation was rising. He had helpers, he had food, he just needed to get free.

Jett had seen this in her rescues as a smokejumper. Someone is so close to safety that they go haywire. Had they been patient and calm, things would probably work out. But no, they get riled and desperate. They do all the wrong things. If Scott were to start yanking on his leg, it might make it swell and make things worse. "What did you learn in your book?" Jett tried to ease Scott toward rational thinking about factual matters. Lower the anxiety levels.

"To be freaked out about bears."

Okay, that wasn't going to lower anyone's stress, Jett thought. "Serious?"

"Did you know a brown bear can weigh up to 500 pounds?"

"Hmm, I thought they'd be bigger." Jett had dealt with bears in the backcountry, but they were usually fleeing the blaze, so they weren't interested in eating her. Besides, she frequently had a chainsaw in hand, and that noise scared everything away.

"The book said I should avoid them."

"Sage advice," Havoc said, one hand clasped around Jett's thigh as she used the lights to gather her own assessment.

"It said to keep human food away, but I don't really have a choice there. I should set up my cooking site away from where I sleep, and it should be downwind. Ditto, no can do. So I was left to heavy metal. I thought easy listening wouldn't offer the same level of protection."

"Probably not. Good call." Jett focused on Havoc. "Thoughts?"

"He's stuck in a crevice," Havoc said with a look toward Jett that told her the situation was complicated beyond immediate resolution.

"Sherlock, your powers of observation continue to enthrall me."

"I also read all of my first aid apps," Scott continued, "that downloaded information onto my phone."

"Anything helpful?" Havoc asked.

"Apparently, there aren't enough folks that land in this particular position for them to have given up any space for it. But I can now talk you through how to remove a fishing hook from someone's face."

"Helpful," Jett said. "Just not today." She turned to Havoc. "Ready to develop a strategy?"

25

———

Chatkal Mountain Range, Kyrgyzstan

Monday, Fourteen Forty-six Hours

Havoc laid on his stomach, aiming the light into the crevice so he could direct Jett's hand. Havoc's arm simply wouldn't fit in the slender space beside Scott's leg.

Jett took off her hoody and sprawled on the rock, trying to slide her hand down Scott's thigh to get to the shoelaces. Scott was right. Jagged rocks lined either side of the crevice.

"Already, I've lost enough weight and muscle tone," Scott called back to them. "I can sort of slap the sides of the rocks, which I couldn't the first week. I had what was left of my First Strike rations. And I had the ones Deepak left behind. Luckily, I had laid those meals out. I was trying to decide what I wanted to eat when all this happened."

"That was at the end of the week, though. A couple of First Strikes didn't keep you in this good of shape for three weeks," Havoc pointed out.

"I like to carry three days emergency rations. It's extra weight and takes up space in my pack, but you know, in case I stepped in a hole…" He was jabbering. Nerves. "To lose weight, I allowed myself one thing at each meal. But two of those things had to be small, so say I had a shelf-stable pepperoni sandwich—big—then I might have a beef jerky for breakfast or a pack of raisins for dinner. And a piece of caffeinated gum as a snack."

Jett caught Havoc's eye and shook her head to let him know she wasn't able to get her hand down as low as the boot. "What do you think, Havoc? Ever seen anything like this before?"

"That, I have not. What are you feeling down there?"

"It's like the jaws of a bear trap. I can't reach his laces, but I have an idea. Sorry for feeling you up," Jett said, pulling her hand back out.

"As long as it's you who's doing the feeling up and not Havoc. Actually, I take that back. Havoc, you can feel me up, too, if you're getting me out of here."

Havoc ignored Scott to focus on Jett.

Jett sat up and pulled her hoody back on. "Scott, how do you tie your laces?"

"I make a loop that I call the tree. I pinch it between my thumb and my forefinger, and I run the other side around it twice like two rabbits being chased by a fox. Bottom rabbit jumps over the top rabbit and pull."

Jett moved up the rock to sit next to Scott's head. "Let me ask you a different way. Once you have your bootlaces in a bow, do you double tie them like this?" She plunked her foot onto the rock where Scott could visualize her laces.

"Three times the charm for me."

Jett tied the third knot in her lace and looked at it, wiggled it, considered it from various angles, sliding her finger in here and there.

"What are you thinking?" Havoc asked.

"That we need some C4 to blow up the rock."

"Might lose the whole foot if we tried that," Havoc deadpanned.

"Meh, he'd be free. You have to take the good with the bad."

"I'm right here listening to this shit. You know that, right?" Scott squirmed around until he could see Havoc. "You didn't pack C4, did you?"

"No," Havoc said. "You're safe from a blast exfil."

"This is obviously a difficult situation." Jett used the kind of soft-toned conviction that she used when rescuing people from dangerous areas. "It's going to take some time, but we've got you. You're going to get out. Gallows humor aside, I want you to know we will not leave you. We're going to figure this out. You're going to go home. Okay?"

Scott's chin trembled as he nodded.

"How is the food sitting?" Jett asked.

"Fine, I think."

"I'm going to hand you your rice and bean packet. Slow though, okay?" She held it out. "If you weren't as well hydrated as you are, I wouldn't allow it. Good job."

"Thanks." Scott accepted the pouch.

"You didn't do that by licking your tent and putting out dew funnels," Havoc said.

"It rained the other day. I laid out all of my clothes, so they caught the water, and I wrung the cloth to fill up anything that could hold it—camel pack, the garbage bags from the First Strike meals. I kept everything to use for whatever. When I couldn't squeeze any more out, I sucked the water from the cloth. But it's been enough water to keep me minimally hydrated. Eating less means needing less fluids."

Jett leaned in, reaching in her bag for a ground cloth.

"Sorry I'm ripe, Jett, I did my best with hygiene, but I've had some pretty intense moments when I was sweating through my clothes for weeks."

"You're fine. You smell like Digger. And since I slept with him last night, I smell like Digger, too."

Jett got busy laying out a tarp.

"The star of this show is Digger." Scott reached for Digger's collar, pulling him a little closer for a rub. "Besides sleeping with me each night, shit, he kept me sane—"

Digger wiggled forward and was lapping Scott's face.

After Digger settled back down to receive his ear scratches, Scott finished, "He brought all of my supplies up piece by piece. It took him all day."

"I bet. Hey Havoc, I'm going to lay out my supplies and Scott's supplies over here and see if I don't have an 'ah-ha' moment."

"You can look through my stuff too," Havoc said. "White packed it, and I haven't pulled it apart yet to see what all she included."

"Keep talking, Scott," Jett said. "Tell me about Digger."

Scott teared up again. "Shows how resourceful he is. Digger brought this stuff to me piece by piece. Luckily, I had been poking around in my pack when I went to investigate the red light. Climbing up here with a closed pack would have been impossible for him.

"How is it that you didn't exfil with Deepak when he got sick?" Jett frowned at their supplies and the distinct lack of space-pirate-laser-beams to just blast the rock away.

"When Deepak got sick, I had to practically carry him out to the road. We started at first morning light, and he was okay to walk. By the end of the day, he was heading downhill fast." Scott stopped to laugh. Then he sputtered out through a new cascade of tears, "See what I did there? All downhill?" He snorted and wiped his snot on his sleeve. "I made it onto the road with him at dusk. I hailed a moped that looked terrified to stop, but I waved a bunch of money in the air. The moped could only carry one of us, so, wing and a prayer scenario. Anyway," he snorted again and used his other sleeve to wipe his eyes, "some of this is my stuff. Some Deepak's. There's bound to be more down there on the plateau if you don't see your inspiration."

"Good to know."

"I have a few pieces missing. My sat phone isn't here. As brilliant as Digger is, telling him to go get those specific things didn't work out. Obviously."

"You said Digger sleeps with you each night?" Havoc walked his pack over to Jett. "I bet him not coming back last night made you nervous. Jett, I'm going down to bring up any equipment I can find. I'll be back."

"He's right. Not nervous, though. *Terrified*."

"After all of this is said and done, I'll tell you how Digger found me and then Havoc. He was definitely out there trying his darndest."

"My tent was set up and pegged in. Still, he got it up to me. I just put it beside me during the day and use the flap as a sun shield, then at night, I take my supplies out, pull it around. If I arch back, I can slide it underneath my torso. Putting my supplies back in protects them from the elements. Scavengers. Those chores don't take long, but it's something to do. That Digger was able to get a whole darned tent up to me probably saved my life. Not probably, surely. It helps keep the wind and dew off me at night. The night it rained was pretty bad, though. It hit my ass as it fell from the sky; it was just painful. And then the cold water soaking my pants. My socks and boots, though, stayed dry, so that's good, I guess."

"I'm wondering what would happen if one of us hiked to the road," Havoc said, coming up with an armful of supplies that he handed down to Jett as she set things out. "How long by horse?"

Jett set the pack down and opened the front pouch. "A day on horseback in this terrain, same as on foot. Another day back with leading a rescue team. If anything happened to the person making the descent on the way, the two in this camp wouldn't know. I'm not a fan of splitting up."

"I'm going to say it, just so it's said." Havoc wiggled the last thing in his arms. "Sat phone."

"No," Scott and Jett said together.

"We just got here," Jett said reasonably. "Let's exhaust all of our options. Peter and Tink are somewhere, and while it might bring us help, it might bring them scrutiny. Either way, we'd have to stop the search. And what the Zorics are up to endangers too many lives. It has to be last-ditch."

Havoc nodded.

There was a whinny that pulled Havoc and Jett's attention down the hill.

"Horse, of course."

"Of course," Havoc sang.

"Old school. How does that song go?"

"The one-roomed schoolhouses of old school," Havoc said. "I don't remember past that much. And I'd rather not get that earworm going."

Scott put his empty rice packet and spoon down. "Hey, how did you get a horse, and my team didn't? It would have saved a lot of work to have a pack animal with us."

"He's not my horse. He's just trying to adopt us."

Havoc picked up a piece of something brown. Holding them up, they were a pair of pantyhose with knots tied above a smooth rock in each leg's toe space. "I'm sure this has a reason."

"Not much I can do for protection lying on my belly with a leg in a hole."

"Other than to blast rock," Havoc said.

"Exactly. So it's like the bolas used by the gauchos of Argentina and Uruguay to catch cattle."

"Clever." Havoc whipped them around, testing them out. "And you just walk around with pantyhose in your pack in case there's a party?"

"There's a lot you can do with a pair of pantyhose, everything from lightweight warmth layer to extra cordage if it's needed."

"Interesting."

"Havoc, focus. We're talking about next steps," Jett said. "Let's not throw out an idea until we follow it to its logical conclusion. Let's play out the idea of one of us going for help. One of us gets to Jalal-Abad. Even gets as far as the apartment headquarters where they've set up the command center. Then what? This is a boulder."

"Jaws of life?" Scott suggested.

"How would they get it in here? How would it be powered? I don't know that the jaws of life would be useful against a boulder. They crush metal. Honestly, Scott, why couldn't you have been trapped face down by a falling tree? We'd have you free by now."

"Sorry. Next time, okay?"

Jett patted his shoulder and drew her lips in, letting the situation settle into her gut so her gut could develop some kind of reaction. "Didn't you tell me your dad was a mason, Havoc? Wouldn't you have seen ways to cut at the stone?"

"Yeah, they can use battery-operated stone cutters that aren't too heavy to heft in, no bulkier than the chainsaws you would take to the backcountry to fight fires. If they have them. But I'm sure there would be people with the hand tools and skills to cut stone. I'm unfortunately not one of them. Brick and stonework were never an interest to me."

"It's an interest to me," Scott said.

"We're still talking days. Two minimum for travel. I'd say at least one for extraction if they're cutting rock. Stress affects on the body. Bedsores from lying in the same position for so long. Pressure issues. I'd rather it wasn't days."

"I'm with Jett on this." Scott's face was tense with panic. "Why don't we save me and just get me the heck out of here?"

Jett and Havoc combed through their supplies. Lifting objects, considering them, putting them back on the tarp.

"Keep talking," Scott whined. "The silence makes me think that you're freaking out. Only one person is allowed to freak out in any given emergency. And I think I earned that right."

"Jett and I were talking about Dunning-Kruger effect," Havoc offered.

"Uh-oh. That's never a fun conversation when that comes up. What were you talking about?"

"Metal in birds' beaks," Jett said, lifting a little bottle of lotion, then rejecting the idea of trying to lube the boot.

"Should I ask how that came up?"

"Not important." Havoc sat opening different blades on his multi knife and considering them. "Applying Dunning-Kruger effect to this situation. I'm confident that we can get you out. On the flight over here, there was a lady stuck in the bathroom, and I got *her* free."

"Did she do a courtesy flush?" Scott asked. "Did you just poke something between her and the toilet seat and pry some flesh up?"

"That's a myth," Jett said. "That never happened."

"Don't say that." Scott drew his brows together. "I like that story. I bet she had a major hickey on her backside. So is that what you did to break the vacuum?"

"Nothing that dramatic. The door was sagging and got stuck," Havoc explained.

Scott rolled his eyeballs. "Such a hero."

Havoc lifted a single brow. "Do you think you're in a good position to throw sarcasm at me?"

"Sorry."

Havoc patted Scott's shoulder. "Hang in there. We've got you."

"I'm thinking about Digger." Jett reached over to *boop* Digger's nose. "It's interesting that he went hunting for help during the day but wasn't willing to go but so far from you. The problem for Digger was that you're not far from a part of the forest that's supposed to be full of evil spirits. People from the area refuse to come here. Havoc and I are probably the first humans he could find in his weeks of looking. And, if Digger was coming back to check on you each night, his range could only be so far."

"Evil spirits? Maybe those rough stones down there *are* Devil's teeth. And look," Scott said with a shake. "I just completely wigged myself out."

"Digger wouldn't allow Devil's teeth near you. Look how calm he is there. Keep telling me about Digger."

"Yeah, that's how it was. He'd run out in the morning when I told him to go get help. Then he'd come back to the camp at sunset to eat. I gave him a small ration. I'm selfish like that since he can hunt. Besides, his kibble tastes like shit. I was protecting him from that."

Digger *absolutely* was a hero dog.

As she thought that, Digger looked her in the eye and nodded. He knew he was a good boy and did a good boy job.

Jett handed Scott a wet nap to clean up.

"Thank you."

Jett had really hoped that something from Havoc's father's job as a mason working with brick and stone would trigger a workaround.

Jett had done rock climbing with her family since she was strapped into a baby backpack as a toddler, going up and down the mountains. In climbing, there was a time and a place for choosing to wedge your foot or hand into a crevice. It was called "jamming." A climber would shove themselves into a crack and then turn the hand or foot, or maybe make a fist in the crack if that were possible. It wasn't the easiest thing to pull off, but it was sometimes the only way to move up.

And from that experience, she knew how powerful and unyielding it felt when trapped between rocks.

This was an unimaginable horror.

26

Chatkal Mountain Range, Kyrgyzstan

Monday, Fifteen Thirty Hours

Jett tugged a silicone utility bag from the thigh pocket on her tactical pants. She pulled out a ferro rod and a piece of fatwood.

"What are you thinking, Jett? Maybe I can help," Havoc squatted by Jett's side.

"If you're thinking of lighting my pants on fire so that you can burn my boot off," Scott's raspy, exhausted voice held both humor and horror. "I've considered it and decided it *wasn't* a good idea."

The last thing Jett pulled out of the emergency fire starter kit was a wire saw, a twenty-two-inch length of braided stainless steel that looked like a simple piece of metallic twine. On either end, there was a circle that looked like a key ring. When using this tool as a survival saw, the user put their finger, or better a stick, into each loop then pulled one side then the other, working the length almost like shining shoes.

"If I could thread this saw through here," Jett stopped and pulled on the triple bow that she'd pulled into her shoelace, "and I could tie paracord through the thumb loops to make this longer so it can reach all the way down the crevice to his foot, then we have a friction saw to cut through the knot."

Havoc reached for the saw, twisting it in his fingers. Testing it, he pushed one of the rings through his laces and scowled. "Maybe. But Scott, you said you got wet the other night during the rainstorm."

"My boots stayed dry."

"But your shoelaces didn't. Even if they're paracord. Unless. . . Did you switch out your laces for bank cord?" Havoc asked.

"Nope, plain Jane shoelaces. But they're a cool red."

"Awesome." Jett nodded. "But if the knots got wet and the shoelace shrank."

"Okay, thanks for this list of doomsday scenarios."

Havoc practiced different ways of pushing the metal circle under the lace's knot and imagined how Jett might accomplish it by extending her arm's reach. "How far were you from the laces when you stretched your hand in, Jett?"

"A good five inches or so. My fingertips were a few inches below Scott's knee."

Havoc pulled out his multi-tool.

"Jezis, it's big. Are you compensating?" Jett asked.

Havoc didn't look up from considering. "Sadly, true."

"Har har, you two. Can you focus, please?" Scott asked. "I can taste freedom, and it tastes like MRE crackers. But man, I'll love every single bite."

"I'll tell you what I saw from my angle. When Scott's foot went into the crevice, and he fell forward," Jett used her hands to demonstrate, "it looks like he shoved his foot under a ridge. And that ridge stabs very closely to his shin."

Havoc looked up and caught Jett's gaze. "Were you thinking

you could tape that friction saw onto a stick and shove it down there to saw his laces free?"

"Exactly." Jett smiled one of her dazzling bright smiles.

Havoc shrugged. "We can try."

"Yes, let's try!" Scott said.

"I'm not going on to a harder scenario until we tried the quick and easy one, first." Havoc pulled up the tool shaped like a fish-hook but with a razor-sharp edge on the inside curve. "I have this strap cutter on my multitool. If we tape it to a sturdy stick, and I can get this under the knot…"

Jett shook her head. "There's no room to turn it and scoop under the lace."

"I'd have to press down into his boot at the tongue about a half an inch. And try to slide it from there."

"Okay," Jett said. "I'll hold the light and help guide you. Once it's in, you stay steady, and I'll grab the top and pop it."

Havoc had prepped his tool in minutes by using his 100 MPH tape to attach the instrument to a tent pole. He added a lanyard that he tied to his belt loop, so if the tool were to dislodge, it wouldn't be lost into the depths of the crevice.

Jett held lengths of paracord at ankle height so Havoc could practice before he attempted the process on Scott.

Then together, they laid next to the crevice and tried.

And tried.

After a long period of focus and effort, Jett and Havoc both exhaled at the same moment, conceding this wasn't going to do the trick.

"Sorry, Scott, that didn't work."

Scott's body was tense with frustration. "Any other ideas? Other than the C4, that is."

"The multitool is too fat to get it past that last jut of rock. You only needed another inch," Jett said.

Scott snorted. "That's what she said."

"Maybe if we did the same thing, but we used a blade?" Havoc used a finger to measure the length of the strap cutting hook, then opened his knife blade. "Or we could use your knife."

"Too risky." Jett shook her head.

"Saw then?" Havoc collapsed the blade and brought up the saw. "I couldn't stab him with this."

"Given the angle of his foot and the rocks around the boot," Jett said, "I can't see getting the blade against something we want to cut without endangering cutting Scott, though."

"Go ahead and cut Scott," Scott said. "Scott doesn't mind you cutting him with your Swiss Army saw. Scott has a first aid kit."

"And he's been studying first aid, he told me," Jett added.

Jett and Havoc squatted on the tarp, looking over their supplies. Once again, hunting for inspiration.

Havoc held up a fishing hook. Twiddling it in the light. Frowning over it.

Jett reached over and took it from him. "I'm with you. Tackling it with fishing gear."

"Jett, stop with the funny," Scott whimpered.

"Lightening the mood."

"I have a rock piercing my appendix. How's that for a lighter mood?"

"Touchy." She turned to Havoc.

"I've got it." Havoc grinned.

Havoc wended his way down the slope and came back with a handful of sticks. "The tent pole was too flexible. These are hardwood, much more rigid."

Scott moaned. "I can't even imagine."

Havoc secured the fishing hook to a yard-long slender stick and set it aside.

"Yep," Jett said. "I think that'll be good." She held out the wire saw.

Havoc tied bank cord to one of the rings and connected that

string to his belt loop once again, so no tool was lost in the crevice. Next, Havoc secured one of the flex-saw's metal finger rings to the stick with dental floss. It was a clever design. He lashed the ring into place then placed a slender twig between the ring and the guide stick. This created a tiny lip that would help to hold the ring at a ninety-degree angle. He bound that into place as well. After testing the device on Jett's boot to see if he could maneuver the ring under a tied shoelace, they developed a workable technique.

"Can you spot for me?" he asked Jett handing her the headlight.

She laid down by the crevice, squinting into the space.

First, Havoc lowered the stick as Jett counted down the inches.

"It's not ideal, but you're going to have to go in from the front of the boot, pushing it under the lace knots back toward his ankle. Nope, too high. Use the stick to press down into Scott's foot a bit."

"Sorry, I don't mean to stab you with this thing."

"Honestly? My leg goes between pins and needles and falling completely asleep. I keep doing isometrics to keep the blood flow. Since you've been here, I stopped with my efforts. I'm numb from hip to toe. Stab away."

"Are you just saying that?" There was concern in Havoc's voice.

"No, that's the state of things."

"Press harder," Jett said. "Yup. Yup. There. Okay. Hold."

Jett rolled onto her back so she could describe what she was seeing and how she thought Havoc should move next. Then, she rolled back over to peer into the crevice.

Havoc stood with both hands on the stick. He stood with his back to Scott's torso. With staccato pulls, he tried to shove the ring under the shoelace.

No go.

Jett pulled off her hoody and reached her hand down to press the stick toward Scott's shin. From this lower point, she had a lot more control. "Bingo," Jett said.

"Bingo!" Scott yelled, then coughed.

Havoc held the stick steady while Jett lowered the stick with the fishing hook attached. Her goal was to scoop into the silver ring that had made its way under the shoelace.

It was finicky. Right away Jett saw the problem. She brought the hook up and using Havoc's multitool, she snipped off the sharp end, so it wasn't catching on flesh or cloth.

Again, she stretched her arm into the crevice working to hook the ring.

Once she got hold of the ring, Jett slowly pulled the stick up, threading the saw under the lace knots.

With one side attached to Havoc, her job now was to thread a second strand of bank line through this second silver ring.

When Jett rolled over, her eyes were wide and unblinking. She held up crossed fingers on both hands.

Now, with the saw under the lace knots and bank cord tied to either finger ring to extend the length of the saw, Havoc wrapped the cord around either fist and worked the saw back and forth until there was a pop and no more resistance.

Jett looked down. "You got it!"

"Got it?" Scot bellowed.

"Scott," Havoc called. "See if you can pull your foot free of the boot."

Scott strained. Havoc pulled on his leg.

"No go." Scott's voice trembled.

Jett leaned over with the light. "Hang on, let me see if I can use a stick to loosen the laces." She worked for a moment then asked Havoc for a stick. "A thick one."

"What I'm doing, Scott," Jett said, "is pushing down on the

back of your boot. Havoc, is there a way you can help Scott? A sling?"

Havoc ran a shirt under Scott's hips. Straddling Scott, once again, Havoc wound the sleeves around his hands, then counted down. "Ready, Jett? On three. One. Two."

"Three!" They all yelled together.

With Havoc taking his weight, Scott piked into a down dog. Out popped his foot.

Havoc and Jett helped lay Scott back onto the rock beside the crevice.

With a cry, Scott turned to lie on his back, gasping for air.

Jett rolled off Scott's sock and pulled up the leg of his pants. Scott's ankle was ugly purple and green. It was swollen from the line above his boot up to his knee.

"The good news is you're free." Havoc wore a shit-eating grin.

Scott raised two fists and shook them in the air.

"The bad news," Jett palpated his injury, "I think your leg is broken."

Scott lifted his head to look down at his mangled leg. "Well, that all kinds of sucks."

27

Chatkal Mountain Range, Kyrgyzstan

Monday, Seventeen Twenty-Three Hours

Havoc pulled Scott over his shoulder in a fireman's carry.

With Jett walking behind the two, gripping Havoc's belt to help counter the gravitational pull of the slope, they moved to the plateau below.

Off to the side, about twenty meters, ran a stream where Horse stood munching grass.

"That water wasn't there when we set up camp," Scott said when Jett pointed it out.

"Plan?" Jett asked.

"I'm pulling all of our equipment down and setting up camp. We're not getting off the mountain today." Havoc held up a hand with his fingers pointing to the side. Each finger represented about fifteen minutes of sunlight above the horizon. "Forty-five minutes or so, and we'll be in civil twilight."

"I'll get a fire going and water boiling. Scott needs a bath and a change of clothes so he can feel human again."

Scott lay on his back, his foot elevated on a fallen log, his head resting on Jett's bunched-up hoody. "You have no idea how good it feels just to be in a different position."

"We need to get your pressure sores treated." Jett pulled a collapsible bucket from her pack to boil water. "While I'm getting set up for you, Scott, I think I'm going to make friends with Horse. Test him out a bit. See what he's used to in terms of human touch."

"I know you know what you're doing," Havoc said. "Just cautious, please. From last night, Horse likes to rear and kick."

Scott burst into tears. "Sorry about this, guys," he gasped between sobs.

"You've been through a hell of an experience," Havoc said gently. "Your system is going to take some time to find its equilibrium again."

THE CAMP SET.

The food eaten.

Both Scott and Horse cleaned, first aid performed.

The three sprawled by the fire, relishing its warmth.

Scott was lying on his back, looking up at the stars. Every once in a while, he'd mutter something under his breath and swipe at a tear.

Digger rested his head on Scott's belly, his eyes closed. A random thunk of his tail told Jett that Digger was feeling contented.

"Since we've got some time here," Havoc said. "Tell me—"

"I'm not going to tell you about all of my childhood pets." Jett held up the bag of candies and tilted the last one into her mouth before crumpling the bag and tossing it into their campfire.

"Have my questions been too personal?" A deep line formed between Havoc's brows, telling Jett that it wasn't his intention to pry.

Jett rolled over on the tarp, pillowing her head on her crossed arms. "I'm giving you a hard time," she said with a yawn. "When I'm tired, my humor doesn't always read as funny. It's kind of dry under even the best of circumstances."

"Like a good champagne?" Havoc canted his head.

Jett turned to him; one eyebrow quirked. "Exactly, bubbly enough to explode the cork across the room, but flat when it's been left out overnight."

"I see what you did there." Havoc laughed.

Jett offered him a gentle smile. She liked their banter. Liked that he seemed to *get* her. Jett particularly liked that he hadn't tried to manipulate her into something she was not. "So your question?"

"You're with the AWG. You know the minutiae of things. What do you think we're looking for? How do you think the Zorics are doing their dastardly deeds?"

"Look at the squirrel over there, hanging from one paw," Jett murmured. "He looks drunk."

Picking up a stick and poking the fire, Havoc created a bloom of sparks. "I met a woman on the plane ride over here who once hid a squirrel in her hoody pocket as she flew. She called the squirrel Pearl."

"As one does," Jett laughed.

"Don't let me interrupt your date, you two. I'll just hang out over here."

"My thoughts aren't on the Zorics." Jett went back to Havoc's question. "One crisis at a time. I'm thinking about next steps for Scott."

"Which is: How are we getting Scott off this damned mountain and into a hospital," Scott said.

"And find him some cheesecake," Havoc added.

"In the morning, I'm going to talk to my horse buddy over there and see if he might be willing to let Scott ride him out. He was comfortable with me cleaning his wounds and dressing them with antibiotic cream. By the way, there was a lot of surface space to cover, and I'm out of that tube. I was able to get him bandaged up. His coat tells me he's used to carrying a pack. He held steady when I threw my body over his shoulder. He didn't mind my dangling feet. I'm not a hundred percent on how he'd do trekking down the slope with Scott. But if we can use him, it would be darned quicker than the two of us trying to carry you out of here, Scott."

"Probably more comfortable than dragging you on a bushcraft stretcher." Havoc stood and stretched.

When he leaned back, his shirt and fleece sweatshirt rose, exposing Havoc's goody trail.

As Jett licked her lips, she turned her back to hide the act. The horse, tied to a tree limb, sleeping, came into view. "It's weird to just keep calling him 'Horse.'"

"I've named him Brownie," Scott said. "Just an FYI. I have zero horse experience."

"What we'll do is put two lines on the ho—Brownie. I'll hold one rope. Havoc, you'll hold the other, and if things go awry, well…"

Scott came up on his elbows, "What do you mean 'well'? Don't I get a say in this?"

Jett and Havoc both turned to Scott and said, "No."

As the fire died, Havoc walked over to Scott and held out a hand. "Come on. I'm going to help you go over there to relieve yourself. It's been a long day, and I'm headed for some shut-eye."

While they made their way in one direction, Jett scooted off in the other. She hurried so she'd have time alone in the camp to get herself changed and her hygiene rituals accomplished before the men got back.

They'd decided that Scott's equipment was too gross for him to use. He'd be sleeping in Jett's tent in her sulfur-smelling sleeping bag.

Jett and Havoc would share his tent.

Tonight, they'd have more legroom and more pleasant air to breathe. Digger would be staying with Scott, where he belonged.

It was a night bright with cold. Even when the fire was going, the wind whipped the heat away.

Jett would be curled up, warm and contented with Havoc again.

Havoc made Jett tingle with every touch, and she'd found herself growing addicted to the sensation. Over the two days that she'd known him, Jett found herself being very handsy when it came to Major Havoc.

Too handsy?

She'd watch and see if her behavior was out of bounds. They weren't colleagues per se. They both worked for the military, but…military people were allowed to be attracted to each other.

And Jett found Havoc attractive. The initial attraction was to his hard body, though hard bodies came a dime-a-dozen where she worked.

What really intrigued Jett was how he kept things low-key, even with things going sideways. That was a quality that Jett had learned to respect in her fellow smokejumpers. It was a quality that she would put on her "vision board" if she were creating one for a relationship—someone who felt emotions but *wasn't* unduly emotional.

Yeah, she'd noticed the tears in Havoc's eyes as Scott's incredulity at help arriving melted into his hitched-breath sobs of relief.

Jett walked to Havoc's tent where her gear was stored and took out her toiletry bag and a pair of thermal underwear she'd sleep in.

Brushing her teeth, Jett thought of other things that she'd like represented on her vision board. One, she and the guy could agree that there was a problem, define the problem, and come up with various ways to consider a solution without ego. Jett preferred pragmatism and solutions-based approaches. Clear-eyed. No head in the sand thinking. Two, someone who had a calling, a passion. That was a trait that she'd learned to respect with the folks she worked with within the Asymmetric Warfare Group. Three, a guy who could step away from narcissism and be empathetic enough to guess how his behaviors impacted others, trying to mitigate the bad parts and increase the good parts. But *not* in an icky codependent 'please, please love me!' way. Four, nice for nice's sake. Kind for kind's sake. Fifth, she'd add thoughtful as in full of thought, ideas, humor, insights.

Jett bent and spat her toothpaste into the grass, swished with water from her mess kit cup.

Yeah, 'thoughtful' was a big deal on this vision of a vision board.

Okay, and pecs.

And abs!

A "Jezis, how many squats do you do in a day?" ass.

All of that made Jett handsy when it came to Major Havoc Whatever-his-name-was.

And tingly.

That all made Jett ready to see if this was more than partners on the ultimate scavenger hunt, finding missing and imperiled operators and the secret something that jeopardized America if not the entire world.

There were worse things in life. Jett smiled to herself as she unzipped Havoc's tent. Removing the shower shoes she wore once she was changed for bed, Jett gave her feet a final brush, then scooted backward into their tent and slid into the sleeping bag.

The only problem with theseDuning 'yes, please' thoughts was that when Havoc completed his leg of the mission, they'd be saying goodbye.

Jett needed to keep a spotlight on that truth.

28

Havoc

Chatkal Mountain Range, Kyrgyzstan

Wednesday, Zero Six Hundred Hours

Over breakfast the next morning, Jett and Havoc huddled over the topo map, deciding how best to navigate their way to the road. The best possible solution was to get Scott on the horse. The second best was to rig a stretcher.

"This is all countryside up through here. If we can get to this spot," Jett pointed, "there's a shop with a phone. Walking a horse, it's another five hours. If we're carrying a litter, it's at least two days."

"Horse!" Scott called, reaching for a second MRE. "Oh, ho ho! Score! I got hash browns and eggs. This is just beautiful. Patriot sugar cookies, tortillas, and cheese. Oh! Granola with milk and blueberries." Tears filled Scott's eyes. "Beautiful. Just the most fantastic menu. Whoever designed this was a genius."

"Slow with the food though, Scott," Jett said. "Your body is in a state of starvation. You want to slow-roll this food consumption."

"I opened it." Scott frowned at the food packets.

"I didn't say don't eat. I'm suggesting you go slow." She looked back to Havoc.

"There's an off chance someone would pass us," Havoc said. "Maybe they could get a car or an ambulance heading our way, and we could meet them on the road."

"Maybe." Jett was skeptical. "Now, from the shop, once we figure out a vehicle, it's about an hour to the hospital. They'll do what they can, but the best thing is for our TOC to arrange an exfil to Germany, so Scott gets the best possible care."

"Amen to that. And cute little nurses in scrubs. *That's* what I'm talking about." Scott poured some water into his granola packet and was shaking it vigorously.

"I want to talk through the sat phone again," Havoc said. "We are two friends that are hiking in the area. We came across Scott, and he's injured. We call for help."

"Right." Jett let her gaze settle on Digger, lying in front of the campfire. It was five in the morning, and the sun wasn't up yet. When daylight hit, they wanted to be on their way. "We make a call to our team in Jalal-Abad. The Russian satellite picks up our position. They listen to the communication. Fine, we script an innocent narrative. The Kyrgyz military analyzes it through AI, very weird to get a signal from this part of their country. Basically, the op is done. We'd have to leave. And we don't want to leave because Peter and Tink aren't accounted for. And, oh, hey, there's an apocalyptic destruction apparatus somewhere that can restructure world order."

Havoc played Devil's advocate. "Coming off the mountain and getting help for Scott, they'll know he's in medical distress. We're not carrying sat phones that use military satellites."

"They're Cradium Global," Scott said. "There are just 66

satellites that group has access to. It covers 100% of the globe's surface."

"Going back to likely repercussions for making a call to our team. Let's say we made a call to our TOC in Jalal-Abad," Jet said. "The Kyrgyz government, they'd know where the call originated and where the call was received. They'd deploy about the same time TOC got a rescue in motion."

Havoc took a sip of coffee, then set the cup by his feet. "They'd have to fold up and move headquarters in case someone knocked on their door to understand the dynamic. The door-knockers go in and see a military-style tactical operations center…"

Jett was silent for a moment. "There's the SOS button. That signal would go to IDECR—International Disaster Event Coordination and Response. They'd look in their directory and send a rescue group to this location. That would sanitize our call. We'd know IDECR sent someone to this GPS coordinate. The problem: How long would it take to mobilize a search and rescue group? Where would they come in from? They wouldn't know the issue, so would they bring in the correct equipment?"

"Yeah, like yours, the SAT phone I was issued doesn't allow for texting, either," Havoc said.

"So we're talking possibly days before we can get Scott to a hospital."

"Scott needs to go to the hospital pronto. Nurses and I.V.s of pain meds. Some green gelatin." Scott scooped up a spoonful of granola in vividly purple "blueberry" milk.

"Do you always talk in third person?" Jett asked.

"I got into the habit when I was talking to myself over the last three hell weeks."

"Got it. Proceed." Jett turned back to Havoc. "Another option would be that we press the button and start down the mountain. We keep pushing it every hour."

"That would confuse the hell out of IRCR. They might even think the sat phone was tossed into someone's bag and is being depressed accidentally."

"The boy who cried wolf," Scott said through a mouthful of granola. "Might even have them call off the rescue."

"Not if we did it at the top of each hour. They'd see a non-random interval," Jett said.

"But we'd also give the Kyrgyz military a trajectory," Scott said. "Where all the police would be waiting for us to take us in and ask some pointed questions instead of taking me to the nurses and the gelatin." Scott lifted his nose to the air. "You both stink like sulfur, by the way. Just like your sleeping bag."

"It's good for keeping ticks at bay," Jett said.

"Seriously?"

"No. Okay, let me think. We get to the road, stop a car. We offer them a hundred bucks to take us to the hospital. We can reach out to the team via cell phone once we're within range." Jett patted her pocket where she usually carried her cell.

"I know," Scott said. "I'm so used to pulling out my phone and calling. It's frustrating to be unconnected."

"Yes, but I was just thinking. The phones Scott and I have are work phones. They monitor the phone for calls and texts at the AWG when I'm in the field. My colleagues call this number and leave voice messages."

"Keep going with that," Scott said.

"What if I record a message telling them the basic sanitized information on my voice mail. I know that everyone who has this number has a high clearance. I tell them to contact HQ and talk to Burnside or Arnold, then I put together a message that gives them the information but not so much that anyone else would know what it means. A string of numbers—our GPS coordinates. Then when they call me, they get my voice mail. They hear the report, they contact whom I asked them to. I don't need connectivity to get my message out. I just need someone to follow through. We wouldn't know if it happened or not—"

Havoc and Jett looked at each other for a long minute, then both said, "Nah, won't work."

Jett grinned. "Jinx. Personal jinx, 1234."

"Stop," Havoc said.

Jett laughed her infectious laugh. "Too late."

"You really want to jinx me out here?"

Jett pulled the laughter back until it just tickled the corners of her lips. "I suck the jinx back and plant it in the ground."

"For some poor guy like Scott to come along and step in it?"

Jett wrinkled her nose. "What would you have me do with my jinx, then?"

"First, be careful with that quick jinx trigger of yours. Make sure the person you're about to jinx is jinxable without the ramifications of that jinx coming back and hitting you."

"Got it." Jett heaved a sigh. "At any rate, that idea won't work unless and until we get into cell phone range, and at that point, I can just whip out a text. So that point is moot."

"How long have you two been dating?" Scott asked.

"We just met looking for you."

"Huh." Scott scooped up a spoon of hashbrowns. "Sounds like you've been tormenting each other for years."

***

It was fascinating to watch Jett work, Havoc thought.

There was a process that she used. She'd look at something close up, then take a step back and assess. Changing angles, heights, and distances. She mumbled as she shifted. He could see the question in her eye, then a calculation, an answer. Not just one, but many. It was like watching a scientist asking hypotheticals and then testing theories, all in short order.

Havoc wanted to be in on the show, part of the conversation, but, at least in this instance, working out the issue of getting Scott on Brownie, Havoc had nothing to add. So it would be selfish to insist that he be involved in the thought processes.

Scott had woken up gritting his teeth and moaning in pain. The pressure from the rock cast had both held Scott prisoner and had also somehow supported Scott's injury. Scott had had no idea that his leg and possibly his ankle were broken until the rescue.

It reminded Havoc of the Taoist story of "maybe."

In the story, a farmer's horse ran away, and the neighbors gathered and told him they were sorry for the farmer's great misfortune. The farmer said, "maybe." The next day, the horse returned home with two wild horses in tow. Reminded Havoc about how Brownie came onto the scene. "Oh!" the farmer's neighbor had said. "What great fortune, now you have three horses." "Maybe," said the farmer. The next day, his son tried to ride the green horses, and he broke his leg. Forever, the son would walk with a limp. "Such great misfortune," said the neighbors. "Maybe," returned the farmer. The next day the military came to conscript the able-bodied young men. Seeing the farmer's son's limp, they left him be. "Such great fortune!" the farmer was told.

"Maybe."

And this line of thought brought Havoc to his relationship with Jett.

It was almost miraculous that Jett had come into Havoc's life. He felt that way— enormously fortunate to have met her. To experience the magnetic pull, the curiosity, the sense that Havoc was fully awake and alive when he was with Jett. Havoc thought about how easy it had all been—knife-wielding, scrotum-grinding fights aside.

Maybe.

Knowing that their lives were destined to go in different directions, how much would he suffer?

How would Havoc's feelings for Jett in this short time they'd be working together create a lens for any possible future relationship?

Another Taoist concept was that you could never step into the same river twice. Everything was constantly changing.

Just like with the farmer, there was always the next thing that happened, the next opportunity for things to go gloriously well, or risk for utter chaos.

Havoc had been in special forces for well over a decade. He was used to the filth, the dark, and the chaos. Those mission experiences made this moment shine.

He stood and went to help Jett as she lifted two of the packs onto Brownie.

They'd found a horse. Under the circumstances, it was a miracle.

Maybe.

Right now, Jett was assembling a means to get them down the slope. It was a complicated rigging. A folded sleeping bag provided a cushion along the horse's spine. Then, Jett lashed Deepak and Scott's backpacks together as saddlebags hanging on either side. A second sleeping bag, folded into the non-slip material of her sleeping pad, became Scott's saddle. Climbing webbing helped hold it securely around the horse's body.

She led the horse over to stand next to a boulder, while Havoc carried Scott over.

Climbing onto the rock with Scott across his shoulders was a challenge.

But Scott, sweat-slick and a little green around the gills, was now up on Brownie's back.

Jett would hike out a pack, and so would Havoc.

They were ready.

29

———————

Chatkal Mountain Range, Kyrgyzstan

Wednesday, Eighteen-Ten Hours

White pushed through the side door at the hospital, looking grim.

"Good to see that the Bermuda triangle mountain range didn't disappear you, too, Havoc."

Havoc stood as she approached. "Yes, ma'am."

White scanned the small courtyard garden where Havoc, Jett, and Digger had planted themselves, waiting for their next commands.

"Scott said you trapped a random horse on the mountain, Annie Oakley. And Scott rode him out." White tipped her head. "What did you do with the horse?"

Jett got to her feet, but White said, "As you were."

It had been an exhausting treacherous time getting Scott off that mountain. Jett had been the rock star, and Havoc wanted her to rest and not stand there at parade rest to show deference.

"When we got off the mountain, we were able to signal a passing motorbike. He knew the owner of the horse."

"Sounds sketchy." White slid her hands into her pockets. "Some guy recognized a horse walking down the road?"

"There was a bit more to it," Havoc offered. "We were waving money in the air to get him to pull over. We're obviously foreigners. Scott and I, at least. When the guy approached, he inspected the lead around the horse's neck. There were complicated knots of colored ribbons. Jett thought it might show ownership, so we'd left it in place."

White pressed her lips together and gave Jett an appreciative nod.

"The motorbike guy said the horse's owner had a car. He went to get the owner and to tell him that we would pay him well to get us to the hospital."

"You guys are in rough shape. You smell like…is that rotten egg?"

"Sulfur," Jett said.

"Is it mission-critical that I ask about that?"

Jett and Havoc shook their heads.

White lifted a large gray bag with rope handles and set it in front of Jett. "I picked up some city clothes for you two. Toiletries." She stopped and scanned the area again for any listening ears. "When you arrived in Kyrgyzstan, Havoc, we sent you a text about the unrest near the capital. People are fleeing south, waiting for things to settle down. Dogs aren't allowed in the building where we set up the TOC. Because of the influx of northerners heading south, there weren't any hotel rooms to get you in. I was able to find a guest house that would allow you to bring Digger with you." White turned her focus to Jett. "Until we can figure something else out, Jett, you're to handle the AWG K9."

"Yes, ma'am."

"Go to the guest house now. For god's sake, take a damned bath. You two are putrid. Get some good sleep. We'll meet at the TOC at zero five hundred. I'll have breakfast for you then. We need to get back up on the mountain and find Peter and Tink. Ty, Rory, and Nitro are on their way in. They should be here by then."

"Where were they searching?" Jett asked.

"They got caught up in the civil unrest up north. They weren't out on a search grid." White turned to Havoc. "Your teammates have had a time of it getting down here. Luckily, you found not only your search target but theirs, too. I'm not a hundred percent upset by the political unrest. It will keep eyes focused elsewhere for a time."

Havoc had shifted to soldier mode. "T-Rex's group?"

"T-Rex is scheduled for communications at twenty-hundred hours. If he doesn't have a lead, I'll get them back here for the morning's meeting."

"Scott?" Jett whispered as if she were afraid for the news.

"Is mangled. The medical staff is making sure he's stable for a trip to Germany. Right now, Scott's loopy on pain meds and keeps asking for green gelatin and an American nurse in blue scrubs. Everything else he's saying is unintelligible. We have Prescott sitting with him, so he doesn't accidentally throw out some classified intel." She nodded toward the four backpacks in a pile by the bench. "Take your packs with you. I have someone coming to pick up Deepak and Scott's things so leave them there."

Jett and Havoc stood.

White pulled out her phone and sent a text.

Havoc's phone pinged.

"That's the address of the guest house. I'll send someone to pick you up in the morning, so the TOC address is not on any electronic device. Now that Scott's in hospital, we don't know if any of the medical staff reports foreigners showing up for care. We need to exercise extreme caution."

30

———

Chatkal Mountain Range, Kyrgyzstan

Wednesday, Twenty Hundred Hours

Their cab ride took Jett and Havoc outside of city limits. It was a cold ride. The cabby had his window rolled all the way down. Probably because they stank.

Havoc pulled up the address on a maps app and watched closely that the cabby was taking them in the right direction. He'd had a run-in with a taxi or two that tried to take advantage of an exhausted tourist as they roamed the roads pushing up the fare. That was on the nicer end of the spectrum. Some taxi drivers were known to shake down their passengers after running up on helper-elves who were heavily armed.

This guy seemed on the up and up.

And he also seemed terrified of dogs. Go figure.

Havoc reached down to scrub a hand between Digger's ears.

The house they pulled up to looked like a family home.

Smoke billowed from the chimney, laundry hung on the line, kids were playing a stick and rock game in the empty lot.

Normal.

Havoc nudged Jett, who had fallen asleep with her head on his shoulder. "We're here, Sleeping Beauty."

"Mmmm. Shower. Bed."

The driver ran around the front of the car to unload their bags from his front seat. Havoc handed him the fare while Jett squirmed out of the car and held the lead while Digger followed.

"This looks nice and neat. And like they have indoor plumbing. Bonus. Maybe there will be a bath."

"Yeah? They didn't have plumbing at Tetushka's."

"Nope. I haven't tub-bathed or showered since I stepped foot in Kyrgyzstan." Jett looked up at him. "If you make one derogatory comment about my hygiene, we won't be friends anymore."

Friends. Ouch.

A woman opened the front door and folded her hand across the front of her apron. "You speak Kyrgyz?" she asked in the language.

"We speak Russian if that's possible for you," Jett replied in Russian.

The woman nodded. "I was having trouble understanding the person who called. It wasn't you, was it?"

"No, ma'am," Jett answered since the woman was looking her way. "A friend was helping me find a place. We've been hiking in the mountains today."

The hostess glowered at Digger. "I knew you would have the dog. He's extra. Many people come right now and need rooms to stay. Me? I book all rooms except the one. I give you extra big room because it's two people and a dog." She pinched at her nose in disgust. "Your room has a bathroom, no sharing with others. You pay one hundred dollars U.S."

"I was told ten per room," Jett said. "Two rooms were reserved…"

The woman shrugged. "I don't have two rooms. I have one room. You want it, or no? I have three people who wish to rent that room, and I can fill it right away. One hundred dollars U.S. in advance." She held out an open palm.

Jett turned to Havoc. "I don't have any money with me."

Havoc dug in his backpack for his wallet. "Yes, ma'am. We want the room." He stood and opened it, hoping that he had enough. He pulled out the cash and counted it out for her in Russian. She looked at it skeptically. "Thank you for your hospitality," he said as he put the last five-dollar bill on her palm.

In exchange, she gave them a key and pointed up the stairs.

"Want to flip a coin to see who gets a shower first?" Jett asked as she made her way up. "Actually, could you go first? That way I won't feel selfish when I spend hours soaking in the tub. Uhm, before I have to listen to the shower water running, can you give me two minutes in the bathroom?"

"You go ahead. I want to call my commander and hear from him what's happening. White is good at her job but very calculating about everything. I want the skinny straight from T-Rex's mouth." He paused. "We use end-to-end encryption."

"You *know* about the Zoric's capabilities," Jett cautioned.

"Sure, but we have burner phones, and no one knows we're here." Havoc turned the key and pushed the door open.

The room was varying shades of pink. There were lots of vases of silk flowers. A table. A single chair. "Weird," she said.

Havoc pulled the curtain to the side to observe the street, nothing doing out there other than the kids at play.

Jett didn't stop her forward movement. She headed straight to the bathroom.

Havoc heard little gasps and groans that he could tell she was trying to stifle. She was probably one hurting puppy after their adventure. Havoc would admit, a piping hot shower, a shave, fresh clothes would make a new man of him.

And food. Something other than an MRE. He'd seen a couple of places that looked like restaurants on the way in. Havoc might think of it as a first date of sorts if they went out to get something. Yeah, that might be nice. Shuck the soldiering and act the gentleman. He'd see how that was received.

Friends, she'd said.

Havoc tried the cell phone, but they didn't pick up. Probably didn't recognize the number. He wouldn't be able to reach out to his team until, possibly, tomorrow at the TOC.

He sat on the chair to take off his boots and socks, then dug around in the bag that White had brought them. There were comfortable-looking clothes for sleeping or hanging out—fleece lounge pants and sweatshirts. There was a set of casual clothes for each if they decided to go out somewhere. She had everything, right down to fresh undergarments and shoes. "White has some fresh clothes for us," he told her as she exited the bathroom.

"Great." She smiled. "All yours."

Havoc took his things in. Showering, changing, shaving, and brushing his teeth, Havoc moved through the steps with the practiced expediency of a man with a seven-minute window.

Jett was quite the opposite.

When Jett slid past him to take her turn, Havoc listened to her shower. Then the drain was shut, and a bath drawn. A half-hour passed and he wondered if the water was still warm.

His gaze landed on the clothing bag. "You don't have your fresh clothes," he called.

"I forgot them. I was so excited by the prospect of hot water and shampoo. Do you mind bringing them in?"

Havoc turned the knob on the unlocked door and stepped through the doorway.

Jett was lying back in the tub. Her feet rested on the lip near the spigot, so she could ease her shoulders into the water. Her eyes half open. Her hair sopping wet. It was how they met, except there was no knife. "Sorry," he said and averted his eyes.

"You really are such a prude. Is that what they do in, where did you say you were from? Rochester?" She smiled at him and shrugged. "If you hadn't already seen me naked, I'd be modest. But that's water under the bridge."

Havoc nodded and stepped back out of the bathroom.

Yup, that certainly sounded friend-zoned to him.

Havoc could hear Jett climbing from the tub, and as if on cue, there was his cock saluting her.

He shook his head, rubbed his eyes, and leaned back with a moan. Meeting Jett was one of the miracles of his life. And he thought of that Taoist farmer and added, maybe.

The burner phone rang.

31

HAVOC
    Jalal-Abad, Kyrgyzstan

Wednesday, Twenty-One Hours

"White here. Is Jett there with you?"

"Yes, ma'am." Havoc looked up as Jett stuck her head out of the door. She was wrapped in one towel and was squeezing water from her hair with the other. She eyed the phone, then sent a searching look toward Havoc.

"Can you put me on speaker?" White asked.

"White, you're now on speaker. Havoc, Jett, and K9 Digger present."

"I was just up at the hospital with Scott. He's in bad shape, as you already know. We're getting a plan together to evacuate him to Germany. However, while he was being assessed, he developed ascending paralysis. Scott believed it was the numbness that he experienced while he was stuck in the boulder."

Jett leaned forward; a scowl clouded her face. "It wasn't?"

"The paralysis reached his diaphragm and diminished Scott's

respiratory drive. I assure you that he's alive and much better. But they had to perform CPR and artificial breathing while they tried to figure it out."

"From his starvation diet?" Havoc asked.

"Ticks. Three of them. Once the doctors found the ticks and removed them, Scott recovered and could breathe on his own again. And that is the reason for my phone call. You both know how to give a thorough tick check. And sorry to do this to you, but that's what needs to happen. The TOC is at full capacity. Havoc, I can't send you one of your brothers to help. Jett, I'm the only female around, and I'm up to my neck in alligators, as our mutual friend Gator Aid likes to say. The hospital is at capacity, and I'd spend time hunting up someone to send your way, but honestly, it's not a big deal, is it? I can depend on your professionalism?"

Havoc and Jett looked at each other.

The pause was long.

"Tick induced paralysis," Jett said.

"Can be lethal within minutes of the ascending paralysis," White said, "but can begin hours to days after the tick is attached. Minutes counted when it comes to lethality rates. This isn't like Lyme's where you can pop an antibiotic. You were in the same places Scott was. If you picked up the same kind of tick, your lives could be in danger."

"Yes, ma'am," Jett said. "We'll get right on that."

Havoc tapped the button to end the call.

"Looks like we're about to get all up close and personal," Jett said, disappearing into the bathroom. "Let me just say this isn't all that uncomfortable for me. When I was a smokejumper, I was the only female on the team. I had to have a fellow jumper look me over." She came back out.

Havoc accepted the comb that she stretched out to him. "Okay."

"Do you want to start with my hair first? Then I'll drop the towel, and you can check the rest of me. Then I'll do you." She caught his gaze. "You've seen me naked a couple times now. I thought, nothing new, right?"

"Right." Yeah, that definitely sounded collegial. Havoc marked "date night" off his evening plans. "I noticed that you had all of the common body parts, and they were placed in the usual order." He brought a chair over and turned it away from the bed. "Want to sit here?"

"You're nervous."

"I don't want to cross any lines." Havoc said, tugging his headlamp from his backpack and pulling it into position on his brow.

"I trust you, and I promise to speak up."

"Thank you." He sat behind her and started by simply combing her hair straight and getting all of the knots out.

"Mmm, that feels nice. I love having my hair combed."

Noted. "Out of curiosity, did you just pick a random guy to help you? How did you pair up?"

"Sometimes that happened to be the case. Then, I aimed for the less pervy ones. But I was dating a guy."

"Still dating him?"

"Nope. That was many years ago, and a different life." She paused, then added with a bit of an uptick in her voice. "I don't have anyone in my life right now."

That was encouraging. "Me neither."

He combed her hair for a few more minutes before starting the process of parting her hair from the left side of her head to the right, observing her scalp, then moving the comb slightly back and creating another part that he pushed forward.

Ticks liked to hide amongst hair and folds in places where it was almost impossible to see on oneself. That meant in a moment,

Havoc was going to have to inspect Jett's private body parts, and that, mmm, that wasn't great.

Yes, he wanted to inspect her private body parts. To fondle her, to pleasure her, to taste her.

What he didn't want was to do it under orders.

For her to comply under orders.

Even if it was a medical inspection for life-threatening reasons.

Yeah, this sucked. And not in a good way.

"Can you dip your chin a bit?" After she nodded her head forward, Havoc asked. "Hey, tell me how you got involved in smoke jumping. Did someone bet against you?"

"I don't rise to that kind of thing. Let's see. I wanted to be a stunt double when I grew up, like my mom. Kind of the traditional role for the women in my family. I took martial arts and gymnastics. I went to a place called Ninja School." Havoc could hear the smile in her voice. "They taught me baby parkour. My parents were really into sports, rock climbing, surfing. There was always the mantra that we should safely do the things that bring a thrill. So protocol and practice were big pieces to my background. I never told them I wanted to be a stunt double, though. I was afraid that it might make them look at what they allowed me to do through a different lens. Like if they thought this was going on to more dangerous things, maybe they should send me to tai chi classes instead."

He combed another section of hair forward. "You changed your mind?"

"I was taking classes in college—chemistry, physics. The stunts are planned around science, and I wanted to understand it and do my own calculations. I was bitten by the fire bug in one of my science classes. I signed up to be a volunteer firefighter and spent the summer in their training center. After that, I focused my engineering degree on fire management. A lot of that had to do with structural fires, but out west, you have to be prepared for all kinds.”

“There’s a degree in firefighting?”

“I changed my physics major to be my minor, and my major became engineering. My emphasis was on fire engineering.”

“Lots of math.”

Jett shifted in her chair. And Havoc handed her a pillow to hug and curl over. “Better?”

“Thank you, yes. I love math. It saves lives.”

“I couldn’t agree more. It also takes lives.”

“Snipers and explosives and such? Yep. Not my gig, though. I mean, they make us learn that kind of thing in the military, obviously. But that’s not my role. They like to parachute me into unfavorable terrains to gather otherwise unobtainable information. Speaking of which, how did you guys get out here?”

“We came over various borders, so we’re in the country legally but under assumed names. I was assigned to find you.”

“Alone?”

“It was Sunday. We thought you’d be at the guest house resting.”

“Mmm.”

He swooped the next section forward and carefully peered. “We divided up. Too many Americans showing up at once might get people gossiping to the wrong ears.”

“That’s for sure. The network of communication in this area is a strong web. People gather and disseminate news with every interaction—the newspapers make their ways in from the city, but—”

“This is an interesting tattoo.” He’d moved the last of her hair out of the way, inspecting the back of her neck and ears next. “What is it? A salmon?” He laughed. “There must be a reason. Something about swimming against the tide?”

“Oh, I never thought of that. I like that. Remote, roadless

areas are my favorites. But the tattoo is in honor of one of my heroes. Sacajawea."

"Of Lewis and Clark fame."

"Yeah, the guys got the fame. Their lives depended on Sacajawea's skills. Her name should be right there in that lineup. But the reason for the tattoo representation is that she came from the Salmon-eater Shoshone, a band of northern Shoshones. She was kidnapped and sold to Jean Baptiste Charbonneau. On the trip, she gave birth and did everything the men did but with a baby on her back."

"Do you have a child? I'm checking your back and arms next."

Jett dropped the towel to her waist. "Not yet. Someday. I have different iterations to my life. In this one, a child would suffer for want of a mother around. But I seem to have a seven-year itch. After seven years fighting fires, I joined the military. Now that I've been seven years in the military, basically doing what we're doing now, I feel like I might be ready to move forward."

Havoc lifted her arm and looked front and back. She had satin skin. Lovely, graceful arms. Strong. And he was working hard at keeping his thoughts and touch platonic. He would continue to be regimented unless and until Jett changed that dynamic. "What does that look like to you? I'm coming around front to check your torso and under your breasts, if that's okay."

"Whatever you need." She held her arms over her head. Yup, she'd gone through this process before. "This gig is coming to an end. I have to look for my next challenge." She stopped and scratched her brow. "I was recently approached about working with special ops, the Rangers and Delta Force out of Fort Bragg."

"Yeah? Doing what?" He was using his headlamp, so the light was bright enough to see any tiny black specs that were looking for a soul to steal. "This checks out. Now I need to do your legs and feet."

"Teaching survival. Not SERE—Survival. Evasion. Resistance. Escape—mind you." She stood, catching the towel as it fell, then spread it on the bed. "Would it be easier if I were here?" Without waiting for a response, Jett crawled onto the bed, lying face down.

Havoc got the full treat of that heart-shaped ass of hers.

Before touching her, Havoc tried to compose his thoughts. But his dick was obnoxious as hell, making this hard for him. "Not SERE," Havoc said, and it had the right effect. No one could think horny thoughts when they remembered the sheer hell of SERE training.

"I am not down with that kind of activity. When I signed up, the recruiter knew I was willing to do what was necessary, but I'm not comfortable being a gun. I wanted to do reconnaissance. I've worked all over the world in every ecosystem there is. I didn't survive. I thrived. I have a lot to teach."

Havoc was looking between Jett's toes. She must wax or something because her entire body was silky soft and hair-free, except for what looked like a bit of a decorative pubic triangle. When he saw her in the tub, he saw that the labia were perfectly clean, ready for licking. That thought was out of bounds under these circumstances. He reached for a way to make that observation more tactical in nature. He remembered a woman he dated years before, a big hiker. She said grooming herself that way made things more comfortable for keeping herself fresh on the trail, fewer women's issues. Though, she never explained what the women's issues were. And frankly, Havoc was cool with not knowing.

This was damned torture. Looking but not touching. "Backside is done. Have you ever been to Fort Bragg?"

Jett rolled languorously over. Her eyes were shut. She bent her knees and parted her feet. "I'm sorry if this is uncomfortable for you."

She had no idea. His dick was so hard he was in pain.

"Fort Bragg. I've taught there before. It's okay. Not a lot to do there. But that would be home base. My job would be doing what I've done countless times before—train Green Berets, Rangers, Deltas, what have you. But I usually take them out on adventures."

"Like what?"

"Oh, I take groups out in the Arizona desert equipped with only a knife, and we have to survive off the land for a couple of weeks." He pressed his hand to her right knee and pushed out a bit and looked on that side. Then pressed the left.

"All done." He stood and turned his back on Jett, so she'd have privacy to stand and go get dressed. Maybe give him a moment to adjust his dick, so it wasn't tenting his pants. "Tick free."

"Good to know I'm not going to die of tick paralysis."

"Would have sucked if I'd woken up tomorrow morning and you were dead beside me."

"Tick. Sucked. I see what you did there."

"What? Oh, ha. Yeah."

She stood and picked up the towel.

"Did you say you go out for two weeks with only a knife? Must be a pretty good knife."

She wrapped the towel around herself, and it skimmed just south of her V. "You've seen my knife."

"Yeah, it's a good knife."

"Anyway, it looks like I'm not going to have much to say in the matter like it or lump it. They're breaking the AWG up in the next year. So I'm pretty much set on accepting that position. Without killing anyone, there aren't a lot of jobs for me. DIA, maybe. Leaving the military to join the FBI or CIA. But again, lots of opportunities when in the field to be called on to remove an obstacle. I'm really trying very hard to live my whole life without outright purposefully killing someone."

"Or even by accident."

"Exactly. Never say never. It's cold in here. I'm going to pull on a sweatshirt." She moved toward the bathroom.

In just a moment, Havoc would have his pants off, and Jett would be searching his dick for ticks. This was absolutely the last way Havoc had imagined things unrolling.

Yeah, he'd kind of thought that things might take a happy turn tonight. But in his mind, there was a restaurant dinner. They'd walk under the moon. He'd tell her how he felt about her. Holding hands, soft kisses. Romance. He'd planned to romance her within the spectrum of what was available and how she received that kind of attention.

It had felt flirty, them together. Scott had picked up on it. But maybe that was all Jett was interested in, some banter to help time pass, to distract from pain and discomfort. She'd never said anything that crossed a line or was even direct. It was tone and posture. It was the length of time that she continued holding his hand. How she slid his arm around her after the viper incident. It was how she tangled their legs as they slept together in the sleeping bag.

He wanted desperately to make love to Jett.

On his own, and without the orders from White, Havoc would have used a mirror to do a tick check to protect from Lyme's, popped an antibiotic just for shits and giggles, and call it a done deal. But tick paralysis was no joke. It *could* be lethal.

They had received orders.

So here he was, with his boner rock hard, and in just a minute, she'd be looking around his pubic hair for bugs.

Kill me now.

32

―――――

JETT

Jalal-Abad, Kyrgyzstan

Wednesday, Twenty-Twenty-Five Hours

Standing behind the chair where Havoc was seated, a towel wrapped around his waist, Jett thought that this situation was absurd.

She couldn't help it. She started laughing.

Havoc looked off to the side, where Digger lifted his head to see what was happening. Havoc gave him a laydown signal, and Digger plunked his head between his paws and went back to sleep.

"This room," Jett said to explain the thought that tickled her, "is like being in some kind of Bismol-pink genie's bottle." She took a step back. "It's just a weird setup. I'll be right back. I'm going to go grab a hair elastic from my toiletries bag."

Jett slipped into the bathroom, wondering if it would be too obvious if she splashed cold water on her face to realign her thoughts. After tying her hair back, she looked in the mirror. Her eyes, like Havoc's, were dilated to almost black. Her skin glowed with a flush of horniness.

Flicking nervous fingers through her bag, Jett found the strip of condoms she carried there. She lifted them.

Should she?

The sweatshirt White had chosen for her had a breast pocket. And Jett thought she looked kind of cute sporting the shirt with nothing on underneath, the hem skimming just past her bottom.

Covered and yet accessible.

No harm in tucking the condoms into the pocket in case Havoc was willing to play.

She knew he was horny and ready. His dick had been like a good soldier, always at attention and ready for a command. She'd slept two nights now with it tapping on her back, "Hey there, wanna play?" Of course, Havoc had been asleep. These were body reactions, not thought processes. Jett had no idea what Havoc wanted.

Though, they had exchanged relationship status reports…

One way to find out.

Jett padded her way back into the bedroom.

Havoc had moved to lie on his stomach, clothes off, a towel wrapped around his waist.

Looking at the broad expanse of Havoc's back, his shoulder, and arm muscles, he was glorious.

Havoc turned his head to see her. "Is this okay?"

Here I go, Jett thought as she licked her lips. "We can start there. I thought—it's up to you—but maybe we could have some fun with my tick scavenger hunt."

He lifted a single brow.

Jett reached into her pocket and pulled the condom pack up just enough, so he had the information. "If you want."

"Definitely. Yes, I want." Not a second's hesitation. Big old grin.

"Well then, soldier, if I do anything that makes you feel uncomfortable, I need you to tell me straight away."

"Absolutely," he said.

She climbed onto the bed, pulling the headlamp into place, then straddled Havoc sitting on his ass. "I'm going to look at your scalp. This will be quick. Your hair is nice and short."

Jett was careful to be methodical because who the hell wanted to be making love and have their partner suddenly be stopped by paralysis. But she also allowed herself to enjoy the sensation of his soft hair. She massaged his scalp with her fingertips and could feel his body relaxing between her thighs. The physical, emotional, and mental stress of the last few days was falling to the side.

For her as well as for Havoc.

She checked his ears, then massaged his neck and shoulders, down his back. Looking carefully, this slow exploration of his body had its benefits. It was his turn to let her do what she wanted. She had a job to accomplish, so there could be no Mr. Grabby Hands that pushed and pulled her to do things as he wanted. Not that she thought that was the kind of lover that Havoc would be. Just this gave her a little freedom that was outside her usual kiss, disrobe, and rumba.

Jett liked it.

When Havoc turned over so she could check his chest, pulling the towel free, she could tell that Havoc was into it too. The tip of his fuck-me-hard dick was slick with precum. This time when she crawled on top of him, they were belly to belly.

She kissed over his face, around to his ears.

When he tried to respond, she pressed his hands back. "Soldier, this is a life-or-death situation. You will *not* distract me from my duties."

He chuckled by way of response and gave her a salute.

She kissed his neck and down his pecs.

Inching backward, she lapped and kissed and massaged her way down either side to his six-pack. She reveled in tracing her fingertips between the ridges.

"Not to distract your life-or-death mission, but if you remember yesterday when Scott warned you about dangling food too close…"

"Fortitude, soldier. Right action."

"Oh, I have the right actions in mind right now. Don't torment me, woman."

Jett laughed as she wrapped her hand around his throbbing cock. She licked the tip.

A hiss of air passed through Havoc's pursed lips. He closed his eyes as she swirled her tongue around the tip. Using the tip of her tongue, she ran it along the ridge, then down the shaft.

Adjusting herself between his legs, she massaged his length while she sucked at the head.

Powerful. Female. She felt like a glowing goddess. She was experiencing something that she'd never imagined before.

Her pussy was slick and throbbing. She really needed to stay focused for a moment more, then she could whip the headlamp off her head. Jett sat back on her heels and massaged his scrotal sack. "No bruises." She bent and kissed it all over, murmuring, "Sorry, guys. I thought you were going to hurt me."

"I will *never* intentionally hurt you, Jett."

"I know," she said as she lifted and inspected his perineum. "One, I wouldn't let you." She tugged lightly at his pubic hair. "Two, it's not who you are." She spat on the tip of his dick and used the moisture to rub up and down the shaft, then put the head back in her mouth. She wanted that salty tang of precum on her lips.

Havoc's hands came down to her head, tugging off the lamp,

pulling the elastic free from her ponytail, playing with the length of her hair. His hands slid under her arms, and when she looked up, he pulled her up his length and rolled her over, so she sprawled beneath him.

"Inspection's done. It's my turn to play."

33

JETT

Jalal-Abad, Kyrgyzstan

Thursday, Zero Five Hundred Hours

Zero five hundred hours, the team gathered at headquarters for a breakfast meeting.

Havoc and Jett had to sneak Digger in.

Holding Digger's lead, Jett made her way around the room, introducing herself.

Damian Prescott wasn't here, and that was a shame. Damian had been at the hospital monitoring Scott, so Scott didn't give away State secrets. The two were now on their way to Germany to get Scott the treatment he needed. But Jett had wanted a few private words with Damian to check on the safety of her friend Anna.

Jett had moved through Ranger School with a woman named Anna Senko. She was destined for work with the Asymmetric Warfare Group, just like Jett. While Jett was working in the back-country, Anna was tip of the spear. Imbedded with her maternal grandmother's side of the family—the Zorics—it was Anna's intel that they were following. Anna identified a family connection in two geographical areas where she thought it was possible for the Zorics to hide their apparatus, here in Kyrgyzstan and the other in the Tatra Mountains in Slovakia.

Both had some kind of Zoric activity going on. Anna just didn't know what.

When Anna was stateside following up on a Zoric family-mandated task last year, she had developed a "relationship" with FBI Special Agent Steve Finley. Finley was on the same joint task force as Damian Prescott.

Finley was a handsome enough guy in the photos Jett had seen. He wasn't Anna's type, though.

Jett was reasonably sure that the Zorics had tasked Anna to date Finley—to mine information about the FBI. The FBI, after all, had arrested and jailed a whole branch of their family. Surely, the Zorics wanted retribution.

The possibility of being ordered by someone into a sexual relationship frightened Jett.

It was one thing to be ordered to undergo a tick check. It was another to feign a relationship and sleep with the guy for tactical expediency.

Jett wasn't that soldier.

She'd probably have said no.

Jett had felt for sure Anna would have said no to such a command, too. But things change in the field.

Jett missed her friend. She had hoped for an opportunity to just ask Damian how Anna was doing.

Since Jett was sitting at the conference table with Digger at her feet, Havoc had gone to get her a cup of coffee and a plate of food from the buffet table. In this setting, without the excuse of monitoring the K9, Jett couldn't have allowed such a boyfriend-like gesture.

Boyfriend? That was such an appealing thought.

Yeah, Jett would be totally down with growing closer to Havoc. His humor, his strength, his kindness…his fuck skills. Yup, she could deal with more mind-blowing sex in her life.

White canted her head. "That's a bright smile you've got on your face, Jett."

"First real bed I've slept in for almost six months. My neck feels better for the first time in a week. Much appreciated, White."

Havoc placed a plate in front of her. "Thanks, things look yum." Jett spread a napkin in her lap, while Havoc pulled out the chair across from her.

They ate the traditional Kyrgyz breakfast of bread and cheese, tea, and some additions of fried goat meat and roasted vegetables.

"All present and accounted for." White nodded as Ty and Nitro walked through the door with Rory. "Let's get started before we're burning daylight." She stood and tapped at the computer. "I'm bringing up an area of interest that T-Rex's group found and brought to our attention." White flashed a grid map onto the screen.

"I have that circled on my map, too," Jett said.

White turned her attention to Jett. "This is Peter and Tink's area. Why were you searching here?"

"I wasn't. The woman who owns the guest house where I am staying told me that there were areas of evil. She circled them on a map for me and told me to stay away from them. I thought those were prime areas to go in and take a look."

"Sherlock 101," Havoc threw in.

"Can I see those?" White stepped closer to Jett.

Jett pulled the map from the silicon sleeve attached to her outer pack and handed it out.

White took a picture and sent it to the computer. The visual popped up on the screen.

"The one in the center, we cleared that. It's a ghost town," T-Rex said.

"The one on the left was cleared as well," Havoc said. "It's a sulfur spring where we found Digger."

"The one on the right is the one you're curious about, T-Rex?" Jett asked. "The story I was told is that the entire town died in the 1912 plague. Because no one was well enough to bury the people, they were just left there to decompose. Evil found the town and moved in, feasting on the bodies. Later, a landslide covered the road, and now there's no passage."

"Which is why this is interesting. We stumbled on what looked like a landslide cutting off the road," T-Rex said.

"Looked like," White repeated.

"It's an optical illusion. You can drive something as large as a dump truck in by coming up the side here." T-Rex moved over to the screen to point. Then there's a tight turn right, and a tight turn left. It looks like it's impenetrable, but it's very much navigable. We didn't follow the road. We didn't want to get into something we weren't prepared for. No weapons. No comms. Better to exercise caution. Since we had a car, my team followed this road to the backside. Here, where there should be an exit to the main road, again, there's the configuration that looks like a solid rock face but is in actuality that optical illusion. I wondered why no one in the area was aware, but if they think it's haunted, they would keep their distance."

"Suspicious, I agree," White said. "And, again, in Tink and Peter's grid. I think this has good possibilities. There's nothing on our satellites at night, so they must close everything down if there are people out there. Also, scanning the images we have from daytime hours, there are no vehicles, no movement that we've captured. Still, I want to mark it off the list, and I'm curious enough that I'm going to send the whole team in. T-Rex, I'd like you to divide the team you've been working with on this mission into two. Alpha goes here along the western side of the road from the back entrance. Bravo continues on the right. Ty's team will be called Charlie and goes left side of the road from the front entrance. Jett and Havoc will take K9 Digger and work the other side, team Delta. I have a van to transport you out. The van will begin a new pass by the front entrance every hour, the van will proceed to the back entrance and be back out at the front entrance again. Like a bus stop, they will look for you here." She tapped the screen. "And here."

"What's the mission window?" T-Rex asked.

"First light to last if there is any kind of activity, I want it monitored and documented and brought out for analysis. The pressing goal is to try to get eyes on Tink and Peter. It's also possible that this is the spot that our imbed sent us to find. Either finding the secret something we're looking for or finding our missing AWG operators would make for a good day. Both would be the golden ticket. While you're on-site, you're also thinking strategically for ways to get Tink and Peter out if we were to find them in this area. If, like the other haunted spot that Jett pointed out, there is nothing and no one, jump in the van, bring the unit back to the TOC, and we'll strategize."

T-Rex stood. "Stay focused. Lives on the line."

34

Jalal-Abad, Kyrgyzstan

Thursday, Zero Five-Forty Hours

Havoc felt a lot less naked now that he had his radio communication system with him.

On the way to their X, Jett looked at the satellite pictures that White had handed out. She said she was memorizing them to leave with the van.

If they were caught by Kyrgyz authorities today, the team's cover story was that they are U.S. citizens on vacation, doing some hiking.

That, of course, wouldn't hold up under scrutiny. Echo had come in under false identities with falsified documents. That and the ghillie suits in their day packs… They'd be held and tried as spies.

When the van let off teams Charlie and Delta, they bumped fists, separated, and moved to their side of the road.

Jett moved like a lynx through the woods. Soundless and alert.

When Jett and Havoc changed their gait, moving from tree to tree, vigilant, Digger seemed to pick up on their cues. He stayed at Jett's heels. When she crouched, Digger crouched. When she hid, he laid flat.

Jett would reward his behavior with a scratch behind the ears, soundless.

The early morning light sifted gently through the evergreen branches. It was bright enough to see their breath clouding in front of their faces, as they made their way to the town.

They assessed the backs of buildings, a mosque, and a string of shops.

Havoc lifted the camera and snapped pictures from different angles.

The first sign of life was the sound of a voice signaling *Fajr.* It was the first of the five calls to prayer for the devout.

Jett turned to him and pointed to a rock outcropping that would get them about ten meters higher.

From there, they could see below.

Women emerged from a school-like structure on Charlie's side of the road.

They wore long tunics over loose pants. Hijabs covered their hair and obscured their faces. They walked two by two.

Sharpening the focus of his aperture, Havoc could see that each pair of women were connected with leg shackles.

Pinpricks slid over his scalp.

If Tink was amongst them, Havoc wasn't sure how they'd be able to tell.

Two men unrolled a carpet. AK-styled rifles dangled from their straps.

The women prayed. They all seemed to follow along with the ritual movements without hesitation. Listed as a Methodist in her paperwork, either Tink had studied and practiced this ritual, or she wasn't amongst those women.

Twenty of them.

After prayer, they were instructed to stand and form a line.

Two more males exited a house with a slender table balanced between them. On the table were stacks of plastic, lidded boxes.

Breakfast?

Each woman accepted her box hesitantly.

So probably not breakfast.

The women were prodded to walk in Havoc and Jett's direction.

Havoc turned to see Jett, she had coaxed Digger up on the boulder, and now she was throwing a ghillie cloth over the two of them. Havoc grabbed his out of his sack.

Jett pointed, then put her lips next to his ear and whispered, "There's a path that looks newly cleaned. I think they're heading to the clearing below us. Let's hope Digger doesn't give us away."

They edged around so that the clearing would be in their view, positioning before the group made their way any closer.

Havoc pulled out a parabolic dish and microphone and set it up, tapping the record feature and sliding an earbud into one ear, handing the other earbud to Jett so she could listen, too.

Both would have one ear that picked up ambient sounds.

Through the magnification of his camera lens, Havoc could see that a man was already in the clearing, lighting a fire against the cold. Around the fire pit were lengths of logs that would serve as seats.

The women arrived and were instructed to sit in a particular order.

Jett looked his way.

"Pashto," Havoc whispered.

Jett shook her head and removed the earbud.

Pashto was one of the two main languages spoken in northern Afghanistan. Havoc could make out *some* Pashto, but his vocabulary had been gathered on the run while deployed. Nothing formal. "Sit," Havoc understood. He also understood the following command, "Swallow."

The women took the lids off their boxes and looked in.

Many of them were crying.

A man worked his way around dribbling what looked like oil into the box. At the first stop, he lifted the box and seemed to show the women how to massage the oil onto the contents. Havoc didn't understand what the man was saying. But then came the command again, "Swallow."

Raised barrels pointed at the back of the women's heads.

Slowly, they began lifting what looked like a small dumpling, tipping their heads back, putting the dumpling into their mouth, and swallowing without chewing.

Shit. Havoc knew precisely what was happening. These women were being used as mules.

A woman clapped a hand over her mouth as her stomach rebelled, trying to vomit up the swallowed balloons. Eyes watering, face bright red, she struggled to keep the drugs in her stomach.

White apprised the team of drug routes coming up from the poppy fields in Afghanistan. Moving so little via mules didn't make much sense.

Once the packets were swallowed, a man collected the empty boxes.

Another man came into the clearing distributing burkas.

A third man had passports. He looked at the picture, searched the faces, and handed the document out.

Four women sat on each log.

Shackles secured every pair of women.

A group of men made their way up the trail to the field. Each man walked toward a log of women, introduced himself, and placed a wedding ring on the finger of each woman in front of him. Then they rose, and walking two by two behind him, they left the clearing.

The clearing emptied.

Havoc and Jett turned on their boulder overlook to observe the women being loaded into an airport courtesy van.

If these men had captured Tink, forced her to mule heroin, and flew her out, they might well be too late.

Tink could be *anywhere* in the world by now.

35

JETT

Jalal-Abad, Kyrgyzstan

Thursday, Zero Seven Hundred Hours

Horror had washed over Jett as she watched the distress of the women below them.

Digger's body had been rigid with concentration. A low rumble started in the back of his throat.

Jett had been terrified that Digger would bark and those rifles would turn in their direction. Jett might be captured and made to sit in the glen like these women.

And who knew what they might do if they found a man. Shoot him in the head was Jett's guess.

They wouldn't want a fit, tactical male working to save his woman.

His. Woman.

Jett set that thought to the side for the time being.

What she needed now was compliance from a K9 that she wasn't trained to handle.

Jett's babushka had taught her to think and communicate with the horses with voice commands, body language, and mental pictures.

Under these circumstances, Jett was left with trying to send "be quiet, be still" pictures to Digger.

He seemed to get it. Though vigilant, Digger laid still, and there were no more rumbles.

They watched the village.

From their position on the boulder, Jett and Havoc had a good view. Team Alpha should have the northern half. Bravo and Charlie should have seen parts of this play out, too.

And that was it for movement.

After the van left, the village was dead.

Silently, they held.

At some point, Jett had rolled away with Digger at her side. They went into the woods to relieve themselves, then sat at the base of the boulder to eat lunch. Jett moved back into position, then Havoc went to take care of his needs.

"Nothing?" he whispered as he pulled his ghillie cloth over him.

"Absolutely nada. I'm not even getting a lens flash from the other teams."

"I walked out a few meters into the forest. From this point, it's too dense to walk easily, and there aren't any visible trails."

"I'm thinking about why they did all of that in this clearing," Jett said.

"I've been debating that, too. The conclusion I've drawn is that they have more prisoners, and they didn't want to let on what would happen to them next. Keep them in the dark to keep them calm and obedient."

"Yup, that was my conclusion, too. No idea about Tink and Peter. We might have missed them. It's been almost a month since their last check-in."

Quiet lay between them.

After a long while, Jett grew sleepy under the cover, with the sun softly warming her back. She needed to talk to stay awake. "Yesterday, White said 'our friend Gator Aid.' That's got to be Gator Aid Rochambeau. Do you know him?"

"I do. Retired Marine Raider working with Strike Force. He was down at Fort Bragg working a mission for Echo."

"Small world."

"How do you know him?"

"Through his sister, Auralia. She's a journalist. She interviewed me back when she was a student reporter, and I was a smokejumper. We got to be friends."

"Nearly eight billion people on the planet, I find it nuts how I can run into someone on the other side of the world and find people in common."

"Six Degrees game."

"Here's an example for you. First step, our team has a K9 named Rory. Second, Rory was handled by Cerberus Tactical K9 Trip Wire when he was with the SEALs. Third, Trip Wire saved a guy's life during a parachuting accident that went way bad but wasn't lethal because of Trip Wire's actions. The guy's name is Jean Louis Roujean. Fourth, T-Rex is Echo's leader. T-Rex is dating Remi Taleb."

"The war correspondent?"

"Exactly. Echo had an assignment to do close protection. Remi was an imbed attached to our team on that mission. And she did it because she was desperate to get to Lebanon and see her friend Jean Baptiste Roujean who was in the hospital after ISIS tortured him."

"Who was Jean Baptist Roujean?"

"A photojournalist Remi worked with and also Jean Louis Roujean's uncle."

"Wow! That's kind of incredible."

"I'm falling asleep," Havoc said. "I hate overwatch when there's no activity, nothing to call out, nothing to document. Would it be okay if I asked you some questions?"

"Depends on how personal, I guess," Jett said.

"Your call, say pass if it's out of bounds."

"K."

"I've never heard of anyone with your unique background, from your grandmother forward to now."

"Meh. Unique, sure, but you haven't heard of it only because you didn't come from Hollywood."

"That's where you call home?"

"Too expensive. We had a family ranch in Montana."

"Where you jumped out of planes."

"Yup, being a smokejumper was a dream come true. I have seen and fought to save some beautiful country. I love to jump out of planes. The peace of it. The views. When my feet hit the ground, then comes the hell and havoc." She smiled at him.

"You told me that you're parachuting into different land-scapes, cultures. Are you alone?"

"Usually not alone. I normally have someone with me. Safety both from a medical point of view, but also to help with a cover story. Few women travel solo. Which is understandable."

"Yes."

"I learned the importance of a few rituals that I do no matter where I am. Otherwise, I feel lost with every culture change. Babushka taught me that from her time traveling with the circus. A new town every few days."

"Rituals?"

"Not religious. More just—you know... Meal rituals. Morning ritual. Bedtime rituals. That means no matter where I am, I have some consistency, bracketing my day. The middle of my day is the adventure. It's not a big deal. It's things like making your bed every morning. Meditate. Stretching exercises. Brush teeth. Simple but consistent. And she's right. It helps."

"How do you get from smokejumper to AWG?"

"Funny story. I approached an Army recruiter. They had started allowing women to try for Ranger school. I thought I had all the qualities needed for that. That I could be useful in that capacity. I asked the recruiter if it were possible to be a Ranger, help out with my skills and not kill anybody."

"He laughed in your face."

"Pretty much. But I laid out my qualifications in front of him. My education, my skills with fire and explosives. My physical abilities. I mean, I basically had everything that they would be teaching me. I don't think he believed I could do what I said I could. He took me to the base and put me through the physical testing. They had me fight, hand to hand and knife. They asked me to shoot, and I do that too. But it was more about being out in the woods when I was off duty and needing to protect myself from animals. I volunteered for the Hunting for the Hungry program. The problem was that I didn't want to kill people, just food."

"The recruiter was impressed?"

"Stoic. But my scores were well in the range for acceptance into Ranger school. The recruiter said he'd do some research and give me a callback. He also said he didn't want to lose me, so that was encouraging. He asked that I not go check in with other branches. Give him a day."

"Recruiting quotas."

"Exactly. The guy calls me and says we'd like you to sign with the Army to become an officer. The contract read that I would be given the opportunity to go through the process to get my Ranger tabs in the first year, and then they'd invite me to join the Asymmetrical Warfare Group. I'd never heard of such an institution. They explained what they did in general and that I would basically be doing reconnaissance work to support their efforts. They'd drop me by a parachute into these crazy places. I'd backpack out. Very similar to what I did as a smokejumper, but without the flames and smoke."

"Walk in the park, then." Havoc lifted his parabolic ear and shifted it around. Aiming it this way and that.

He shook his head.

"Your turn: How did you join Echo?" Jett asked. "And I know you're Delta. Damian Prescott and I are friends—friendly. At any rate, I know his background, and you said that you had served together. So no need to obfuscate."

"Okay."

"To be a Delta Force operator, you had to have skills. Not just trained in a classroom, but real-world experience. That meant none of the team was a spring chicken. How old are you?"

"Thirty-two. You?" Havoc asked.

"Thirty-four."

"I was in the reserves while I was in college and then went full-time," he said. "At seventeen, my parents signed permission to allow me to join the military right out of high school. With my track and field records, the recruiter tapped me for the Rangers from the get-go. But I had to promise my parents to hold off and get my college done."

Jett remembered how his muscles felt under her hands the night before. He had a wiry toughness to his body that was made for Iron Man races and extreme marathons.

"Ranger to Delta Force Echo."

Their gazes held for a long moment.

"I was thinking of the Edwardo Mellon novel Trifecta," Jett said.

"I've never read it."

"There's a quote that kind of stuck with me. The passage asks,

'How did you get yourself here?' and the character responds, 'I took a step, then I tumbled.'"

Jett had to counsel herself to be brave. She hated the heart on her sleeve bit. But she wasn't willing to just say goodbye to Havoc after this mission without testing the waters. And you never knew what the next minutes, hours, and days might bring.

"Okay."

"Not to freak you out," she said.

"I'm a warrior. Books don't freak me out."

"Do I, though?"

"Freak me out?" He chuckled.

She took in a breath. "This is spiraling out of control. Let me say it a different way."

"Good. Yes."

"I'm talking about my feelings for you. I've been taking steps toward you since we met."

"And then you tumbled?"

"Yes. Then I just tumbled." She stopped to laugh. "Nerves."

He nodded.

"I feel connected to you. Affection for you. I really enjoyed last night. All of it from the tick check to the booty call." She laughed again. "I think we work well together. Communicate well. And then there's the chemistry of us."

"The chemistry of us." Havoc smiled. "I like that."

36

Jalal-Abad, Kyrgyzstan

Thursday, Fourteen Hundred Hours

Jett took in a deep breath. It seemed a bit craven to have this conversation while they were both staring through binoculars. But there it was. She wasn't sure when she'd have another opportunity. In the field, things changed fast.

"I wanted to speak to you about going forward with a relationship," Havoc said. "I'm glad you brought this up. For sure, I don't want to lose you."

"Ah, but I refuse to talk about a relationship with someone when I don't know their name."

"I'm Timothy Nathan Hale, a descendent of the Hale family in Coventry, Connecticut. I go by Timothy Hale when I'm not operating or with my brothers."

"Havoc Hale?"

"Havoc is my military name. I don't introduce myself as Havoc Hale. I'm Havoc, or I'm Timothy Hale."

What's the evolution of your name? Why Havoc?"

"In boot camp, I was known as 'X'."

"Exhale? Ha!"

"Yeah, my fellow recruits weren't that inventive when it came to names. They went for the low-hanging fruit. I had gone along to get along. There were other more important things to focus on."

"Like?"

"My career trajectory. I wanted to be in The Unit. I arrived on base thinking that getting to Ranger school was going to be a piece of cake with my athletic background. What I wasn't prepared for was the mental fortitude that I needed to build. The in-your-face stress was something else. The smells and noises. The suddenness of change. The utter chaos."

"Exactly," Jett said. "I experienced that as a smokejumper. So I was lucky in that regard when I got to RASP1 for those first eight weeks of training. So high school star Timothy Hale, then Private X, and now a seasoned Delta Force operator called Havoc."

"Yup, the Rangers, I made it in and did my duty. It had been a good fit for me as a younger man. Then I needed more. The challenge wasn't as inspiring after a decade of work."

"You seemed to have worked through the physical and mental stuff."

"I'm always training. I like rubbing my psyche over a whetstone to sharpen my senses."

"So you put yourself out for The Unit?"

"Getting onto Tier One Team Echo was a dream come true."

"The 'Long Walk' is I guess a lot like the SEALs Hell Week. How did you do on yours?"

"Second man over the line. We weren't given much by way of an explanation of the challenge. A seventy-pound pack, a topo map, and a whistle blow. We had no idea how fast we needed to get the job done or get cut. The course was forty miles of back-woods crazy. I sprained my ankle about three quarters of the way through."

"No! *Shit*."

"At one point, when I thought the only way I could finish the course was to do it on my hands and knees, I cried out the Shakespeare phrase, 'Cry havoc and let slip the dogs of war!' It was the only thing that came to my exhausted mind. I remember it vividly. I was leaning over a boulder much like this one, trying to figure the easiest way to crawl down. My voice hit just right, and it echoed out over the valley."

"Cool!"

"Others heard and took heart. Drew power from it. By the time the last man was down, my name had been changed from X to Havoc."

"I like it much better. What role do you play for Echo?"

"My main function is as Echo's sniper. I spend most of my time hidden in the shadows, waiting for the shot, or in this case, any kind of movement and intelligence gathering. I wish someone would show their face so we could count heads."

"Maybe from a different vantage point?" Jett suggested.

"From here, we've got our area covered. Maybe one of the other teams has more."

"Yeah, this is a lot of how I spend my days. It's good, though. Contributions can come as information or lack of information. Both add to the knowledge pool. Something's there. Something's not there. Most days, I'm happy with my role."

Havoc leaned over for a luxurious kiss. "Mmm. What do you like about it?"

"Oh, you know, the things I like are also the things I dislike." Jett smiled at him then turned her attention back to her binoculars.

"Yeah?"

"I like being a minimalist. I don't need things. I prefer experiences."

"Same."

"But by being a minimalist, I always experience a sense of scarcity. Electricity, communication, even water and food. It makes me feel humble and appreciative. Those are good things." She drew in a deep breath. "I glory in the outdoors. It's where my soul wants to be. And yet amongst the dirt and pines, I'm dirty and pine covered. Mud in my teeth. Days without bathing. When I was fighting fires, I could go down to the base camp. They had people there that filled our needs. They provided delicious hot meals. Showers with soap. They washed and folded my clothes for me while I slept in my tent. But I'm rarely clean. Clean is a luxury."

"It is indeed. Scott can certainly attest to that. Being alone like that, brutal."

"He had Digger most nights. That's good. I don't ever want to be in Scott's predicament, for sure. But I have hermit tendencies. I like to be alone and have my thoughts. To contemplate and to own an experience without others' input. It's mine for the good or bad. Yin Yang. I also have a deep longing for connection. For support when things turn bad. Or when a sunset is so glorious that it hurts. And I want to stand shoulder to shoulder with someone and bask in the pain. I mean, I meet people along the way. I can have intense connections. But those relationships are fleeting, I've learned."

"You take from them what is offered. You give what you can, and then you wish them well and part," Havoc said.

"There's the inevitable relationship hangover when they're suddenly gone. The longing to have the connection back. But it's ephemeral. Fleeting."

"You have a poetic soul. And you have a lineage of strong, courageous, athletic women standing behind you."

"It's shaped me. Yes. The relationship we have between us—"

Havoc lowered his binoculars to focus on Jett. "To me, this feels like one of the intense ones you mentioned. But I don't want it to be ephemeral. I don't want to think that you're gone from my life forever. Just a memory I pull from my back pocket to contemplate and feel nostalgic over from time to time."

"That's not who we are," Jett countered. "We're the kinds of people who go to the ends of the world, who face obstacles and conquer them. If the objective is essential, we find a way and don't give up."

"We can apply that to an *us*. We can persevere, be creative. Jett, I *want* to find a way to make it happen. I'm seeing our lives like a Ven diagram. You like math."

Jett's grin was wide and happy.

"Don't laugh. Hear me out. You have your way of doing and being, and I have mine. We can enjoy the spaces that allow an overlap. I'll give you an example. The Asymmetric Warfare Group is disbanding. You told me that you'd been offered a job training special forces worldwide but could be based out of Fort Bragg. I'm based out of Fort Bragg."

"If I worked there, we might be at the same place at the same time."

"More, you said that you seemed to be on a seven-year cycle. Seven years jumping out of planes to fight fires. And you're at your seven-year mark in the military training for and then being part of the AWG."

"Yes." Jett lifted her binocular back into place. "Close your eyes to rest them. I'll take the next fifteen minutes watch."

Havoc laid his head in the crook of his elbow and closed his eyes. "If you were to spend another seven training special forces, I'd have my twenty years in. Did you want to stay in until retirement?"

"That was my plan. But I'm not going to spend my life doing something I hate."

"I hope not. My point is, I guess that we have options."

"You're talking about years of this Venn diagram overlap."

"I am." He popped his eyes open to catch Jett's gaze. "I'm talking about a future without permanent goodbyes."

"That's aspirational." She leaned in for a kiss and let her lips linger there, soft and buzzing. "Hopeful," Jett whispered.

"Possible?"

37

Havoc

Jalal-Abad, Kyrgyzstan

Thursday, Nineteen Hundred Hours

The room was silent.

The teammates shoveled food into their mouths with downcast eyes.

Exhaustion came at the end of a day where everyone held themselves at Code Red. Ready to fight for their lives at any moment while lying very still, focused on their sections.

As the team rose to put their dishes in the bus bins, White came to the front of the room. "I just got word that AI gives it a 97% that Bravo captured Tink's image. We have nothing on Peter."

The team shuffled quietly to their seats, attentive.

"I'm going to play a section for you from Havoc, Jett, and Digger's recordings. This happened at their arrival. From their vantage point, there was no other activity."

The scene of the women swallowing their balloons was played.

"Mules," was whispered throughout the room as the woman tipped her head back.

"Go back, White, to the point where the first woman tips her head back." T-Rex paused while White rewound and played that section again. "See how they do it? Going one woman to the other making sure they eat it and giving it time to settle before they have them do the next. This has been going on for a while and has been fine-tuned."

At the conclusion of their video, White said, "This next section is from Bravo."

The screen showed the airport transport driving down the road. The women all hidden under their indigo burkas.

After they left, the men with the rifles stood in the road yelling. Women came out of three houses and lined the roads.

"This is a selection process," White narrated what they were seeing. "The women are shackled two-by-two as were the women in Team Delta's video. The women were lined up, and another twenty were chosen, Tink amongst them. There." She circled her laser light on one of the women in a hijab.

"Bolt cutters for the shackles," Nitro said.

White paused and listed that on the whiteboard.

"Obviously, the men know that the women would want to run before they swallow the balloons," Ty said. "Once they've swallowed the balloons, that's money to be made."

"Next, after the selection, we see that the women are brought to the yard between the houses. Guarded by men with semi-automatic rifles, they are stripped down, and they bathe using a plastic swim pool and water heated over the fire. On this woman," White circled her pointer again, "there's a tattoo that seems to be of a Marine bulldog on her back. This is the tattoo listed in Tink's medical file. It's honoring her late father. That helped the AI make its determination."

The film continued.

"These women, once they were all cleaned and had fresh, ankle-length dresses from the pile, all moved into this house through a side door. Twenty is the same number as the group this morning. The women—cleaned and dressed similarly as the women this morning and no longer in the loose pants and tunics the other victims are wearing—tells me that in the morning light, these women will move into the clearing to swallow their heroin packets."

White leaned her hips back into the table. "So, how do we get her out? And more importantly, how do we get Tink out and protect Peter's life if he were being held in a different building."

"Or even in a building off-campus," T-Rex said.

White planted her hands on the table. "Go through that."

"It's hard for me to believe that a woman who has moved through SERE school hasn't tried to get free. Rifles, yes, but this group looks like they're basing their power on threat. Threat alone shouldn't keep Tink there. What if she was threatened that if she were to escape that Peter would be killed. Or worse, sold to insurgents."

"She might be biding time," Jeopardy said.

"Almost a month?" Nitro asked.

"There was no other movement from Alpha's or Charlie's grids. All we know is that Tink is in there. We're going to have to go with what we have. We can have comms in this area. Thanks to the shape of the terrain, radio signals were loud and clear. We have zero in the way overwatch. You're on your own out there."

"Night vision?"

"Some of you have a monocular, some binoculars. All of them are night vision with thermal. That's it."

"Weapons?" T-Rex asked.

White pressed her lips together. "That gets complicated."

"There are at least a dozen armed men in this camp, according to my count," T-Rex said. "Are you suggesting we go in with bear spray and knives?"

"I'm saying that it's complicated. We don't know the political associations that this group has with the police. I'm assuming that they pay them very well. I'm working the problem."

"We need to get Tink out," Jett said.

"Agreed." White's mouth tugged into a frown. "As bad as it is for the other women, those other women aren't the mission. For now, we need to focus on Tink. Then we can see what can be done for the others."

"Do you know where the bus went?" T-Rex asked.

"To the airport," White said. "They flew to Dubai."

"Five men, each with his four wives, arrive with the heroin," Dice said. "I bet that's lucrative."

"Dangerous, though," Ty said. "One of the women has a balloon split. She'd die by overdose—maybe. That would put security's eyes on the group flying in. Dubai has zero-tolerance for drugs. If you're caught consuming them, it can be life in prison. It would be a death sentence for a woman functioning as a mule."

"Using mules to get drugs into Dubai means a lot more money for a lot less product," White said. "I'm going to assume that those men have an association with people who could make charges disappear. And that they fly in and out at regular intervals. They have the process down to a science, too. We saw that in Delta team's video."

"I wonder if they just go around kidnapping random women." Jeopardy crossed his arms over his chest. "And if they just went around kidnapping women, wouldn't the number of women from this area be noticed?"

"No, actually. It's a norm to kidnap young women in Kyrgyzstan," Jett said. "Half of the married women in the country are married to men who kidnapped them."

"What?" All of Echo (except for Havoc) leaned forward, dumbfounded.

"Trust me, it's a thing," Jett said. "No one is looking for a kidnapped woman. It regularly happens that they're kidnapped in the streets."

"This is the perfect country to set up such a program," White agreed.

"What do you think they do with the women after they've passed the heroin packets out of their systems?" Nitro asked. "Is it possible to track Tink and snatch her back at the airport? Maybe even in Dubai? I know it's a risk to allow her to swallow the balloons, but it might be the lesser risk if Peter is being held."

"To answer your question about next chapters for these women, I'd imagine that they're sold into slavery, forced into prostitution," White said. "All of the women are young and attractive. I'm sure that's a part of the picture. Extra cash flow. We have no idea if Peter is in the area. Rescuing Tink is our immediate goal."

T-Rex stood and moved to the map. "Looking at the setup, we need to get to them before this point."

"Agreed," Jett said. "Before Tink swallows the heroin."

"It would be best if we get Tink before sunrise," Havoc said. "In the dark, we'd have a better chance against these guns. It would be a bloodbath to have a gunfight around these women. They might even target them to keep them quiet should the law get involved."

Ty asked. "Given our capabilities with our present equipment, what options are we considering? How do we handle it?"

T-Rex drummed his pen on the table. "I'd love more time observing. And I'd insist we take it—"

"Except there was a selection," Jett said.

T-Rex pointed her way. "Exactly."

"White, can you go back to the close-ups of the houses in the section the women are held?"

White pulled up the images.

"We could light the building on fire," Jett said. "Here, along with the chimneys. The chimney would create a buffer. The corner creates another, mmm, not block. It will slow the flame slightly. It's a risk. But humans flee fires. I would guess the men would save themselves. You guys could handle the squirters. I could run in with bolt cutters, lead the women into the forest. Hike them to safety."

"There are a lot of 'what ifs' in that scenario, Jett," White said.

"What if we burned out uninhabited buildings?" Nitro said, and the team chuckled. Nitro loved to explode things and set them on fire. The opposite of Jett, who liked to put them out. "Would the drug smugglers come out to see what was going on? It might give us cover to get in and sneak the women free."

"We didn't map who was where. We're not sure that any of the buildings are empty."

"In the dark," Uncle said, "we only have the monoculars and binoculars, and that makes it tough to run and gun."

"Guns aren't available," Jeopardy said.

"I'm working the problem," White clarified. "We should have word soon. I'm hoping to get you full headgear with snap-down optics. Even if I'm unsuccessful, chances are still good for success. The others don't seem to be well equipped. We own the night just…holding up a monocular and taking a few steps at a time."

The men laughed.

"How do we pick out Tink in the crowd?" White asked.

"We have Digger and Rory," Ty said. "We could give them a scent and have them chase it down."

White's phone pinged. She looked down at the readout. "All right, gentlemen, let's fine-tune this plan as much as possible."

T-Rex canted his head. "Was that about weapons?"

"I have a message from Damian Prescott. He's just made it over the Uzbekistan-Kyrgyzstan border at Dostyk."

"That's near Osh, less than a three-hour drive," Jett said.

"He met up with DIA and is bringing in the normal Unit battle rattle. You'll be suited up with the equipment you're used to working with. But you will not have American flags on your uniforms. You will not have ID. And god help you, you will *not* get caught. Because you *will* be disavowed."

38

Havoc
Jalal-Abad, Kyrgyzstan

Friday, Zero Dark Thirty

The plan had been pared down to the simplest possible components.

Before they knew that White was able to get equipment in, the fires seemed to have been the best bet. The more questions Jett asked about the flammability of heroin and other components, the more her math made smoking them out too hazardous. This was especially true since they didn't know what chemicals lay where. There was a high probability that fire or any explosives could make things go *BOOM.*

They'd have the cylinders of their noise cancellation suppressors screwed onto their rifles. That lowered the chance of the gunpowder flare impacting the flammable environment.

Caution, though, was the word.

The men would silently breach the house where they saw Tink go in. The guards would be dispatched, hand to hand if possible.

With her uncanny sense of direction, Jett would bolt-cut the shackles if the woman wore them to sleep. Jett would then hold out a line of climbing webbing for the women to hold on to, and with a pair of night vision goggles, Jett would lead the women out to a waiting van that would take them to the hospital for a medical check.

Echo would hold the line while the women escaped, then they'd slip back into the woods for an exfil in a different direction.

It was simple, in theory.

You didn't land on Delta Force Team Echo without understanding the truism: "No plan survives the first contact with the enemy."

"Breacher up," T-Rex whispered into his comms.

Jett was back in the tree line with Digger, waiting for her call to action.

Nitro steamed forward, turned the knob, cracked the door.

Easy day.

On signal, the team ran in to clear the house. On silent feet, rifles at the ready, they moved. Room to room. Closet to closet. The only sign that there had been human life was a pile of skeletons dumped into the corner of an upstairs bedroom. A family still dressed in dry rotted nightclothes a century-old, seen in eerie array through the green field in Havoc's night vision lenses.

The vivid story of how this village turned into a place of evil paused Havoc for a nanosecond.

But the evil in this village came from the acts of living men, not demons.

Looking around, there were no packed bags. No stacks of

fresh clothing for the journey. Nothing to show that Tink or anyone had been in here.

Havoc would question that they'd landed on the correct building except that Jett hadn't said this was wrong. And she had that internal compass and distance tool in her brain.

This had been their opportunity to sneak in and walk away with their prize.

"White. Echo, there's a delivery truck that's moving in from the south entrance. The back door is open. The truck appears to be empty. A driver and a shotgun."

"T-Rex. Good copy."

On to Plan B.

Things were going to get loud.

"T-Rex. Jett, can you get eyes on?"

"Jett. Wilco. Moving."

Havoc wasn't a fan of Jett moving unilaterally toward the enemy with her unwillingness to kill and a K9 that she didn't know how to handle.

Ty pulled a bag from beneath his breastplate with a scent source. He signaled Rory to smell the T-shirt pulled from the guest house where Peter and Tink had stayed on the weekends. It had been collected by the operator who had gone in to investigate the lack of postcards.

Rory's nose went up in the air. He sniffed around and sat on a spot near the window. A signal. Tink had been here.

But where was she now?

"Men, watch your night vision if that truck moves in our direction with headlights on." T-Rex reminded the team. "We're going to split up. Havoc, Ty, and Rory work the scent trail. The rest of Echo will clear house to house. We'll start with those where Bravo documented the hostages."

After the team stacked and moved from the building, Ty gave Rory a signal.

Havoc followed as Ty worked with Rory. They tracked out to where the women had bathed. The ground was damp. This was indeed the correct house.

Havoc stood downwind as Ty offered Rory the scent to track. Havoc's rifle at the ready, his head on a swivel. While Ty focused on Rory, Havoc was their eyes and ears and their first line of defense.

Rory's nose was to the ground.

Over the comms, Havoc followed his brothers' progress as they moved to the house where Bravo had filmed a group of women emerge.

"Jett. I'm at the paneled truck. It's parked by the entrance to what looks like a community hall to the south of the mosque. Two fighting-age males are sitting on the bumper, smoking. They are facing north. If you are moving up the road, you will eventually be in their line of sight. Proceed with caution."

Havoc tapped his comms. "Havoc. Copy."

From his comms Havoc tracked the progress. House after house, breached and cleared.

House after house stood empty.

They were burning moonlight.

With night vision, they owned the battlespace. But as soon as the sun rose over the horizon, they'd lose that advantage.

Havoc, Ty, and Rory had made their way toward the mosque. There was a white paneled truck exactly as Jett had described.

Without a moment's hesitation, Havoc leveled his rifle and shot each man between the eyes. The *pop-pop* of the subsonic rounds passed almost noiselessly through the suppressor.

"Havoc. Two Tangos dispatched at the vehicle."

Undisturbed, Rory continued his way. He snuffled up the stairs to the door where he sat.

Stepping back, Ty gave Havoc a moment to assess. The

windows were covered in black-out paint. Light pooled from under the door.

Havoc put his ear to the door, nothing.

He tried the knob, unlocked.

The last thing he was going to do was pop it open and run in guns blazing. Havoc circled the perimeter. Finding a ladder hung from hooks on the back wall, Havoc radioed to Ty. Together, they silently put the ladder in place.

Havoc climbed the rungs to an upstairs window. Here, the glass had been left transparent. He searched the room and, seeing no one, tried the window. Locked.

From the side pocket of his mission pack, Havoc drew a suction cup and a glass cutter. Spitting into the cup, Havoc pressed it to the glass, creating a seal. He used the glass cutter to score around the circle. In a single practiced move, Havoc pressed hard into the glass then tugged it back. The glass released as a circle. Havoc handed it off to Ty.

Reaching his hand through the opening, Havoc unlocked the window.

It didn't move. The stuck bathroom scene on the plane came back to him. Havoc pulled his knife, and he scored around the edge of the window in case it had been painted shut. He jiggled the pane a bit then pushed it up. The opening was just big enough to squeeze through without his pack and body armor.

Havoc pulled off the equipment, handing it to Ty, who balanced on the ladder just below him. Havoc turned to look behind him just in time to see Jett scooting back into the tree line, one hand on Rory's collar the other on Digger's. He hoped she moved well back and hid amongst the boulders as she provided watch.

Havoc slid into the empty room and on silent feet made his way to a balcony overhang.

The room below was a grid of tables, four women at each

station. They were weighing and packaging heroin. Surgical gloves on their hands. White jumpsuits. Hair tied back in scarves. Over their nose and mouths were respirators that filtered out fine particles. Lab goggles protected their eyes.

Each quartet of women was covered by a man similarly dressed. Beards protruded from around their filtering masks. Each man had a rifle in hand. As Havoc watched, he videotaped the proceedings, sending the information on to the team.

Crawling backward away from the balcony, Havoc crossed through the room and down the ladder.

"Havoc. By my count, there are eighteen tables. Each table has four women stationed in the heroin packaging effort. That equals seventy-two women. Each table is guarded by an armed male. There are two males at the entrance, and I surmise there would be at least two at the back door. I couldn't get a full visual from my range. Minimum of twenty tangos."

Those odds weren't stellar for all the good guys to walk out healthy.

39
———

Jalal-Abad, Kyrgyzstan

Friday, Zero Dark Thirty

"White. Were you able to pinpoint Tink?"

"Havoc. Negative."

"White. Anything on any captured males in the village?"

"T-Rex. Negative. House by house complete. Looks like all hands on deck for packaging. I'd surmise they've got to make a delivery deadline. And before Havoc dispatched the drivers, they seemed to be waiting for the load."

"Prescott. Doubtful that they'd give Peter a gun to monitor the women."

"White. Never say never. If his wife were threatened, he would do it. It simply takes the command, 'Do this job, or the man standing behind Tink ventilates her brain.' He'd do it, for sure, thinking he wasn't really adding to the harm and might be winning friends. And that's a problem since we can't see faces."

"T-Rex. How shall we proceed?"

"White. Take out everyone holding a gun. All of them. We aren't getting Tink out otherwise. Daylight is an hour away. If Peter has a gun in his hand, he's now the enemy. Sucks, but there it is."

"T-Rex. Wilco. Echo gather at Jett's location."

Havoc was glad to get over to Jett and see how she was faring. She wore a ghillie cloth like a superwoman cloak.

In a circle, they took a knee.

"Havoc, what have you got?" T-Rex asked.

Havoc took a moment to draw the situation into the dirt. "The lights are here and here."

"Any way to shoot them out from the balcony?" Nitro asked.

"Negative." Havoc drew a line in the rectangular representation. "They're positioned just below the balcony. There's no line of sight."

"All right, we're going to clear this systematically. Echo will slide along the south-side wall. Havoc, as our sniper, you're in first. Your job is to take out the lights. I want you back in this corner out of the way. Here." T-Rex whirled the dirt in the south-western corner. "We're calling this line of tables A, B, C moving south to north. Nitro, you're the second man in. You have the hostiles along line A, Jeopardy. B is Dice. C that's yours, Uncle. D, Nitro. I have E. Jett, you're not in my command. If you're willing, I'd like you here behind the truck engine for safety, looking out for any squirters. We don't want anyone to get to comms and call in back up. When we have the room cleared, Havoc will radio to you. I'd like you to be the one who comes in and addresses the women. Do not identify as American. Do not call out Tink's name. Just ask the women to pull off their goggles, masks and headscarves."

With a nod, the team moved into place.

Jett and the K9s positioned behind the truck. Jett held her rifle at the ready.

Echo stacked. Standing to the side of the front entry, T-Rex slowly turned the knob and slid the door a fraction of an inch, assuring the team that it would open. Holding up a hand, he counted the team down, three fingers, two, one. The door was thrown wide.

With his night-vision goggles clicked out of his way, Havoc focused his rifle on the two men at the door who turned at the noise. Working the trigger, Havoc took out the two lights, aiming for the bulb of the high-lumen battery-powered lights.

Two shots.

The room plunged into darkness.

Havoc pressed himself out of his teammates' way as the women's razor-sharp screams filled the air. He dropped his night vision into place. Crouched below table height, Havoc watched the methodical precision as Echo cleared the room.

T-Rex had just passed him, last in the stack, when the back door popped open, and the room was flooded with a bright light that seared Havoc's retina, blinding him.

Havoc stretched his hand to the wall to follow it to the door and out where he could regain his sight. A small hand pressed him back. "Stay back," Jett called.

There was a *pop, pop, pop* of a suppressed rifle by his ear. The light went out.

As the room fell dark, Havoc clicked his night vision back in place as he squinted and blinked, trying to find enough visual acuity to find the men with the rifles and put them down.

Jett yelled, "Get him, Digger. Go. Go, Rory. Go! Eat the bad man."

Fur missiles launched. Albeit in an unorthodox way.

Male screams filled the room.

Pop. Pop.

"Clear!" T-Rex called into his comms. "Jett, you're up."

Gasps and sobbing filled the room.

"Women," Jett called out clearly in Russian. "Rescue. Rescue. Rescue."

It was going to take a moment for that to sink in.

Echo set up a lighting system.

Jett repeated. "Women. Rescue. Rescue. Rescue. I need you to line up at the front door. Take off your scarves and safety equipment. You will be exiting one at a time."

40

JETT

Jalal-Abad, Kyrgyzstan

Friday, Zero Dark Thirty

None of the women rose to their feet.

It was possible that none of them spoke Russian.

Jett tried again. "AWG. AWG. AWG," she called in English then switched to Russian to ask the women to come forward.

One woman crawled out from under the table. Shackled together, she dragged another woman by the arm.

Uncle ran forward with bolt cutters and separated the two.

"Tink. I'm Tink." She piked her hips into the air but scrambled on hands and feet like a bear. It took several tries before she was upright and running toward the door where Jett stood with her battle balaclava obscuring her face.

Throwing herself against Jett, Tink clung there gasping, "Here! Here! Oh, my god! I'm Tink. I'm here! Thank you! God, thank you! I'm Tink. I'm here!"

Jett pulled the respirator and goggles from Tink's head and whispered into her ear. "We're here to save you. Is Peter here?"

"No. No."

"Do you speak the language the other women understand?"

"Pashto, yes."

"Turn and tell them to take the things off their faces and heads. We will cut the shackles, then they are to exit the building for safety. Do *not* mention America. Do you understand?"

"Yes. I will." Tink turned and called to the women. After several tries and much coaxing, the women crawled forward, stood, and removed their headgear.

Jett hauled the trembling Tink out the door and around to the back of the building. "Jett," she called into her comms. "White, I need you at the rear of the building stat."

The night was softening into a new day.

The ground glistened with hoarfrost.

Shapes emerged from the darkness, though the details were still obscured.

The women were sobbing and ululating, the sounds carried by the wind back to where Tink trembled in Jett's arms.

Havoc came around the corner, he stood guard over the women, his head sweeping the area.

Jett simply held a shocked Tink.

Soon, White was by their side crouching on the ground so she could look Tink in the eye. "Hi Tink. Glad we finally found you. Are you hurt?"

"No. Not hurt. So relieved. So grateful. You have no idea." She clung to Jett's jacket with a white-knuckled grip.

"We need to find Peter. Is he here? Do you know where they took him?"

Tink's eyes stretched wide. Her lips flattened and disappeared as she nodded, then shook her head.

"You don't know? He's not here in the village?" White asked.

"He's dead."

"Dead?" Jett repeated, horrified.

"Take a minute. Breathe." White used her hand to emphasize the movement as she drew a noisy breath in through her nostrils, then let the air blow through pursed lips.

Tink worked to join in. After a few stumbles at a full inhale, she got it.

White had her phone out recording. "Tink, what happened to Peter?"

Tink audibly swallowed, licked her lips, sent a searching glance around her then said, "We discovered this ghost village. We watched it all day. Nothing happened. We saw no one. Peter and I—" Her voice hitched. She took a noisy breath in, expanding her nostrils. "We decided to look around a bit, then camp in one of the buildings. It had begun to drizzle, and we didn't want the tent wet." She sucked in another deep breath. "We were captured at gun point. Held. They were considering ransoming Peter. I was going to be kept. Along the way, about three weeks ago, Peter managed to get to his pack, the sat phone was gone. He dug out the flare gun he had in a hidden pocket in the kidney strap and shot it. He thought there was an off chance that one of the other AWG operators would see it and come to our rescue."

Scott had, Jett thought. That was the light that Scott had seen. Hoping to follow the trajectory, Scott had scrambled up the rock face when his leg slid into the crevice.

Stepping into that crevice, not able to follow through, *that* might have saved Peter's life.

Wow, what a thought.

Havoc had been telling her along the trek about a Taoist farmer's tale. In this story, when things went badly, the farmer would reply, "maybe."

Scott was trapped for three weeks, what a terrible event. *Maybe.*

And maybe it was a terrible event that kept him from much worse.

"Our captors heard the whistle of the flare. They dragged all of us into the forest where we were held, with no shelter, for days until the men felt that the danger of detection had passed. That morning, they had us make a semi-circle. They dragged Peter to the center. 'This is what happens to those who try to escape.' And they shot him. No other warning. The shot came from a rifle behind me. I felt the heat of the bullet fly past my cheek. I saw the sudden red hole in Peter's head. I watched him collapse." She shook her head back and forth.

Jett gathered Tink tighter in her arms. But the woman pressed herself away from the comfort.

Tink swiped at her eyes. "They left his body in the clearing behind the packaging center." She pointed through the woods. "I have to go to the authorities to get his body home. I won't leave these women to wander down to the road. They were brought up from Afghanistan. There is nowhere for them to go. They will die in the streets or fall prey again. I have to go to the authorities."

White nodded. "I agree. First, calm the women and ask them to stay here in the village while you get help. We'll get you to the nearest village. You will tell them you found a ride once you got to the road. You will say there was a gun battle over the drugs. The rivals came and shot up the others. Ask them to take you to the hospital. There, call the embassy. I will work with our diplomats to make sure that America brings pressure to treat the women well and to follow up. We weren't here. Only the rival drug traffickers."

Tink nodded. "I can do it."

"Of course you can," Jett said softly. "You can get the women to safety, and you can bring Peter home. This will be over."

EPILOGUE

THEY STOOD ON THE RUNWAY AT DOVER—ECHO, JETT, TINK, Scott, Renée, Deepak, Prescott, and White.

The plane rolled to a stop with precision.

Jett put her arms around Tink.

This day had been a long time coming.

It was a secret repatriation. No one knew that Peter had been in Kyrgyzstan trying to save the world as we know it, and no one ever would know. This story was destined for the black hole of history.

With the U.S. ambassador by her side, Tink had led the Kyrgyz officials back to the site to help the women and retrieve her husband's body.

The Kyrgyzstan government had kept Peter's body for over a year as they investigated the drug smuggling activity in the abandoned village.

They never knew who came in and killed the drug runners.

With this flight bringing Peter's remains home, Echo's mission to find and bring back all AWG operators was complete.

But the Zoric threat was still very much ongoing.

The team waited while Peter was unloaded without ceremony. No flag draped his coffin.

Echo, dressed in civilian suits, lifted and carried the coffin to Tink.

Tink rested one hand on the silken wood; her other hand gripped at Jett.

With a stilted gait and a grief-crumpled face, Tink walked forward with Echo as they moved to the waiting hearse.

Tink had opted to ride with her husband to the funeral parlor.

Echo stood at attention until the hearse disappeared down the road.

"I would have liked a different outcome on this count," White said.

Havoc wrapped his arm around Jett and tucked her in tight.

White focused on Havoc and Jett's fingers interlaced at her shoulder. "I see wedding rings. When did that happen?"

"It's been a month," Havoc said.

"Difficult times to feel happy. But I had a good feeling about you two. Congratulations. Less than a year might seem fast to some, but in the world we live in," White turned and looked down the road where Tink and Peter rounded out of sight, "we have to be brave enough to grab at what goodness and love we can find."

Havoc turned to Jett. "That's our plan—to balance some of the dark with light."

Jett looked into her husband's eyes, in a world filled with upheaval and pain, here was her fun, her adventure, and her peace.

The End

Thank you for reading about the very beginning of Jett and Havoc's relationship. Their story will continue in future Iniquus Security world novels.

If you are reading Iniquus Security in chronological order, up next is, *Fear the REAPER*, a Strike Force Romantic Suspense Mystery Thriller.

Reaper Hamilton's backstory as experienced through his wife Kate's point of view is available to read now in the *Kate Hamilton Mysteries*.

READERS

Readers, I hope you enjoyed getting to know Havoc, Jett and K9 Digger. If you had fun reading Danger Close, I'd appreciate it if you'd help others enjoy it too.

Recommend it: Just a few words to your friends, your book groups, and your social networks would be wonderful.

Review it: Please tell your fellow readers what you liked about my book by reviewing Danger Close. If you do write a review, please send me a note at hello@FionaQuinnBooks.com so I can thank you with a personal e-mail. Or stop by my website www. FionaQuinnBooks.com to keep up with my news and chat through my contact form.

Please, turn the page to find a list of Iniquus novels in chronological order.

THE WORLD of INIQUUS

Chronological Order

Ubicumque, Quoties. Quidquid

Weakest Lynx (Lynx Series)

Missing Lynx (Lynx Series)

Chain Lynx (Lynx Series)

Cuff Lynx (Lynx Series)

WASP (Uncommon Enemies)

In Too DEEP (Strike Force)

Relic (Uncommon Enemies)

Mine (Kate Hamilton Mystery)

Jack Be Quick (Strike Force)

Deadlock (Uncommon Enemies)

Instigator (Strike Force)

Yours (Kate Hamilton Mystery)

Gulf Lynx (Lynx Series)

Open Secret (FBI Joint Task Force)

Thorn (Uncommon Enemies)
Ours (Kate Hamilton Mysteries)
Cold Red (FBI Joint Task Force)
Even Odds (FBI Joint Task Force)
Survival Instinct - (Cerberus Tactical K9)
Protective Instinct - (Cerberus Tactical K9)
Defender's Instinct - (Cerberus Tactical K9)
Danger Signs - (Delta Force Echo)
Hyper Lynx - (Lynx Series)
Danger Zone - (Delta Force Echo)
Danger Close - (Delta Force Echo)
Fear the REAPER – (Strike Force)
Cerberus Tactical K9 Team Bravo

Coming soon, more great stories from the ex-special forces security team members who live, work, and love in a tightly knit family.

ACKNOWLEDGMENTS

My great appreciation ~

To my publicist, Margaret Daly who named Jett.

To my cover artist, David Berens.

To my friend, Michele Carlon, for being the BEST sounding board.

To my Beta Force, who are always honest and kind at the same time, especially Elisa Hordon, Susan Bishop, Michele Carlon, and Kim Schup.

To my Street Force, who support me and my writing with such enthusiasm.

To B Boswell for her story of the true-life Pearl the Squirrel (not injured in any airplane incident)

Thank you to the real-world military who serve to protect us.

To all the wonderful professionals whom I called on to get the details right. Please note: This is a work of *fiction*, and while I always try my best to get all the details correct, there are times when it serves the story to go slightly to the left or right of perfection. Please understand that any mistakes or discrepancies are my authorial decision making alone and sit squarely on my shoulders.

Thank you to my family.

I send my love to my husband. Every day I wake up knowing my life is blessed by you. Thank you.

And of course, thank YOU for reading my stories. I'm smiling joyfully as I type this.

I so appreciate *you*!

ABOUT THE AUTHOR

Fiona Quinn is a six-time USA Today bestselling author, a Kindle Scout winner, and an Amazon All-Star.

Quinn writes action-adventure in her Iniquus World of books, including Lynx, Strike Force, Uncommon Enemies, Kate Hamilton Mysteries, FBI Joint Task Force, Cerberus Tactical K9, and Delta Force Echo series.

She writes urban fantasy as Fiona Angelica Quinn for her Elemental Witches Series.

And, just for fun, she writes the Badge Bunny Booze Mystery Collection with her dear friend, Tina Glasneck.

Quinn is rooted in the Old Dominion, where she lives with her husband. There, she pops chocolates, devours books, and taps continuously on her laptop.

Visit www.FionaQuinnBooks.com